KNOT READY FOR MURDER

"Can you see how the police might conclude the marriage thing gives you a motive to arrange for Mrs. Levy's disappearance?"

"Don't be ridiculous. I'm more interested in who might inherit the business if Hadas is dead and Yossi were in prison for her murder. Do you know?"

"Yes."

"I suppose it's futile to ask you for names?"

"Yes, but I will share this with you. The business will stay in the Uhrman family."

"You mean Ze'ev Uhrman's family?"

He remained silent in a response I could only interpret as assent. Finally he spoke. "One word of caution, Martha. The people behind Ze'ev Uhrman's death and Mrs. Levy's disappearance are your worst nightmare. I can't emphasize too much that any inquiries you make may prompt them to return to your house. And next time, they'll be coming for you . . . ."

Books by Mary Marks

FORGET ME KNOT

KNOT IN MY BACKYARD

GONE BUT KNOT FORGOTTEN

SOMETHING'S KNOT KOSHER

KNOT WHAT YOU THINK

KNOT MY SISTER'S KEEPER

KNOT ON HER LIFE

KNOT OF THIS WORLD

KNOT READY FOR MURDER

Published by Kensington Publishing Corp.

KNOT READY
FOR MURDER
A QUILTING MYSTERY

MARY MARKS

KENSINGTON
PUBLISHING CORP.

www.kensingtonbooks.com

KENSINGTON BOOKS are published by

Kensington Publishing Corp.
119 West 40th Street
New York, NY 10018

All Kensington titles, imprints, and distributed lines are available at special quantity discounts for bulk purchases for sales promotion, premiums, fund-raising, educational, or institutional use.

Special book excerpts or customized printings can also be created to fit specific needs. For details, write or phone the office of the Kensington Sales Manager: Attn.: Sales Department. Kensington Publishing Corp., 119 West 40th Street, New York, NY 10018. Phone: 1-800-221-2647.

The K logo is a trademark of Kensington Publishing Corp.

First Printing: August 2021
ISBN-13: 978-1-4967-2052-8
ISBN-10: 1-4967-2052-0

ISBN-13: 978-1-4967-2055-9 (ebook)
ISBN-10: 1-4967-2055-5 (ebook)

10 9 8 7 6 5 4 3 2 1

Printed in the United States of America

For my grandmother, Amy Rachel Doud,
who created in me a love of quilts.

ACKNOWLEDGMENTS

A huge, heartfelt "Thank you" to everyone who helped make this Quilting Mystery Series: my mentor and writing coach Jerrilyn Farmer, my agent Dawn Dowdle, and my editor at Kensington, John Scognamiglio. Thank you for believing in me and in Martha Rose.

And to my fellow writers in the Friday workshop, thank you for all your valuable suggestions and feedback.

And to my husband, Timothy Gale Palmer, who gives me undying support and love every minute of every day.

CHAPTER 1

Using the side of my dinner fork, I concentrated on cutting neat, little squares in the potato kugel on my plate. *Should I say something now or wait until everyone leaves?*

My stomach fluttered with anxiety as I thought about my options. *As much as everyone at the table will probably approve, shouldn't Crusher be the first person to know? He's been so patient . . .*

I'd managed to reduce the kugel, a potato and onion casserole, to nine bite-sized pieces when my daughter, Quincy's, voice dragged my attention back to the Sabbath table. "Earth to Mom. Come in, please." All conversation stopped as seven pairs of curious eyes focused on me.

Embarrassment warmed my cheeks. "Sorry."

Quincy continued to probe. "Is everything okay?

You've hardly touched your food. Are you ill?" Since becoming a mother herself, my daughter had become keenly aware of exposing her infant daughter to germs.

I gave my daughter a tight little smile. "No, I'm fine." Actually, I was more than fine. My name was Martha Rose, and at my age—still in my fifties but marching toward sixty—I had made an important decision regarding my future.

My sister, Giselle, lowered her fork and pinned me with laser eyes. "Then if you're not having a stroke, give it up, Sissy." Giselle was long on smarts but short on tact.

I learned I had a half sister only a year ago. Together we discovered the fate of our father, who'd gone missing more than thirty years before.

"What's going on with you?" she asked.

Everyone sat at attention, eagerly anticipating my response. I sighed with resignation. Obviously I wasn't going to be able to discuss this first with my fiancé, Yossi Levy, aka Crusher. I reached for his hand.

He encouraged me with a slight nod of the head. "Go on, babe. Whatever it is, I've got your back."

I cleared my throat, found my voice, and gazed into his impossibly blue eyes, into the face of the man who waited patiently for me to overcome my fear of failure. "No more waiting, Yossi. I—I'm ready to get married."

The table erupted into a chorus of "mazel tovs."

He lifted my hand to his lips and kissed it tenderly. "It's about time."

The rest of the evening he avoided looking at me. Something was wrong. Crusher had been proposing marriage almost every day for years. Now I was finally willing to become Mrs. Yossi Levy, he looked miserable.

Everyone began to chatter about having a wedding at

Giselle's estate in Beverly Hills. My sister and daughter vied for which of them deserved to be my maid of honor. Giselle plopped her back against the chair. "Fine. We'll both be maids of honor."

"And Uncle Isaac can sing the seven blessings," Quincy said.

Crusher remained unusually quiet. *I should've listened to my gut and said something to him first.* For the rest of the evening, I sat on *shpilkes*, waiting for everyone to go home.

Quincy and Noah were the first to leave, bundling their sleeping baby girl in the sweet pink-and-white quilt I'd sewn for her. Uncle Isaac and his helper Hilda prepared to leave with Giselle and her fiancé, Harold. My eighty something uncle patted my shoulder with a hand wobbly from Parkinson's disease and whispered, "You've given me such *nachas* tonight, *faigela*."

I loved it when he called me *little bird* in Yiddish.

"I'm glad I lived long enough to see you settle down with a real mensch."

Apparently, my anxiety didn't pass unnoticed. My sister waited for everyone else to walk out the door, grabbed my arm, and took me aside. "Something's not right. You've been twitchy all evening."

I lowered my voice. "Not now, G. I'll call you tomorrow."

I closed the door behind my sister and paused for a breath. Water splashed in the kitchen sink, an indication Crusher was washing the dinner dishes, according to our well-established division of labor. If one cooked, the other cleaned.

With my heartbeat pulsing in my throat, I headed toward the kitchen, compelled by both curiosity and dread.

"I should've warned you first, Yossi. I'm sorry for blurting it out like that."

Without looking up, he scraped table scraps off the plates and stacked them on the counter. The white Sabbath china was a family heirloom we carefully washed by hand to preserve the delicate cobalt blue and gold bands on the rim. "I couldn't be happier, babe. But I wish you'd spoken to me first. There's something I need to tell you."

I moved over to the sink, stood next to him, and gently touched his arm. "What is it, Yossi? You know you can tell me anything. I won't judge you."

He turned off the stream of water and turned to face me. I'd never seen him that tortured. "We have to hold off on the wedding for a while."

"Why? Have you changed your mind about wanting to be married?" A seed of anger took root in my brain, and I took one step backward in order to peer at his face. "Because if you have . . ."

"I haven't changed my mind. It's just that I've got to do a couple of things before we can make it legal."

"Like what?"

"Like get divorced."

I wasn't sure I heard him correctly. "You're *married*?" Sour heartburn shot upward from my insides. "You told me when we first got together you'd never been married. You lied to me?"

Crusher dried his hands on a towel and gently held my shoulders. "Not really. It's a complicated story. I've never been married—in my mind, at least. But there was a wedding years ago. The marriage was never, uh, consummated. I was helping out a friend."

"You mean like helping someone get a green card?"

He sighed. "I wish it was that easy."

"Well what, then?"

He grasped my hand and led me to the cream-colored sofa in the living room, where we sat facing each other. He squirmed on the seat and coughed nervously. "Back when I was a student in the yeshiva, there was a girl, the sixteen-year-old sister of a friend of mine. Her name was Hadas. She got pregnant. Unfortunately, the father of her baby was already married to someone else."

"How did you get involved?"

"One day when I was visiting my friend Ze'ev, we found Hadas sitting at their kitchen table, crying. She blurted out the whole story. She said everyone would be better off if she and the baby were dead. That's when my friend concocted the idea of me marrying his sister and pretending I was the father. I mean, it was a lie, but under the circumstances, it was a matter of *pikuach nefesh*." He referred to the principal in Judaism in which the laws could be ignored if—in doing so—a life could be saved. If he could prevent the girl from committing suicide, two lives would be saved.

I slowly understood the enormous mitzvah my future husband performed for the sake of the girl and her child. "Okay. I get it. You married her out of compassion. What happened next?"

"I left the yeshiva and took a construction job to support the two of us. That's where I got the name Crusher. From working the rock crushing machine."

"So, she's the reason you never completed your studies?"

"No way. She was my excuse for dropping out. The truth is, I wanted to leave anyway. You know me. I'm not the kind of guy who can sit all day. We found a tiny, one-bedroom walk-up on the fourth floor in Brooklyn. She slept in the bedroom and I slept on a sofa bed."

"Oh, come on. You want me to believe you never slept with her?"

"That's exactly what I want you to believe because it's true."

"I think we need a drink." I went into the kitchen and poured two glasses of wine from the half-empty bottle left over from dinner. I returned to the living room and handed him a glass. "I'm not criticizing you, Yossi. After all, this was a long time ago. Right?"

He took a sip from his glass and set it on the coffee table. "Right. A very long time ago. Like almost thirty years."

"And the baby? What happened to it?"

"Hadas miscarried at five months. The baby didn't survive."

"Wow. You went through all that for nothing."

"It wasn't 'for nothing.' I got to leave the demands of the seminary life and she and her family got to maintain a good reputation. After she lost the baby, Hadas moved back in with her parents. Her brother Ze'ev, my friend, was grateful for the way I helped the family avoid a scandal. He gave me his solemn promise he'd help us with an annulment. The family got a lawyer to draw up the papers, which I signed and returned to them. At that point, my involvement ended. And that's it. You have the whole story."

I swallowed the last of my wine and stared into the bottom of the empty glass. "Not quite the whole story. How did you find out you're still married? What happened to the annulment?"

He groaned and closed his eyes. "I don't know why Ze'ev didn't keep his promise, but those papers never made it to court. They were never filed. My sister, Fanya, knows the family. She was the one who broke the news to me about the annulment. She's flying in from New York tomorrow afternoon. I tried to discourage her, but she can be stubborn."

Crusher came from an Orthodox family, who wouldn't dream of travel on the Sabbath.

"Something must be really important if she's willing to fly on a Saturday."

He raked his fingertips through his beard and looked at me sideways. "She's not coming alone."

My ears started to buzz. I thought I knew the answer before I asked, "Who's she bringing?"

"Hadas."

CHAPTER 2

I spent a restless night fretting over having to guess the reason for Fanya's visit. My tossing and turning didn't faze Crusher as he snored softly. *Why is she bringing Hadas? Does Hadas want Crusher back after all these years? Why didn't she get an annulment? How much of a threat will she be?*

Had Crusher been totally honest with me? Even though my rational mind told me this present situation wasn't his fault, he should have followed through with the annulment years ago. Bitter resentment crept up my gut and landed in the back of my throat. I finally fell into an exhausted sleep around three in the morning.

When I opened my eyes again, the clock read eight. The curtains were drawn shut, but they couldn't totally defeat the gentle morning light from creating a warm glow in the bedroom. Every muscle and joint ached with a painful flare-up. I threw aside the down comforter, rolled out of bed, and hobbled to the bathroom to take my fibromyalgia meds. The face staring back at me from the mirror looked pinched and drawn with pain. Puffy bags sat under my eyes, testifying to a night with little sleep.

I raked a wide-toothed comb through my gray curls. *Oh great. Crusher's "wife" Hadas will still be in her forties. She probably has a perfect figure, perfect hair, and a creamy complexion. How can I compete with her? She might be younger than me, but I'm not going to let her waltz in and grab my future husband. If she wants to fight, I'll give her a run for her money.*

Saturday was supposed to be a day of rest. But I knew I wouldn't relax until the house was clean and sparkling. I wanted my home—Crusher's home—to be above reproach. God forbid Hadas should find a reason to criticize!

By the time I shuffled into the kitchen for my first cup of coffee, I was primed for combat mode. It must've shown on my face because Crusher came over to me and gave me a hug. "Morning. Are you okay?"

I stuck out a defiant chin. *Does he think he can drop a bombshell about his marriage and expect me to welcome his wife in our home?* "Hardly slept at all." I brushed past him and walked over to the coffee maker sitting on the apricot-colored marble kitchen counter. I poured myself a large mug of Italian roast and plopped down at the kitchen table and glared at him.

Crusher reached into the oven and pulled out a plate of pancakes and scrambled eggs. My favorite breakfast. "I kept these warm for you." He placed the plate in front of me in an act of contrition.

His strategy worked. The more I ate, the more benevolent I became.

Between mouthfuls of fluffy scrambled eggs, I managed a question. "Tell me about her. Hadas. Tell me what to expect."

"I haven't had contact with her since she moved back in with her parents."

"Oh, come on. Didn't you ever wonder what happened to the annulment? Didn't you ever try to find her on Google or Facebook?"

He shrugged. "She's not on Facebook. But my sister, Fanya, is friends with the family."

I'd talked to Fanya on the phone a few times but never met her in person. She'd never once mentioned Crusher's wife. "Since your sister was friends with the family, didn't you ever ask her to find out about the annulment?"

"Once I asked her to find out why I never received the final papers. Hadas assured Fanya everything had been taken care of."

"Well, how was Hadas back then?"

"Wild and rebellious, considering the community we lived in." He referred to the Jewish enclave in Brooklyn.

"Was she pretty?" I watched his discomfort as he navigated through a minefield of possible wrong answers.

He eyed me carefully and, from his expression, I guessed he was contemplating the wisdom of making comparisons. "She was . . . uh, attractive, yes. But," he added hastily, "definitely not my type."

I laid out another minefield for him to walk through. "What is your type?"

He closed his eyes and scrubbed his face with his hand. "You're enjoying this, aren't you?"

I smiled, taking pleasure in his discomfort. "You have only yourself to blame. So? What is your type?"

"You're my type. Smart, funny, and beautiful." A slow grin curled his mouth. "And sexy. Very sexy."

I threw back my head and laughed. "Right answer. I guess we can still be friends. What did you do to the pancakes? They're extra-good this morning."

"Cinnamon."

"I've only talked to Fanya over the phone. Tell me what to expect."

He sipped his coffee. "You can't tell we're siblings because she got all the good looks in the family. She's smart and she's tall. Us Levys tend to be tall." He wasn't kidding. At six feet six inches, he was the tallest person I'd ever known.

"Is she religious?"

He shook his head. "She is fiercely superstitious, but not religious. Contrary to our parents' expectations, she chose not to marry. She loves her independence too much. Fanya's a lot like you, in that respect."

I finished my breakfast and put the dishes in the dishwasher. Even though work was strictly forbidden on the Sabbath, we spent the bulk of the morning doing laundry, scouring the bathrooms, dusting, and vacuuming. I wanted Hadas to know she was up against a balabusta, a skilled Jewish homemaker. After an inventory of the inside of our refrigerator, I sent Crusher to the market. Buying and selling was also forbidden on the Sabbath, but this was an emergency. Fanya and Hadas didn't have to know what day the food was purchased.

By two in the afternoon, we'd finished our labors and I was about to take a shower when my sister, Giselle, called. "You know, Sissy, I've been waiting for hours. You were supposed to call me today, remember?"

Oh crap. "The day isn't over yet, G." I'd been too focused on making my house sparkle to remember my promise to call my sister.

"Well, I can't handle the suspense any longer. You were antsy and distracted all evening. Yossi, too. Harold agrees. Something's troubling both of you."

I told her about Crusher's marriage to Hadas.

"Shut the front door! He's *married*?"

"In name only. Yossi signed the papers and trusted his friend to do the legal stuff, but apparently that never happened. His sister, Fanya, is flying to LA as we speak, and she's bringing Hadas."

"Why now?"

"Excellent question, G. I won't find out until they arrive. I think Yossi means for them to stay with us."

"Are you going to let that happen? Are you going to let his wife, for God's sake, stay in your home?"

"Actually, G, it'll be easier for me to keep an eye on things if they do."

Little did I know how much I would grow to regret that decision.

CHAPTER 3

Crusher left Encino at three to meet the five o'clock arrival of Fanya's flight from New York. In LA, one always hoped for the best traffic conditions, but the smart driver added extra time in case there was a major delay on the freeway. I calculated he wouldn't return with our guests for another four hours.

While he was gone, I ignored another Sabbath prohibition. According to the strict rules of Orthodoxy, kindling a fire (such as cooking or operating a vehicle) was one of the thirty-nine types of work forbidden on the day of rest. Food must be prepared before the Sabbath began at sundown on Friday. I chose to overlook many restrictions imposed by such a strict practice of Judaism. My personal observance fell somewhere between the traditional or moderate branch and the Reform or liberal branch. I had plenty of time to cook dinner and get dressed before Crusher returned with our two houseguests.

Around seven, the sound of the automatic garage door opening indicated Crusher had arrived. Perfect timing. I'd finished dressing in an Eileen Fisher long-sleeved gray tunic and matching wide-legged trousers. I walked with measured steps toward the front door and waited until I heard their voices. I took a deep, calming yoga breath and plastered a pleasant smile on my face.

Fanya kissed the mezuzah on the door before entering. She towered over me by at least ten inches. Enormous golden hoop earrings about the size of a child's bracelet dangled from her ears. Tortoiseshell combs kept her long chestnut curls from falling over her face. She wore a fisherman's sweater, stonewashed blue jeans, and what appeared to be Doc Martens boots. She looked much younger than her forty-five years.

"Martha!" Fanya crushed me in a bear hug, smashing my face against her boobs. Then she grabbed me by the shoulders, took a step backward, and appraised me from head to toe. She flashed a smile wide enough to see a gap between her two front teeth, just like Crusher's. "I'm so glad to finally meet you in person. We always seemed to miss each other those few times you came to New York." The grin vanished as she leaned toward me and whispered, "Be careful."

Oh no. Was Hadas going to be a problem? I nodded once to acknowledge her warning. "Wonderful to see you, too."

Fanya stepped aside, allowing me to greet the other woman. I sipped a quick breath when I saw Hadas. She reminded me of the exquisitely gorgeous Penélope Cruz;

dark, luxurious hair and golden skin. Her blue, almost-violet eyes were made more intense by her purple sweater. Hadas definitely took care of herself in the intervening years. She raised her chin to literally look down her nose with a smile as real as a cobra's. "You must be Martha."

I offered my hand to shake, which she ignored. The smile I returned was equally insincere as her own. "Not only must I be Martha, I insist on it."

En garde.

Crusher stood in the doorway with two rolling suit-cases and looked like he was about to throw up. The battle line had been drawn, and he knew it. "Martha's prepared a nice dinner for us. I'll take your bags into our guest room."

Hadas stepped over to Crusher and purred, "I'll go with you, Yossi. A lady always likes to freshen up after a long journey." Hadas placed a proprietary arm through his and tittered as he awkwardly rolled the luggage. "Are you nervous? Don't be. After all, you're still my husband."

I watched in disbelief as they disappeared together down the hallway.

Fanya waited until they were out of earshot. "She means to get him back, Martha. I tried my best to discourage her, but *gornisht helfen*." Nothing helps.

"That's not going to happen!" I growled through my teeth.

Fanya wagged her head. "I've known Hadas since we were schoolgirls together. When she gets something in her head, she's relentless. Believe me, she's always shown such chutzpah."

"Maybe so, but I'm just as relentless. Anyway, I'm

puzzled. Why is she coming after him now? And why didn't she go through with the annulment?"

"You'll have to ask her about the annulment. As to the other, I believe she's always had a crush on Yossi. Even before their so-called marriage."

"Still? Almost thirty years have passed since then."

Fanya shrugged. "Some people never get over their first love. She couldn't stop talking about him. Believe me, she was *hocking a chinek* for five hours straight on the plane." Fanya used the Yiddish expression for someone who rattled on and on like a boiling teakettle on top of a stove. Footsteps approached in the hallway from the bedrooms. "Shh," Fanya warned.

"You two must be hungry after all your traveling. Dinner's prepared. Take a seat there." I gestured toward the dining room. "Yossi, honey, will you help me bring out the food?" I pulled him into the kitchen while our two guests sat on opposite sides of the table. "Did you ask her want she wants?" I hissed.

He closed his eyes and shook his head slowly. "Something about a business proposition."

I wouldn't let it pass. "You'd better set her straight about your divorce." I turned on my heel and shoved a platter with slices of cold baked salmon in his hands to put on the table. I followed with the other dishes of deviled eggs, green salad, and slices of challah, while Crusher opened a bottle of Baron Herzog kosher white chardonnay.

As Fanya reached for a deviled egg, I noticed a red string tied around her left wrist. It wasn't uncommon to see people walking around Israel wearing a bracelet of red string, but one rarely saw them in the US. Those strings had been taken to Kever Rachel (the tomb of the matriarch Rachel) and consecrated with prayer. Once transformed by the holy place, the strings became an amulet to ward off the evil eye. Some strings made their way to the USA. Red was the color thought by Ashkenazi Jews to protect against the evil eye. Blue was more the color for Sephardi Jews.

"This is delicious, Martha." Fanya took three more eggs but declined a serving of fish.

Hadas moved the leaves of lettuce around on her salad plate. "This would have been perfect if it hadn't been for a piece of overripe tomato."

I ground my teeth. "No problem." I reached over, grabbed her salad plate, and put it in the kitchen. When I came back to the table, I caught her batting those blue eyes and aiming a triumphant smile at Crusher.

I waited until my pulse rate slowed to normal before I dared to speak. "You know, Hadas, I'm concerned about your comfort. Fanya will sleep in the double bed in our guest bedroom. The only other place to sleep is on the sofa. I'm sure you'll be more comfortable in a nearby hotel."

"How sweet of you to be concerned, Martha, but I'm happy to sleep on the sofa." Her eyes flicked in the direction of my chair. "You may find it a tad too narrow, but I'll fit without a problem."

A red haze closed in on my vision, and my heart rate soared once more in response to her insult about my being overweight. Fanya's eyes grew wide.

Crusher drained his wineglass and poured himself another full glass of Baron Herzog chardonnay. "Martha's right about couch surfing, Hadas."

She reached over and rested her fingertips lightly on his hand. "Remember after our wedding how you insisted on sleeping on the sofa? It's the least I can do to return the favor."

"It's okay." Fanya dabbed the corner of her mouth with the napkin. "Hadas and I can share the double bed."

The next morning, Sunday, I woke at six. Crusher's side of the bed was empty. I threw on a bathrobe and headed toward the laughter coming from the living room. I yawned. "Everyone's up early."

Hadas waved a dismissive hand. "We're still on New York time. It's nine for us."

Crusher wore jeans and a red plaid flannel shirt. He had tied a blue bandanna on his head, his preferred religious head covering. He brought a cup of coffee and cream from the kitchen and handed it to me. "We were reminiscing about the old days, babe."

Hadas flinched when he called me by such an affectionate term. She refused to make eye contact with me and made a big deal out of smoothing the pleats on the skirt of a pink linen dress.

"What about the old days?" I thanked him for the coffee.

This morning my future sister-in-law wore stylish jeans torn at the knees and a blue *Save the Whales* T-shirt. "Oh, you know. People, family, the sequestered life of the Orthodox community. We've each managed to break away."

"It's obvious you no longer adhere to the strict dress code for women, Fanya, but in what other ways have you forsaken tradition?" I asked.

"For one, I've solved the kosher thing by becoming a vegetarian."

So that's why she didn't eat the fish last night.

"I've also made the choice not to *pru urvu*." Fanya referred to the first of the 613 commandments in Torah to be fruitful and multiply—a mandate many Jews took very seriously, especially after the decimation of the Holocaust. "I make a nice living hanging wallpaper. Flocked, metallic, plain, grass cloth, and even fabric; homes, businesses; uptown, downtown—I do it all. And before you ask, yes. As tall as I am, I can sometimes reach the ceiling without a ladder. Owning my own small business gives me the freedom and the means to travel when I want to."

"I suppose all those things are a lot easier when you don't have to take care of a family."

She smiled. "I love the life I've chosen. I've never really felt the need to have a traditional family of my own." She held coffee in one hand and made a grand gesture with the other. "The world is my family." She glanced around the living room. "You know, I bet I could transform this room into something sensational. If you want, I could easily paper this living room in a day. I recommend using an understated geometric. Like stripes. Or you could totally go in the opposite direction. Like a very detailed William Morris nineteenth-century leaf and bird print."

"I'll keep it in mind. Thanks." I eyed my rival over the rim of my cup. "What about you, Hadas? How have you broken from tradition?"

"Parts of the tradition I keep." She sniffed and looked at Crusher. "Some of them have been very useful. For example, being a divorcée or widow would've automatically invited interest from single men. My father would've

forced me to marry one of them. But being an agunah created a boundary against such annoying attention."

She referred to the laws of divorce in Judaism. A man
could divorce a wife, but a woman couldn't divorce a
husband. An *agunah* was a woman who had been abandoned by her husband but was chained to a marriage because he hadn't given her a Get, a bill of divorcement.

"Of course, a lot of men have wanted me," Hadas
boasted. "More than one married man promised me the
world if I became his mistress. But I'm no *nafke*." She
used the Yiddish word for "whore."

"*Has v'halilah!*" Fanya cried. God forbid!

Crusher shook his head. "Ze'ev promised me he'd
make sure we got an annulment. When Fanya asked, you
led her to believe you'd taken care of it. Why did you
lie?"

An enigmatic smile softened her lips. "Don't blame
poor Ze'ev. I didn't want an annulment from you, Yossi.
As an agunah, it was easy to justify working in my father's business. I was quite happy and fulfilled there."

What I wanted to say was *monkey business*. What I actually said was, "What business is that?"

"*Shmatas*. Garment manufacturing. I started with supervising the workers in the pit, the place where all the
machine sewing goes on. I reorganized the workspace to
make it more efficient. I modernized and digitized the
business records next. When I saw how much money we
could save by sending the work overseas, I negotiated
great deals with our Mexican, Vietnamese, and Chinese
suppliers."

With every statement, Hadas became more adamant,
speaking to Crusher as if he were the only one in the

room. "I've increased sales every year. I must say, I'm as good as any man at making hard decisions."

"*Pu, pu, pu.*" Fanya pantomimed spitting three times behind her hand, to ensure Hadas's boasting wouldn't attract the attention of the evil eye.

Hadas continued: "You can't be afraid of making people angry if you want to be successful. I couldn't have achieved everything I've done if I'd remarried and raised a family."

"What about your brother?" I asked.

"After my father died, may he rest in peace, the business went equally to me and my brother, Ze'ev. We ran the company together. Ze'ev was the numbers guy. I was the salesperson. We worked well as a team. Unfortunately, Ze'ev was killed six months ago. I've been running the company alone ever since."

"Killed?" Crusher carried a pained look. "How?"

"Hit-and-run driver. Never caught." She paused for maximum effect. "I've written a new will. In the event of my death, Yossi, ownership of the business will revert to my closest next of kin. You."

Fanya erupted with another fresh bout of spitting. "You should live a long life, *halevai.*"

And there it was. The whole reason for her visit. She wanted to lure Crusher back to New York, using a thriving business as bait. It didn't take a genius to see she also wanted to live as husband and wife.

Fanya clasped and unclasped her hands in her lap.

Crusher's jaw dropped. "I don't think you understand, Hadas." He pointed to the floor. "I live here. In this house. I'm in love with Martha. We're getting married. We're happy."

Hadas's eyes narrowed. She reminded me of a snake getting ready to strike and kill. "Think about how much easier your life can be, Yossi. I'd continue to run the business and you could either join me or pursue something else you enjoy."

I knew my fiancé well enough to be alarmed at his continued silence. Why didn't he stop her? Dear God, was he taking her proposal seriously?

He finally broke the silence. "I am doing what I enjoy, Hadas. I'm a federal agent." Yossi Levy, aka Crusher, worked for the ATF. His job sometimes required him to operate undercover. Those were dangerous assignments, but he loved the work and was good at it.

"Yes, but how much longer before you're too old?" She briefly glanced at me. "There are millions of dollars involved. We could have a beautiful life."

I placed my empty cup on the coffee table. "I've got another idea, Hadas. Once you and Yossi get a divorce, you'll be free to look for a more suitable man to help you run your business."

"I don't need *help*!" she snapped. "I'm more than capable of running the business by myself."

I crossed my arms. "Then why did you fly all the way to LA?"

Hadas continued to ignore me and spoke as if I weren't in the same room. "I'm thinking of moving our headquarters to Los Angeles, Yossi. Even if you want to continue in your present job out here, we can still be together while I run the business. Trust me. I've thought of everything."

"Not everything, Hadas." Clearly, the woman was delusional if she thought I would sit quietly while she attempted to steal my fiancé. "When you were a teenager, you behaved like a *nafke* and got pregnant." I ignored her furious stare. "Yossi was kind enough to rescue you and your family from the shame you deserved. But this is thirty years later, and he's moved way beyond your situation. Get over him. He's with me now."

She shrugged off my words. "Things can change."

CHAPTER 4

Later that morning, Crusher suggested we take our houseguests to the Pacific Ocean for an alfresco meal. I loaded a picnic basket with cheese, deviled eggs from the night before, baguettes, olives, grapes, and a large thermos of homemade iced tea into the trunk of my Honda Civic. As we headed out the door, Hadas's phone rang.

She looked at the number and told us to go without her. "I've got to take this. Besides, I feel a headache coming on."

What I wanted to say was, *I hope it's an aneurysm!* Instead I said, "I'm sorry. Would you like a Tylenol?"

Sunday traffic would be heavy with beachgoers, so we chose a lesser-used route and drove west through Topanga Canyon to the Pacific Coast Highway (known as the PCH locally). As we crested the last hill, we viewed the deep blue waters of the Pacific stretching toward the horizon. Dozens of sailboats fanned out from the marina to the south and dotted the dark waters with colorful sails. Unblemished by clouds, the azure dome of sky stretched to the infinite distance. Seagulls glided on the currents of air above the beach, screeching to each other. I rolled open the window and filled my lungs with the salty ocean air.

"Ah!" Fanya also took a deep breath and sighed. "No wonder hordes of New Yorkers flock to California. This smells like heaven."

Sunday traffic crawled on PCH, but we managed to transition north at the traffic light and stopped at our destination, Point Dume State Beach. We hiked on top of the promontory and eventually found our way to the sandy beach below the cliffs. I spread out an old cotton blanket on the sand. I would never treat a quilt as roughly. Crusher opened the picnic basket and handed iced tea all around. We watched a towheaded youngster toddle toward the water as fast as his short legs could carry him. A blond woman wearing a black string bikini ran after him.

Something about Hadas's story felt incomplete, but I couldn't quite put my finger on what was bothering me. "What do you think about Hadas?" I asked Crusher. What I wanted to ask was, *Do you have feelings for her? Are you tempted by her offer?* But I purposely left the question vague to see what he'd come up with.

He glanced at his sister. "Why is she interested in me, Fan?"

Fanya took a sip of tea. "The Uhrman Company has

been her whole life. I'm convinced her enthusiasm for the business was a substitute for raising the child she lost. When Ze'ev died, she was left alone in this world with a big corporation to run. I think she's afraid to be alone. As her husband, you're now her next of kin. She's not going to let you go without a fight. I know her."

We spread out our food and began to silently eat lunch, each wrapped in our own thoughts. Finally, I realized what it was about Hadas's story that bothered me. "Did Hadas ever mention who would inherit the business if Yossi refused?"

Her large gold earrings swung gracefully as she shook her head. "Nope."

I plucked some fat, red grapes from the stem. "I wonder who is next in line after Yossi."

We finished our picnic, trudged back onto the cliffs, and took the scenic route home. I sat in the back seat and let Fanya ride shotgun so she could enjoy looking at mile after mile of beautiful homes lining both sides of Sunset Boulevard.

After five minutes, she gasped, "These houses must be worth a fortune. Yet there are thousands of them. Who are these people? Where does all their money come from?"

I often wondered the same thing. "The country's wealth is held by the top two percent. There are roughly three hundred thirty million people in this country. Two percent would equal six million, six hundred thousand. All those people have to live somewhere. What nicer place than right here in Southern California?"

"Yeah," Crusher scoffed. "As long as you don't mind the earthquakes, wildfires, mudslides, flash floods, and occasional small tornado . . ."

Fanya laughed. "We don't get earthquakes in New York. I wouldn't mind experiencing one just to see what it feels like."

"I'll try to arrange one for you," he said.

We transitioned onto the 405 Freeway north and pulled into my driveway in Encino a half hour later. While Crusher retrieved our picnic basket from the trunk of the Honda, Fanya and I headed for my front door.

My orange tabby Bumper ran to greet me and meowed. I became alarmed because he didn't use his normal happy greeting. This was a plummy, full-throated yowl.

"What's wrong, little guy?" I bent to scratch him on his jaw and behind his ears, but he pulled away and yowled again.

Crusher deposited the picnic basket on the kitchen island and joined us in the foyer. "What's wrong with him?"

Bumper didn't wait for guesses or explanations. He walked toward the hallway, looked over his shoulder at us, and yowled a third time.

"I think he means for us to follow him." I moved toward the cat.

When he saw me walking his way, he turned back around and headed down the hallway.

"What is it, Bumper?" I crooned.

He got as far as the door to the guest bedroom, stopped, and meowed one more time. I approached him and looked at the closed door. "What's the matter, sweetie? Did you leave something in there?" Bumper loved his three stuffed toys: a little gray mouse made of suede, a long turquoise snake with a felt tongue, and a white bunny rabbit made of faux fur.

I knocked softly on the door. "Hadas?" Nobody answered. I knocked a little louder. "It's Martha. Do you still have a headache? Can I get you anything?" Still no answer. I opened the door and screamed. "Oh my God! Yossi!"

The sound of size fourteen boots came clopping in the hallway in prompt response. "What?" He frowned.

I stood mute and pointed inside the bedroom. Clothes were scattered on top of the dark mahogany sleigh bed and tossed around the room. Drawers hung open in utter disarray.

I walked through the room, being careful not to disturb the scene. I stuck my head inside the en suite bathroom and smelled a sweet, chemical odor. I gathered a rag lying on the floor. It smelled of ether and cut grass and even a small whiff made my head spin. I held the rag at arm's length and approached Crusher. "What is this, Yossi?"

"Drop it. I can smell the chloroform from here." I hurriedly tossed the rag back into the bathroom.

Fanya came to see what all the fuss was about. She stopped abruptly when she saw the condition of the room and grabbed Crusher's arm. "Look over there!" She pointed to the cracks in a hand mirror someone had hurled across the room. "That's seven years of poverty for whoever broke it." She rubbed her arms. "Where's Hadas?"

Crusher pushed us out of the room. "Don't know, Fan. Looks like she was chloroformed."

Fanya spat a heartfelt *pu, pu pu*. "*Oy va voy and three sholem aleichems!*" She began to search the house. "Hadas! Hadas! Where are you?"

She got silence in return.

Crusher motioned for me to wait in the living room. "I'll check the garage and backyard."

Something sitting on the hall table caught my eye. *Don't call the police, or she dies. Wait for instructions.*

Crusher said, "We need to call the police."

"But, Yossi, the note says not to."

"Ignore it. We'll have a better chance to find her alive if we involve law enforcement. They're experienced in this sort of thing." He headed for the backyard and returned two minutes later. "Not there. Did you call the police?"

I shook my head. "I wanted to wait for you, in case you found her outside."

Fanya paced back and forth, her Doc Martens clomping as loudly as her brother's boots on the hardwood floor.

Instead of 911, I called my son-in-law Noah Kaplan. He was an LAPD robbery/homicide detective assigned to the west side of the San Fernando Valley, where we lived. "Noah, something awful has happened." I told him about the missing Hadas. "We found a note. She's been abducted. We also found a rag soaked in chloroform."

"Besides your friend, is anything else missing? Jewelry, electronics? Have you called the police yet?"

"You *are* the police, Noah. Remember?"

He released an impatient breath. "I mean, have you filed a report? Talked to anyone else?"

"No on both counts. Are you coming over? Do you want to talk to Yossi?"

"Not until we get there. He knows how to secure a crime scene. I'll be over soon with my . . . *partner.*"

"I was afraid of that." Noah's partner in robbery/homicide was Arlo Beavers. My ex-boyfriend.

Noah huffed. "Believe me. He'll be even less enthusiastic than you are. Don't leave. We'll be there in about ten minutes."

Beavers's new white Camry parked in front of the house ten minutes later. I opened the front door as they got out of the car and moved up the walkway. Noah wore a brown suit and tie. Beavers wore his usual gray suit, white shirt, and blue tie. He also sported a shock of silver hair, a white mustache, and the woodsy cologne I remembered from our time together.

Noah reached me first. "Are you okay, Mom?" He put a slight emphasis on the word *Mom*.

"Yes, thank you, Noah. We're fine."

Beavers rolled his eyes at Noah's familiar greeting. "Here we are again, Martha. You keep popping up like a boil on my—"

"Hey!" Crusher growled.

Beavers ignored him. "So, where is the crime scene this time?"

"Guest room."

"What have you done with the chloroform?"

"I left the rag on the bathroom floor where I found it."

"Stay here while we have a look."

Noah and Beavers made a quick tour of the house and came back to us in the living room.

I explained why Hadas came to LA with Crusher's sister, Fanya. "Yossi and I wanted to take them for a picnic at the beach, but Hadas complained of a headache and stayed home. Just the three of us drove to Point Dume."

"What time did you leave?" Noah looked at his watch, a gold Rolex given to him by his wealthy father.

"Eleven?" I looked to Crusher and Fanya for confirmation and they both nodded.

"It's three right now," he said. "When did you return home?"

"Only minutes before I called you. After two-thirty."

"We'll work the case as an abduction, not a missing person. It would help if you could give us a picture of Mrs. Levy."

My gut clenched when he used her full name.

Fanya pulled her cell phone out of the back pocket of her jeans. "We took a selfie in JFK. Give me your number and I'll send it to you."

I glanced at Beavers, who seemed to be fighting a smile. I was sure he enjoyed the juicy details of Crusher's past.

Finally, he broke his silence. "Let's see if I understand you correctly. If something happens to Mrs. Levy, her husband," he pointed to Crusher, "will inherit a successful corporation?"

I immediately guessed where he might be going with his line of questioning. "If you're thinking Yossi has a financial motive to hurt Hadas, you're wasting precious time. You need to look elsewhere for her kidnapper. He was with the two of us, and we were all at the beach."

Beavers trained his dark eyes on my face. "So you say."

Crusher snarled. "That's a crock, man, and you know it."

Fanya watched the conversation bounce back and forth like a ball at a tennis match. "I'd like to say something, if I may."

We each turned to her.

"We don't know where Hadas is at the moment. We don't know if this is—God forbid—an abduction or worse.

All I can tell you is none of us are responsible for whatever happened here." She rapped her knuckles three
times on a wooden table. "Hadas was fine when we left
her at eleven."

"Or," Beavers continued, "you're all involved in Mrs.
Levy's disappearance and are providing alibis for each
other."

"Whatever happened in the bedroom took place during
the hours we were gone: eleven to two-thirty. Fanya,
Yossi, and I were out during those hours. End of subject."

Beavers opened his mouth to speak, but I held up a si-
lencing hand. "Please let me finish. Judging by the fren-
zied disarray in the bedroom, somebody was looking for
something."

"Think about it, dude." Crusher spread his hands.
"Why would any of us trash the bedroom? Someone with
motive did that."

"Or," said Beavers, "it could have been staged by you
to look that way."

Crusher scowled. "Could've but wasn't."

Noah's phone chirped. "I got a text. CSU is on its way.
Until they're finished, the three of you will have to find
someplace else to stay. Probably won't be for more than a
day."

"Well, if we can't stay here, we need to get a change of
clothes," I said.

"You and Yossi can go in your bedroom, but I'm afraid
nobody is allowed in the crime scene." He looked at
Fanya. "Sorry. And just so you know, Mom? I'm sure to
be pulled from this investigation because we're closely
related. However, it's likely Arlo will remain the lead detective."

Did I die and go to hell? Working with my ex-boyfriend would be torture, especially if he suspected us of foul play. Which was ridiculous, considering we weren't even here when Hadas was taken. And there was one more thing. Although it was ancient history, the rivalry for my affections between Beavers and Crusher could interfere with Beavers's objectivity. This investigation could very well devolve into a pissing contest between them.

I plopped my hands on my hips. "Arlo, I think you should also recuse yourself from this case. Especially in view of our past association and all."

"Don't flatter yourself."

I narrowed my eyes. "You know deep inside none of us is responsible for Hadas's misfortune. You're having fun yanking our chains when you should be trying to find her."

He ignored me and addressed Fanya. "You're visiting from New York?"

"Yeah. Yossi's my brother and Martha will soon be my sister-in-law."

I cringed. Fanya had no way of knowing she'd stepped on a sensitive nerve. Beavers also wanted to get married, but I chose Crusher.

"Don't leave LA."

"Well, when can I go back home?"

"I'll let you know." Beavers looked at the three of us. "You need to go to the station now and give formal statements. We want to keep this from the press for as long as possible. Aside from the police, don't talk to anyone about the abduction. If Mrs. Levy is still alive, we don't want to spook her kidnappers. Miss Levy, once you reach the police station, you'll have to give a set of your prints for the purpose of elimination."

He handed Fanya his business card. "In case you need to reach me, Miss Levy. Martha doesn't need my card. She and I have been down this road many times. I suspect she has me on speed dial." He raised an eyebrow. "Remind me again. How many times have you shot someone in this house?"

CHAPTER 5

We parked the Honda in front of the West Valley police station and walked inside the lobby.

A young officer in a dark blue uniform sat at the desk, filling out a form the old-fashioned way, with a pen. He didn't look at me. "How can I help you?"

"Detective Beavers sent us to each give a statement about a missing person."

He scanned our faces. His eyes stopped at Crusher. "Don't I know you from somewhere?"

Crusher dug his ATF badge and ID card out of his pocket. "It's likely we may've worked a case together."

A grin of recognition blossomed on the cop's face. He leaned over the desk and offered his hand. "Yeah. Now I remember. Gun bust in Reseda. Aryan Nation. Right?"

Crusher shook the young cop's hand. "Nice to see you again, bro." He explained why we were there.

"Right. I'll get someone to help you. Please take a seat."

We moved to the gray plastic bucket seats lined in orderly rows facing the desk. All the surfaces in the station were washable: tile floors, plastic seats, laminated front desk. The police served all kinds of humanity in the daily course of keeping the peace. Victims, offenders, and witnesses weren't always neat and clean. Only a few months ago, a homeless man brought the MRSA bacteria to the station, and three officers became infected. The process of sterilizing the place was made easier by the washable surfaces.

After a ten-minute wait, Fanya was the first to be escorted into a blue interview room to give a statement. I was the last to be called.

The officer introduced himself as Detective Jarvis and handed me a small, clear plastic bottle with a rendering of snowcapped mountains and *fresh, mountain spring water* written on the label. "Tell me in your own words what happened this morning, Mrs. Rose."

I went through the facts methodically, painting a detailed picture of the day from the time I woke until the time I discovered the rag soaked in chloroform.

"What is your relationship to Mrs. Levy?"

I cringed when he called her by Crusher's last name. "She knew my fiancé many years ago."

"Your fiancé being Yosef Levy?"

"Yes."

"She's married to him, right?"

"Well, technically, I suppose."

"So, let me get this straight. Your fiancé's *wife* is a guest in your house?"

"Yes. That's what I said."

"You didn't object?"

"Not out loud."

"And she wanted him to leave you and return with her to New York?"

"Correct."

"I see. How did she make you feel?"

"How would *you* feel if someone was trying to seduce *your* fiancé right in front of you? I wanted to slap the arrogance right off her face. I wanted to pull out her hair. I wanted to roast her in the oven. I wanted to—"

I stopped when I realized he was writing down my every word. And he wasn't smiling. "Wait. Stop writing. I didn't actually do any of those things. They were just figures of speech. To illustrate how she made me feel. I mean, you asked."

"You had reason to see her harmed?" Jarvis didn't wait for an answer. "That's called 'motive,' Mrs. Rose."

"Maybe so, but she disappeared before we got home from the beach. Like I told you before, when we left the house at eleven, Hadas was very much alive and healthy."

He continued writing for another couple minutes, then shoved the papers across the table. "Please check this for accuracy and sign at the bottom."

I reviewed the statement, crossed out the part where I said I wanted to bake Hadas, and signed my name. "Can I leave now?"

Jarvis gathered the papers, tapped them neatly on the table, and stood. "Mrs. Rose, I'm telling you what I told your friends out there. Don't leave LA."

I joined Crusher and Fanya outside the station and puffed out my breath as if I'd been holding it for hours. "Can you believe it? He said I had motive to hurt Hadas and told me not to leave LA."

"You hurt Hadas? God forbid!" Fanya leaned over and rested her hand on my shoulder while studying my face. "But he does have a point, Martha. I mean, all three of us know you didn't do anything to Hadas. But the police might see it differently. Am I right, Yossi?"

He grunted. "Maybe."

On the walk back to the Honda, I called Giselle and explained the situation. "Can we stay at your place tonight? Noah told us CSU would probably let us back in the house tomorrow."

"Of course, Sissy. Anyway, I'm dying to meet Yossi's sister. What's she like?"

"Delightful. You'll see for yourself soon."

"Great. I'll have Aria cook dinner. Unless Yossi's sister only eats kosher." Aria was Giselle's live-in Guatemalan housekeeper.

I was proud of all my Catholic half sister had learned about Judaism while maintaining steadfast in her own faith. "Fanya's a vegetarian, G. I don't think you have to worry about kashrut. We can stop on our way to your house and grab two veggie pizzas. If you prepare a salad, I think we'll be fine."

"Sold!"

We paid for two pizzas from Bucca Di Beppo and made our way over the Sepulveda Pass to Giselle's house in the Pacific Palisades. Fanya gasped when we turned left on Napoli Drive and pulled into the driveway of a massive two-story French chateau-style home with gray stucco and a copper mansard roof. Dozens of lavender bushes filled the front yard, sending fragrant blue clusters on long, delicate stems.

As we got out of the car, she said, "Oy vav oy! Your half sister is in the top two percent?"

I smiled at her reaction. She seemed genuinely awed in the face of such ostentation. "Actually, Giselle's probably in the top one percent. But she's down-to-earth and very generous. Plus, she's anxious to meet you. Let's go inside before the pizza gets cold."

Giselle greeted me with a brief kiss on the cheek and shoved me aside. Fanya stood right behind me. She was the one my sister wanted to meet. "Wow! I wondered if you'd be tall like your brother, and you are. Not as tall, but well above the average height for women. Thankfully you don't look a thing like him. If you had his build and a beard, you'd be a lot less attractive." She laughed at her own joke, but Fanya stared. Giselle rolled on, blissfully unaware of the confusion she stirred in her guest. "Are you hungry? Come in."

Giselle ushered us into the dining room, where Fanya's gaze landed on three portraits of the same woman: one as a naïve eighteen-year-old, one as a young mother in her twenties, and one in her forties. "Are those paintings original?"

Giselle glanced at me. "Yes. Our father, Martha's and mine, painted these. He was a famous portrait artist before he disappeared." There was much more to the story, and someday I'd tell it to Fanya. But not tonight.

A cheerful red-and-mustard-yellow jacquard cloth covered the dining room table. Stripes woven with acorns defined the borders, while pears, apples, and birds were woven into the middle. Only four places were set.

"Where's Harold?" Crusher asked.

Harold Zimmerman, Giselle's fiancé, was the CFO of Eagan Oil, the company she owned.

"He flew to Dallas for a couple of days."

"I love your home," Fanya said. "You've managed to

make a large space feel cozy. Your use of the primary colors is very French country. But have you considered having plain white walls is a bit too safe? What if you put up a French-themed paper? You could go with a traditional toile or do flowers, landscapes, even a mural on the big wall where those three pictures are. Of course, I'd have to cover the texture that's presently on your walls. It's too bumpy to hang a decent paper."

"Wallpaper?" Giselle burst into laughter. "These walls were hand-plastered by the famous Boris Budinoffski. I flew him and his helper Dyann all the way from London in my private jet because I wanted a handcrafted texture on these walls. Budinoffski's the best. There's no way I'd cover his work. That would be like painting over the Mona Lisa because you've run out of canvas."

Between the four of us, we managed to eat one-and-a-half vegetarian pizzas. We also went through two bottles of chilled pinot grigio. At ten, I pushed my chair slightly away from the table. "This has been an exhausting day, G. I need to crash."

"Of course, Sissy. Let me show you all to your rooms."

Fanya cleared her throat. "The police wouldn't let me go inside the bedroom to retrieve a change of clothes for tomorrow. I'm forced to wash what I'm wearing and hope it dries overnight. I hate to impose, but do you have a bathrobe I can borrow? Martha's was way too small for me."

"Hmmm." Giselle studied my statuesque future in-law. "Harold has one I think will fit. Give your clothes to me and I'll have Aria wash and dry them." She pointed to the artfully ripped-at-the-knee jeans Fanya wore. "Is it safe to wash your pants? Won't they unravel more being tossed around in the washer and dryer? Forgive me for not knowing this, but I thought this style of torn jeans was strictly for schoolgirls."

Fanya tilted her head. "Are you saying I'm too old to wear these jeans?"

"Oh, of course not. I mean, if you feel like a teenager, well, good for you."

I could tell by Fanya's expression Giselle had finally begun to annoy her.

"I'd be grateful if you fetch the robe and point me to the washer and dryer. I'll do my own things. I wouldn't dream of asking anyone else. And no, the pants don't ravel or fray in the wash."

Giselle shrugged. "Suit yourself."

At ten-thirty, Crusher and I climbed into a king-sized bed and met in the middle.

"Yossi," I yawned and snuggled close to him. "Where do you think Hadas is right now? Do you think she's still alive?"

"Hard to say. They'll examine her business and personal affairs. Like, did anyone else in her life know she was traveling to LA? They'll also check her credit cards, bank statements, and phone records for any activity up to the time she disappeared."

"Even though she's trying to steal you away, I hope she's okay. I feel guilty for wishing her harm."

I closed my eyes and began to doze, my mind slipping in and out of that nimble place in between sleep and wakefulness. I replayed the scene where Hadas complained of a headache and couldn't go with us. Suddenly, I opened my eyes and shook Crusher awake.

"Oh my God, Yossi. I totally forgot about this. I know

Hadas begged off the picnic because of a headache. But right before we left, she received a phone call. What if the call is connected to her disappearance?"

"The police will check her phone records. It's routine."

"Yes, but I don't want the police to think I deliberately hid information. The detective taking my statement said I had a motive to kill her. I don't want to give them even the smallest reason to suspect me."

"You'll be okay." He muttered "good night" as he turned on his left side and seconds later began to softly snore.

I slid out of bed and padded across the room to the dresser, taking care not to wake him. I unplugged my phone from the charger and tiptoed outside our bedroom through the hallway to the living room. All the lights were extinguished for the night, except one. A small lamp with a Tiffany stained glass shade cast a pool of golden light on an end table. The house was silent except for the faint sound of the clothes dryer two rooms away. I plopped on the chair next to the lamp and called Beavers.

Beavers's voice was sleepy and gravelly. "What is it now, Martha? Did your missing friend show up?"

I told him about the phone call Hadas received. "I wasn't trying to hide anything, Arlo. I would've said something in my official statement, but I only now remembered. I want it on record that I'm cooperating fully with the police. Hadas's phone records should tell you who called her at eleven this morning."

"I'm one lucky SOB."

"What?"

"It's not every cop who has someone like you to remind them of standard police procedure. I mean, who knows how much time it would've taken me to remember to check her phone? I don't know how I'd solve anything without your special insights, Martha. It's been a pleasure speaking to you late at night. It evokes such nice, warm memories. Good night."

Beavers ended the call.

Was he flirting with me?

I tiptoed back through the hall to the bedroom and slipped back into bed without waking Crusher. I tossed and turned for another half hour until I finally fell asleep.

CHAPTER 6

I woke Monday morning while the sky was still black and Crusher snored softly beside me. I moved to the en suite bathroom and quietly closed the door. Hot water in the walk-in shower cascaded over my neck and back, soothing my sore muscles. By the time I dressed, the first morning light had turned the sky from black to gray. I left him still snoring while I made my way toward the smell of fresh coffee, coming from the other end of the house.

Aria, the Guatemalan housekeeper, smiled as I entered the kitchen. "Good morning, missus. I get you coffee?" Her dark eyes twinkled, and a warm smile creased her young face.

I guessed from the smooth skin on her arms and hands and neck that she hadn't yet reached her forties. She wore a simple blue cotton dress and her long, black hair hung in a careful braid down her back.

I moved toward the coffeepot, where Aria had laid out delicate porcelain cups and saucers, cream, and sugar. "I'll help myself." I inhaled deeply. "Something in the oven sure smells good!"

"Five more minutes, missus. *Galletas con mantequilla.* Hot biscuits with butter."

"Great!" I took my coffee to the living room sofa and sat with my feet tucked under me, staring out of the tall windows overlooking the greens of the Riviera Golf Course a little way beyond the backyard. After a good night's sleep and hot shower, I was ready to face the task of going back to my house and cleaning the mess Hadas's kidnappers made.

What could've happened to Hadas? How did someone manage to get inside my house and chloroform her, ransack the bedroom, and spirit her away? Did she know them? Did she let them in the house? If the intruders didn't find what they were after, would they come back?

I'd already decided there must've been more than one person involved to be able to take an unconscious woman from the house and put her in a vehicle. Maybe one of my neighbors saw something. Even if the police already went door-to-door, I'd canvass the neighborhood.

Yesterday's red-and-yellow tablecloth in the dining room had been replaced with a starched and ironed white linen cloth. Aria brought the silver coffee service to the dining room and set the table with four places. Then she brought out a large plate with a pile of hot, steaming biscuits. "For you, missus." She added dishes of whipped butter and boysenberry jam.

I wasted no time relocating myself to a chair nearest the goodies. "Wow. Thank you!" I cut a hot biscuit in half and spread it with soft yellow butter that melted almost immediately. I smeared a generous spoonful of sweet, dark jam on top of the buttered halves. A few minutes later, I repeated the process with another biscuit.

When I swallowed the last bite of my second biscuit, Fanya entered the room, dressed in yesterday's clean clothes, knees poking through the shredded jeans. Her long, chestnut hair hung without restraint in waves around her face. She poured a cup of coffee and helped herself to one of Aria's *galletas*. "Mmm. This is delicious."

"How'd you sleep last night?"

She sighed. "Not very well. I kept thinking about Hadas and wondering who wanted to hurt her and why."

"And did you discover anything?"

Fanya shook her head, hair sweeping her shoulders.

I urged her on. "Even if something seems insignificant, it could lead to a major clue. At this point, between you, me, and your brother, you're the one who knew her best."

"Did I hear someone talk about me?" Crusher's heavy boots echoed on the wooden floor as he entered the dining room. He walked over to his sister, kissed her forehead, and ruffled the top of her head.

"Stop it!" Fanya batted his hand away and sighed. "I'll never be a grown-up in his eyes. I'll always be the kid sister!"

Crusher chuckled and bent to kiss my lips. "Morning."

"Good morning. We were talking about Hadas."

He poured a cup of coffee. "Not surprised. Come to any conclusions? Insights?"

I shrugged. "Not yet. But I'm going to ask around. Maybe one of the neighbors saw something."

Giselle padded into the dining room on softly slippered feet, wearing a pink silk dressing gown tied around the waist. She greeted us with a cheerful smile. "Good morning, everyone. I see Aria has already started you off with a little prebreakfast." She helped herself to the last cup of coffee in the pot. "If everyone is up for it, I'll ask her to make a frittata with mushrooms and veggies."

"Count me in." Crusher took a giant bite out of a biscuit and washed it down with a gulp of coffee.

Giselle disappeared for a moment to the kitchen and returned. "Aria's amazing. I didn't have to tell her anything. A frittata is already baking in the oven. She says it'll be ready in fifteen minutes." Then she checked out Fanya and smiled. "I'm glad to see you managed to launder your clothes last night. So," she scanned our faces. "What is everyone planning for today?"

"I'm going to canvass my neighbors," I said.

Giselle scrunched her forehead. "Do you know who would want to hurt Hadas?"

"That's the problem, G." I licked a drop of boysenberry jam from where it spilled on my finger. "We don't really know enough about her to dig into her personal life. Not yet, anyway."

"I thought you two were friends, Fanya." Giselle worried the corner of her lip. "Surely you must have an idea about who could've come after her. Was she wealthy? Do you think the kidnappers took her for ransom?"

Aria appeared in the dining room with a new pot of coffee.

Fanya lifted her cup for a refill. "I don't know. Wouldn't they have contacted us already?"

"Maybe you're on to something," I said. "I mean, let's take another look at this. If someone wanted to kill Hadas, they could've done it right there in the house. But they didn't. They drugged her with chloroform, probably to keep her from resisting, and took her away. Which tells me they want her alive. At least for a while."

"Yeah, but aside from me," Giselle said, "none of you has the kind of money a ransomer would demand."

"Maybe she's being held for something other than money. I mean, they ransacked the bedroom looking for something. If they found whatever it was, they could've left her behind, either alive or dead. But they abducted her, which suggests to me that if they didn't find what they wanted, they would try to force her to give it up. Of course, as soon as she gives them what they want, they're going to have to kill her. She could ID them."

Everyone at the table grew hushed. The silence was broken when Aria appeared with plates of frittata, an eggy omelet baked with onions, mushrooms, spinach, and tomatoes topped with dollops of sour cream.

As I enjoyed the subtle flavors of the food, I wondered if Hadas was still alive, would she be hungry? I felt almost guilty for diving into our breakfast with such gusto. Almost guilty, but not really. Although I didn't wish her any harm, I didn't want Hadas back in our lives. Why couldn't she just give Crusher a divorce and get on with it? Was there something else behind her coming to California? Was there a hidden reason she needed Crusher's help?

Out of courtesy to the others, I'd put my cell phone on vibrate, which it was now doing in the pocket of my jeans. I looked at the caller. *Beavers!* I excused myself from the table and moved to the living room to talk. "Hello, Arlo. Have you found her?"

"No. I called to tell you CSU has finished with your house. You can go back inside."

"Did you find anything useful you can tell us about?"

"No."

"*No* you found nothing useful or *no* you're not telling?"

"Right."

I clenched my teeth. "God, I hate when you get this way. A crime was committed in my house and I want to know what you are doing about it. I have a right to know."

"I'll only give details to her next of kin. As far as I know, that would be Yosef Levy. Am I correct?"

"Are you saying you will only talk to Yossi?"

"Yosef Levy is her *husband* of thirty years, right?" I could tell by the lilt in his voice he was enjoying every bit of this conversation.

"Only technically. But not for real."

"Well, technically, he is the one I'll talk to."

"Yet you called me, not him."

"You're the homeowner. I called to let you know I'm releasing your home back to you. By the way, I enjoyed our little chat last night. We must do it again sometime."

I ignored his little flirtation. "Tell me this. Have you gone door-to-door in the neighborhood to find out if anyone saw anything yesterday?"

"There you go again, Martha. Rescuing me from my own ignorance. Thanks for the tip."

"Never mind, Arlo. I'll get my answers another way."

"You wouldn't be the Martha everyone knows and loves if you didn't try. But I should warn you. From the looks of things, the ones who abducted Mrs. Levy yesterday meant business. Don't start poking around. You'll be way out of your depth."

I returned to the dining room and resumed eating.

"Arlo Beavers called to tell me we can go back to the house."

"Did they find anything?" Giselle asked.

"He says he'll only discuss the details of the case with her next of kin."

"Who's that?" My sister seemed puzzled.

I sighed and jerked my thumb toward Crusher. "Her husband of more than thirty years."

Crusher rolled his eyes.

Fanya reached for the dish of jam and accidentally knocked over the saltshaker, spilling a small amount onto the table. Her eyes grew wide. "Oh no. Bad luck." She pinched some of the spilled granules with the fingers of her right hand and threw them over her left shoulder. *"Hamsa, hamsa, hamsa."* She murmured a chant against the evil eye.

I cleared my throat. "You should call Beavers, Yossi. He said he will only talk to you."

"He's playing some kind of manipulation game. I'll wait for him to call me."

Crap! "I knew this would turn into a pissing contest between you two. What's more important here? Finding Hadas or being the alpha male?"

"Hmmm. Hard choice."

Fanya slapped her brother's shoulder. "Not funny! Martha's right. You need to take the high road and ignore his game. If Hadas is in danger, you're not doing her any favors by turning her rescue into some kind of macho sporting event."

I wiped my mouth with the white cloth napkin and placed it on the table next to my empty plate. "We didn't have time to take inventory before the police barred us from the house. I want to go back and see if anything of ours is missing. I also want to talk to the neighbors before any more time passes. Memory fades with time. It doesn't become sharper."

"Sounds like a plan, Sissy. Do you need some help? I'll get dressed and drive to your place."

"I appreciate the offer, G. I know how you hate coming to the Valley. But before we start questioning people, I want to check for missing items in my house. I'll call and let you know when I'll be ready to walk the neighborhood."

The traffic headed north on the 405 Freeway was unusually light and the three of us reached my house in Encino in forty-five minutes. I inserted the key to the front door and discovered it was already unlocked. "Oh great!" I frowned. "The police forgot to lock the door when they left. I'm going to give Arlo heck for this."

"Wait!" Crusher held out his arm to prevent us from going inside. He reached into the holster strapped to his ankle and pulled out a gun. As an agent for the ATF, he carried a weapon, even when off duty. "Let me make sure no one has broken in. Step back."

I grabbed Fanya's hand and pulled her away from the front door. Crusher poked his head inside long enough to look around, then stepped through the front door into the house. "Federal agent!"

We heard the door off the laundry room slam as someone bolted from the house. My property sat on a corner, so I ran across the front lawn to the side of the house in time to see a figure dressed in a black hoodie jump over the fence into a black Jeep Cherokee idling next to the sidewalk. The driver didn't wait for his passenger to close the car door before speeding off. The whole thing happened too fast, and I only managed to see part of the license plate: 8BZN.

Crusher barreled out the front door and around the corner, but he was too late to stop the getaway. "Damn! Did you get a look at the perp? The car?"

"Only a partial on the plate."

Fanya looked at me curiously. "You sound like a law enforcement pro."

"Yeah, kind of. Except I'm not official, of course. But I do have a lot of experience."

Crusher called 911. Five minutes later a black-and-white appeared, with blue and red lights flashing on the roof.

One of the uniforms approached our little group of three. "You called in a burglary?" Crusher nodded and showed the cop his ATF badge.

Ten minutes later, Beavers parked in front of the house. "I heard. Have you been inside yet? Do you know if anything is missing?"

Crusher's response was a terse "Negative."

"Have you secured the house?"

Crusher nodded.

Beavers called someone at the station and asked them to run the partial plate of the black Jeep Cherokee. He ended the call and inclined his head to the door. "Let's go inside and take a look around." He instructed the uniforms to search the outside of the house, including the backyard, while we led the way into yet another crime scene.

CHAPTER 7

As I stepped through my front door and scanned the inside of the house, my stomach dropped to my knees. Books had been flung to the floor from the tall bookcase in the living room.

Fanya gasped. "Oy! *Achalaria* on them!" She cursed them with a case of cholera.

I could barely speak with a mouth made dry by shock. "Did your people do this?"

Beavers's voice was gentle. "You know that's not how we work, Martha. CSU finished at three this morning. Your house must've been vandalized after they left. My guess is the same people who abducted Mrs. Levy came back to finish their search. We can check the rest of the house. Try not to touch anything."

Fanya covered her mouth with her hands. "Is it even

safe to be here?" She looked at her brother with wide eyes.

"As long as you're with me, you're safe, Fan." Crusher playfully reached for the top of his sister's head.

"Don't!" Fanya pushed his arm away before he could ruffle her hair.

Beavers answered his phone. He listened and then turned to me. "We got a match to the partial plates you saw on the getaway car. Unfortunately, they belong to a black Jeep Cherokee reported stolen yesterday."

"What does that mean?" I couldn't stop wringing my hands.

"It means since you caught them in the act, they'll probably ditch the car and torch it to get rid of any trace evidence leading back to them."

Crusher grabbed my worried hands in his and held fast. "Someone was determined to get something they thought was hidden in this house."

Beavers peered at me with concern. "Do you think you're ready to look at the rest of the house now?"

I swallowed hard. "Let's get it over with."

We walked past the mess in the living room and through the hallway.

I heard a faint meow. "Did you hear that?" I squeezed Crusher's hand and stopped. "Bumper."

My fluffy orange tabby must've heard my voice because he meowed again, only louder. "Sounds like it's coming from the linen cupboard." Generous built-in cabinets for sheets and towels lined my hallway. I began pulling out drawers and opening the cupboard doors. We found Bumper sitting on a pile of blue towels. I lifted him out and held him in my arms. He immediately began to purr. I scratched under his chin and buried my face in his silky fur. "How in the world did you get in there?"

Crusher reached over and stroked his back. "Perps probably stuck him there to get him out of the way. He's lucky. One of them must've been a cat lover."

Beavers started moving toward my sewing room. "I'm glad the cat's safe, but we need to press on."

I stared at the floor, reluctant to look, afraid all my beautiful fabrics and sewing notions had been pitched like the books in the living room today.

Beavers indicated I should enter the room. "Is anything missing?"

With a sigh of great relief, I scanned my sewing room. Nothing seemed disturbed. My fabrics sat folded neatly on the shelves, separated by color. My Bernina sewing machine rested on the sewing table. Even the scissors and sharp rotary cutter—potential weapons—lay undisturbed on the cutting mat. "Thank goodness they didn't have time to toss this room. It would take me the better part of a day to put it back together. I don't think anything is missing in here."

Fanya whistled slowly. "So many fabrics! You should live to use them all, *keinehora*." She used the Yiddish expression meaning *no evil eye* said to ward off any jealousy or bad luck. "I'm in love with your quilts. I'd like to make one. Can you teach me how?"

Nothing makes a quilter's heart sing more than finding someone new to welcome into the sisterhood. "Yes! As a matter of fact, tomorrow is quilty Tuesday. You'll get to meet my friends."

While Fanya and I spoke, Beavers took a couple of pictures of the room with his smartphone. "Okay. Let's move on." He walked toward the bedroom I shared with Crusher. "What about your bedroom?"

We stared at the queen-sized bed neatly covered the day before with an Ohio Star quilt.

"Looks like nothing's been touched in here." Beavers squinted his eyes and gave me a look saying, *I clearly remember when you once welcomed me onto that bed.*

Warmth rose from my chest to my cheeks, and I avoided looking at either man. I scanned the bedroom before stepping inside. "Everything looks normal." I checked my jewelry box. "Nothing's gone."

Crusher opened his gun safe, a strongbox with a heavy lock. "Nothing's missing here, either."

The guest room was the last room to check. Fanya seemed reluctant to move across the hall to yesterday's crime scene.

I took her hand. "It's okay. I'll go in with you."

The room looked the same as it did the day before. Clothes were strewn all over, where the bad guys had thrown them. Fingerprint dust from the good guys covered most of the smooth surfaces of both the bedroom and the bathroom. I peeked in the bathroom, relieved to see CSU had taken the cloth soaked in chloroform.

Fanya took a small plastic sandwich baggie from her pocket filled with salt and poured some into the four corners of the bedroom and the four corners of the bathroom, all while reciting the protective phrase *keinehora, keinehora*.

Beavers, the only Gentile in the room, looked at me with confusion. "What is she doing?"

"Exorcising demons," said Crusher. "They don't like salt."

I took a deep breath and puffed it out again. "I guess we should pick everything up."

"On one condition," Beavers said. "CSU will return today to check for new fingerprints. Don't touch anything else. Just the clothes. Keep your fingers off any hard surfaces."

With Beavers watching, I gathered the pieces on the floor while Fanya carefully sorted and folded them. When we finished, her face carried a puzzled look. "I couldn't tell yesterday because of the mess, but these are all my clothes. There's nothing from Hadas in this pile."

"I don't see any laptops, tablets, or smartphones. Did Mrs. Levy bring any electronics?" Beavers asked.

Fanya swiveled her head as she scrutinized the room. "Hadas brought a laptop and cell phone. I don't see either of them here."

Beavers moved toward the bathroom. "What about in here?"

Fanya brushed past him and briefly scanned the toiletries on the bathroom counter. "All these are mine. Thank goodness they didn't take my little bottles of Ayurvedic oils."

"Oils?" We all spoke at once.

"Oh, yes. They're an important part of natural medicine developed by the Hindus. I can't do without them. I brought only the basics on this trip: lavender for stress, bergamot and grapefruit for sore muscles and female things, and frankincense for when I meditate."

The guest room was now tidy enough to take a closer look at what might have been taken. I walked slowly around the room, looking for clues, and crossed my arms to keep from touching anything. "I can't shake the feeling something else should be here, but I don't know what."

Beavers announced, "I've requested another sweep for fingerprints. They shouldn't take more than an hour or two. We'll stay until they come. Then we need to leave them to their job. I'll let you know when they're finished. Probably by this evening."

We headed back toward the living room. Bumper stayed so close to my feet that I stumbled over him and almost fell. Crusher caught me and kept me upright while I hung onto his arm and regained my feet. An unwelcomed vision popped into my head of Hadas hanging onto Crusher's arm as he wheeled their suitcases to the guest bedroom on Saturday.

I stopped in the middle of the hallway. "Of course!"

Three curious faces stared at me.

"What?" Beavers asked.

"I've been struggling to remember. I know what's missing."

He nodded. "Go ahead."

"One suitcase!"

Crusher asked, "What did you and Hadas do with your luggage, Fan?"

She gasped and tapped her fingers lightly on her mouth. "Oy. You're right. We kept them on the bench at the foot of the bed."

"Arlo, could you check with CSU . . ."

He was already speaking on the phone. "You sure? Right. Thanks." He ended the call. "I'm reluctant to admit this, but it looks like you hit on something, Martha. CSU says they only saw one piece of luggage."

Fanya shivered slightly. "So those men took Hadas, along with her suitcase, all her clothes and electronics? Oy, *Gottenyu!*" She went into a paroxysm of spitting on the evil eye.

Crusher put a comforting arm around his sister's shoulders. "We can safely assume they thought something was hidden in her suitcase. When they didn't find it, they came back for a second look."

"But why would they look through my stuff? I don't own anything professional thieves would want."

"Well," I said, "maybe they didn't know which was yours and which was hers, so they took everything."

"Hadas could've told them."

"Not if she were unconscious," I said. *Or dead.*

While we sat in the living room waiting for the fingerprint guys, I called Giselle and told her we were postponing our house-to-house. Crusher and Beavers remained silent, each making a point not to look at the other. Fanya broke away from our little group. I could hear her banishing the demons as she salted the corners of every room in the house.

CHAPTER 8

"Martha." Crusher gently shook my shoulder. "Time to rise and shine."

I groaned and snuggled deeper under the duvet.

"It's eight in the morning, babe."

"Go away," I mumbled.

"Isn't Tuesday your quilting day?"

I reluctantly opened my eyes and yawned. "Right. Thanks." My whole body ached from the cleaning we did the evening before. I moaned as I forced myself to move. My neck and shoulders hurt from scrubbing off fingerprint dust. My hips and back throbbed from bending over a million times to retrieve the books and return them to their shelves in the living room. Even the bottoms of my feet hurt as I shuffled to the bathroom and headed for my meds.

Fifteen minutes later I was dressed and in the kitchen pouring coffee.

Crusher took one last gulp from his cup and kissed me. "Gotta go now. Have fun today." He reached for the top of Fanya's head but pulled his hand back. "Bye, sis."

Fanya sat at the kitchen table and slowly paged through an *American Patchwork and Quilting* magazine. One of a dozen such publications on the market.

She smiled at me. "Good morning, sleepyhead. I didn't know quilting was this popular!" She rattled the magazine at me for emphasis.

"You're too young to remember the American bicentennial in 1976, but it was a big deal. Quilting and other American crafts enjoyed a revival. Since then, the demand for beautiful cotton prints, sewing notions, and specialized quilting machines grew into a huge multibillion-dollar marketplace. And as the marketplace grew, so did the number of quilters. And as the number of quilters grew, so did their appetite for inspiration and information. Hence the books and magazines, like the one you're holding."

"I see a lot of notions and stuff advertised here." She flipped the magazine to show me a picture of some major equipment. "What's a longarm machine?"

I sat next to her and leaned over to read the full-page ad. "Those are seriously commercial quilting machines. The machines can function in two ways. The operator can program in a design and walk away, knowing the quilt in the frame will be finished in a few hours. Or she can guide the machine with her own hands to quilt a custom design."

"If I took up quilting, I'd want one of these."

"Are you sure? Some of those longarm machines can cost thirty-five thousand dollars."

Fanya's mouth fell open. "For a *sewing* machine?"

I laughed. "And it isn't even made by Rolls-Royce. Of course, you can buy one for much less. Maybe a thousand dollars. Or you can quilt by hand like I do. There's a difference in the *hand* of a quilt, the way a quilt or piece of cloth feels when you hold it. To me, machine-stitched quilts feel a bit stiffer. But goodness knows a skillful longarm machine operator can produce beautiful quilting patterns. Anyway, I'm glad you're looking at my mags. Have you seen anything to inspire you?" I sipped my coffee.

"These are all beautiful, Martha. They all inspire me. How do you decide between every possibility?"

"How does anyone choose which wallpaper to hang? As a paper installer, you must see thousands of patterns and prints in the course of your work. How do your clients decide which ones to use?"

"They usually want a particular color and-or style, so I show them sample books from specific manufacturers. I don't waste their time looking at designs that don't meet their criteria."

"Designing quilts isn't much different. Nowadays, if you visit a quilt store, you'll find a kaleidoscope of hues and prints to choose from. A finished quilt is something new that is greater than the sum of its parts."

"What do you think about this one?" Fanya pointed to a photo of an Ohio Star quilt. "I could see this done in many different colors."

"Ohio Star is a perfect block for beginners. I have one

of those on my bed right now. It's not too hard to construct. Especially for someone with your skills as an artisan. I think you're going to like our little group of quilters."

At ten sharp, the others began to arrive. Jazz Fletcher, a successful menswear designer and business owner came with his Maltese Zsa Zsa Galore. The fifty-something Jazz wore a pink linen shirt with a mandarin collar and tan linen trousers with pleats in front. As usual, he dressed Zsa Zsa in a matching pinafore of pink organza. I introduced him to Fanya and a smile lit his face.

"So you're Yossi's sister? A pleasure to meet you."

Giselle breezed in carrying an aqua-blue leather tote bag and a pink cardboard box tied with white string. "Chocolate éclairs from Benesch." The wind tousled her normally perfectly coiffed hair. Hands full of stuff, she jerked her head to the side, trying to coax a stray lock of auburn off her face.

Lucy Mondello, my best friend, came in next with her across-the-street neighbor Birdie Watson, also my friend. Lucy was in her sixties, with orange hair, courtesy of L'Oréal, and carefully drawn eyebrows. She was nearly six feet tall and walked like a runway model in black-and-white houndstooth check slacks and a black cashmere pullover.

In contrast, Birdie was in her seventies and dressed in denim overalls, a white T-shirt, and Birkenstock sandals. Her long, white hair featured a turquoise streak and a purple streak undulating in and out of the braid hanging down her back.

Lucy, Birdie, and I were the original members of the Tuesday Morning Quilters, meeting every week for two decades. Then we welcomed Jazz into our midst and most recently, Giselle.

After introducing Fanya, I put the éclairs on a plate, served coffee, and settled in the living room for a morning of quilting and noshing.

Lucy gave Fanya a knowing smile. "It's nice to meet another woman as tall as I am."

As I threaded my needle to help Lucy piece her blocks, Fanya said, "Martha, you need to put some thread in your mouth to chew on."

"Did I hear you right? Chew on some thread?"

Everyone stopped what they were doing to listen.

She nodded vigorously and looked at the others in the group. "Oh, yes. You all should do that to make sure you don't accidentally sew up your wits."

Giselle wrinkled her forehead. "Sew up your wits? What does that even mean?"

Fanya seemed unfazed. "Some say it's an old *bubbe meiser* to chew on a piece of thread while you're sewing, but I know for a fact a tailor in our neighborhood was taken to a mental hospital because he forgot to chew!"

"Whoa." Jazz broke off some thread from his spool of green thread and put it in his mouth. Then he broke off four other pieces and handed them to each of us. "Better not to take any chances."

I reluctantly accepted the thread. "My uncle Isaac was a tailor. I'll have to ask him if he ever chewed on thread."

"Listen up, everyone." Giselle raised her voice for attention. "We have two big things to tell you. One happy, one bad. Which should I start with?"

"Give us the good news first, hon." Lucy's jaw muscles worked as she chewed her piece of green thread. "I always like to be fortified by the good news before hearing the bad."

"Okay. So, first of all, Martha told Yossi at dinner on Friday night she's ready to get married."

"What?" "When?" Birdie and Lucy spoke at the same time.

"For real?" Jazz asked.

Everyone began speaking at once. Jazz looked at me over the rims of his magnifying eyeglasses with a big smile. "Our little Martha? It's about time! *Mozzle tov*!" he said in a near approximation of the Hebrew words of congratulations. "I'll make your wedding dress. I might even make matching outfits for all of us. We can be your bridesmaids and bridesman. Where's the ceremony going to be?"

"At my house, where Quincy was married." Giselle had hosted the wedding of Quincy and Noah Kaplan at Giselle's late grandparents' lavish estate in Beverly Hills. The Eagan estate, as it was known, could accommodate five hundred guests. Quincy and Noah didn't have even a fraction of that many guests. My wedding would be even smaller. A lot smaller.

Birdie delicately nibbled on the thread. "I was sorry to miss Quincy's wedding. Lucy's description of the whole event was most intriguing. I hear your parents' estate is gorgeous, Giselle dear. Like a museum. This is one wedding I won't miss." She beamed at me. "Martha dear, will you have a color theme?"

"I haven't actually thought very far ahead. White dresses and color themes all seem inappropriate for a divorcée in her fifties. Yossi and I will be married by a rabbi, and we'll ask Uncle Isaac to help officiate. I'll have to think about what I want to wear."

Of course, the question of a wedding would be moot if we failed to find Hadas and get a legal divorce.

Lucy reached for an éclair. "You said two pieces of news, good and bad. What's the bad piece?"

Giselle gave me a look saying, *You tell them*.

CHAPTER 9

I broke the shocking news to my friends about Crusher being married and Hadas being missing.

Birdie stopped sewing and grabbed the end of her long, white braid. "What do you know about her, Martha? Why was she abducted?"

"We don't know. But I don't trust Hadas one little bit. Not after she announced she wanted to take Yossi back to New York and resume their married life." I filled the group in on what had happened since Fanya and Hadas's arrival the previous Saturday evening. "So far, that's all we know."

Lucy frowned. "Correct me if I'm wrong, hon. Yossi was married about thirty years ago and never told you?"

"Well, he thought the marriage legally ended back then when he signed the papers for an annulment. He only recently discovered the documents were never filed."

"Who dropped the ball?"

"Hadas. Turns out she used the marriage as a convenient excuse to stay single and have a career. She devoted herself to running her father's *shmata* business."

"Wait," Fanya said. "In Hadas's defense, she genuinely has feelings for my brother. She's not as mercenary as you're making her out to be. I think she's lonely."

Jazz waved a dismissive hand. "Well, let her be lonely with someone else's fiancé."

Too distracted to work on my own quilt, I helped Lucy stitch together the curves of four-inch square Robbing Peter to Pay Paul blocks. Each block featured a quarter circle of contrasting fabric in the corner. The quarter circle had a convex curve and the background square had a matching concave curve. The secret to creating a curved seam was to clip the edge of the inner curve so it would bend enough to fit around the outer curve.

Lucy knotted a new length of thread. "Let me get this straight. You're saying your ex, Detective Arlo Beavers, is in charge of finding your fiancé Yossi's wife of thirty years so Yossi can get a divorce and marry you?"

Jazz shoved Fanya's arm with his elbow and snorted. "This is better than the Byzantine twists in the reality show *Angry Housewives of Van Nuys*! Have you seen it?"

"I live in the big apple. New Yorkers don't know from Van Nuys."

"Oh dear." Birdie tugged her braid. "If finding Hadas alive is the goal, don't you think Arlo has a conflict of interest? He may still have feelings for you, Martha. Until

Arlo finds Hadas, Yossi won't be free to marry you. At least not for another seven years. Isn't that how long you have to wait to declare someone legally dead?"

"First of all, I doubt Arlo has 'feelings' for me anymore. However, I did suggest to him that he recuse himself because of our history. But he insisted on leading the investigation."

Giselle cleared her throat. "Well, we're doing some investigating of our own. I asked Shadow to see what he could find out about Hadas and the Uhrman Company."

"Giselle . . ." I said in a warning voice. "Do you think that's wise?"

"Who's Shadow?" Fanya looked around the circle of faces.

"He's a hacker Giselle keeps in her employ," I said.

She corrected me. "A *former* hacker, Sissy. Now he's my IT guy and head of research. He sometimes stumbles across useful information not readily available online."

"Sounds like a hacker to me," I said.

Giselle sniffed. "I don't ask. He doesn't tell."

"Did he find anything useful?" Fanya asked.

Giselle sat a little straighter and cleared her throat. I knew my sister well enough to know she was about to say something juicy. "A year ago, the Uhrman Company dipped in the red because of large cash withdrawals. About six months ago, the situation reversed. Uhrman began operating in the black again. Big money comes and goes on a regular basis."

An alarm went off in my head. "Six months you say? Hadas's brother Ze'ev Uhrman was killed by a hit-and-run driver six months ago."

Fanya paled and gasped. "Are you suggesting the two things are connected?"

"Think about it. The business is failing, largely because it was bleeding cash every month. Then Ze'ev dies, and suddenly the business is thriving again. What if his death wasn't an accident? What if it was deliberate?"

Birdie tugged her braid. "Murdered?"

A high squeak of horror escaped Fanya's open mouth. "God forbid! *Pu, pu, pu. Has v'halilah* and three oy gevalts."

Giselle frowned. "What is she doing?"

"It's a precaution against the evil eye," I explained. "Anyway, I don't like coincidences. At the very least, I think his death is worth looking into."

Giselle stopped chewing her thread. "Speaking of investigations, Sissy. Weren't we going to go around and talk to your neighbors?"

"I'd be glad to help." Birdie said. "I've been watching a lot of British detective shows on Amazon Prime lately, and I've learned a few pointers about interviewing perps. Of course, the British system isn't exactly the same as ours. I noticed right off that their Miranda warning is different. Plus, they have solicitors and barristers, not plain lawyers. And their DAs are called 'silks.' And everyone wears those silly white wigs. They don't even try to hide their real hair. They just plop on the wig like a curly white hat and away they go."

"Are you calling Martha's neighbors 'perps?'" Jazz chuckled.

I sighed. "I thought I could canvass the neighbors today after we've finished sewing. It's not necessary for everyone to help, Birdie. Although, I appreciate the offer.

I'm only going to question my immediate neighbors. Chances are, people living farther down the street wouldn't have seen anything from that far away."

I'd also seek out the Eyes of Encino, our neighborhood watch that patrolled the streets at night. It was a long shot, but maybe one of them saw something in the early morning hours.

CHAPTER 10

At three in the afternoon, Lucy, Birdie, and Jazz said their goodbyes, but Giselle insisted on staying.

"Really, G, I can question the neighbors on my own. Don't you have an oil empire to run, or something?"

My sister gathered her sewing and stowed it in her new aqua-blue leather tote bag. "I won't intrude, Sissy. I'll record the interviews with my smartphone. No one will even notice me."

Like that would ever happen. My forty-something sister was beautiful in face and in body. Because she inherited an oil company to run, she was very wealthy and dressed like she'd just walked off the pages of *Vogue* magazine. With all her diamonds and expensive clothing, she'd not only be noticed, she'd be the focus of attention.

"No way. You can't record someone without their consent. The last thing I want to do is alienate my neighbors."

She rolled her eyes. "So how are you planning to take notes if someone tells you something important?"

"Okay. I get your point. You can bring a notepad and pen. But that's all."

"What about me?" Fanya stepped closer. "I want to come, too. I need to do something to find Hadas, besides sitting and waiting."

Our first stop was across the street to talk to Sonia Spiegelman Fuentes. She'd been Mick Jagger's girlfriend for five minutes back in her groovy days. Now, in her very early fifties, she'd recently married Hector Fuentes, Crusher's colleague in the ATF. Hector's street name was Malo, which meant "bad" in Spanish.

Don't ask.

Sonia painted her house a light turquoise and her front door purple. She believed the colors offered some kind of cosmic protection I never quite understood. Some of the neighbors were vocal in their disapproval of nontraditional colors until Malo moved in. One warning look coming from the Latino with a long black ponytail and tattoos on his face was enough to silence Sonia's critics.

She must've seen us coming because she opened the door before I could knock. "Martha. Giselle." She grinned and gestured for us to follow her inside. "How nice to see you both." She offered her hand to Fanya. "Hello. I'm Sonia Fuentes."

Fanya seemed fascinated by Sonia, the former hippie flower child with long graying hair and thick green eye shadow. She looked around the living room as we sat down. "Have you ever thought of putting up wallpaper? I install wall coverings for a living. I could show you something funky and psychedelic in an iridescent foil."

"Puhleez!" Giselle made a face.

Sonia formed an "O" with her mouth. "Oh my God. Iridescent? Can you show me something in a lime green?"

"I sure can."

"How much do you charge?"

"It goes by the number of rolls."

Giselle interrupted. "Are both of you crazy or merely having an attack of mutual bad taste? Why don't you hang a mirrored disco ball from the ceiling while you're at it?"

Sonia ignored her and reached for my hand and gave it a little squeeze. "I've been dying to ask. What's going on at your house?"

I told her about Hadas. "We've been waiting for the kidnappers to contact us, but so far they've been silent. Did you see anything?"

"We left the house to visit friends on Sunday around noon. I saw a blue SUV parked in front of your house but thought you were having company. The car was gone by the time we got back."

"Did the police ever question you?"

"Oh, yes. We didn't know anything was wrong until the cops came knocking at our door Sunday evening. I told them about the blue SUV. Then they came back the next day and asked about a black Jeep Cherokee. What's going on?"

"The forensic team worked in the house from Sunday afternoon until about three Monday morning. Sometime between the time the police left my house and the time we came back a few hours later, we found the house had been ransacked a second time."

"Whaaat?" Sonia's jaw dropped. "They came back again?"

"We're pretty sure it was the same people. We actually surprised them in the act, but they got away before Yossi could stop them. I only got a partial on the license plate. It was a stolen car. No help there." I could always count on Sonia, the neighborhood yenta, to collect stray bits of harmless gossip. "Have you talked to the other neighbors, by any chance?"

Sonia pursed her lips. "Um, not really. Hector and I have been pretty busy with DCFS lately, training to qualify as a resource family for foster care. The rules for becoming a foster parent changed recently. Hopefully this new system will keep people who have no business being around children from qualifying as providers." She fanned the air in front of her face. "Oh man. Don't get me started!"

I tried to steer her back on track. "What about the Eyes of Encino?" Years ago, Sonia organized a local group of retired military vets and others to patrol the streets in two-hour shifts at night. During the summer, when the air was balmy, they all wore yellow T-shirts with an eyeball logo printed on the back. "Do you know if the police questioned them?"

Sonia stood and walked to the kitchen to retrieve her smartphone. "I'll call Ron Wilson and ask. He keeps track of the patrol schedule and logbooks. You remember him from before, don't you?"

I'd worked with Ron briefly a few years ago when murder paid a visit to our neighborhood. "Sure I remember. The Eyes saved my life."

We decided to walk to Ron's house since it was on the next street over, not far away. The streets in our area were lined with mature trees, some of them over fifty years old. They provided leafy shade, especially in the heat of summer. However, the invasive roots of those lovely liquid ambers buckled the sidewalks, making them look like scattered decks of cards.

Fifteen minutes later, we knocked on a red front door. The tan doormat under our feet read *WELCOME* in black letters.

Ron's petite wife opened the door and smiled. "Hi, Sonia. He's waiting for you."

Ron Wilson was a veteran of Korea and Vietnam. Now, in his later years, he'd turned into a big teddy bear of a man with a head of short white hair resembling a large scrub brush. Suffering from severe mobility problems, Ron didn't rise from his adjustable chair to greet us. "Martha!" he boomed. "Trouble at your place again? We have to stop meeting this way." He laughed at his own joke.

I walked over to his recliner and gave him a peck on the cheek. Then I introduced Fanya and Giselle. "Can we see the logbook for Sunday night and early Monday morning?"

"Way ahead of you." He reached for a blue spiral notebook next to his chair and turned the pages to the most recent handwritten entries. "Okay. What do we have here? Hm. Oh yeah. Tony Di Arco took the two a.m. to four a.m. shift on Monday morning. He logged an LAPD van in front of your address at two-fifteen a.m., two-thirty, and again at two-forty-five. At three-fifteen a.m. he noted the van was gone." Ron looked up from the notebook. "There's nothing else."

"Well, what about the four a.m. to six a.m. shift?" I pointed to the logbook. "Anything?"

Ron shook his head until his jowls waggled. "Nope. That's all she wrote."

Darn! I hoped to discover a clue in the logbook. The kidnappers knew what they were doing. If they'd returned in the wee hours of Monday morning, they'd have to turn on lights to search the house. A light might've aroused the curiosity of any witness who happened to be awake then. But arriving after daybreak helped them appear to be visitors or workers parking on the street. By being bold enough to be seen, they became invisible.

"Thanks for your help, Ron. I guess we'll have to interview the neighbors individually. Can you tell me which Eye took the last shift of the night? I know it's a long shot, but maybe he saw something that seemed so insignificant he didn't bother to log it."

Giselle clicked open her pen and held it poised over the notepad. "Anytime you're ready, Sherlock."

Ron flipped the sheets of the logbook all the way back to the beginning. I peeked over his shoulder and saw the first two pages contained the names and contact info for each watchman. He moved his forefinger over the names until he found what we needed. Giselle noted the information and we left.

On the short walk back to my house, Fanya suddenly veered ninety degrees to the right. She waved her hand at Giselle, Sonia, and me. "Quick! Follow me." She crossed the street, mumbling and spitting.

We glanced at each other and crossed the street, trotting right behind her.

"What's wrong? Where are you going?" I asked.

Fanya stopped and pointed back across the street. Sauntering slowly toward the spot where we once walked was Hucklebee, a neighbor's black cat. Fanya let out a big puff of air. "Phew. That was a close call. You should never let a black cat cross your pathway. You're only asking for something terrible to happen."

Three doors away from mine we stopped.

Giselle looked at her notes. "This is the address Ron gave us."

Built in the mid-1950s, my housing tract boasted four different floor plans to choose from. The person we were about to interview lived in the "Rancho" model. It was five-hundred-square-feet larger than my own model, the "Cottage." Over the decades, many of the houses had been remodeled, obscuring the original floor plan.

Melroy Briggs lived in the house his parents purchased new in 1956, before he was born. He continued to live with them even after earning a degree in animal husbandry from the local community college. After the death of his parents, Melroy was the sole inheritor of all their earthly goods. He now owned the mortgage-free house and, it was rumored, a large amount of money from a trust—freeing him from having to work for a living. He answered the door today and stood almost at eye level with me, about five feet three inches. His thin gray hair was parted on the left side and carefully combed over his bare skull. Creases had been ironed into his brown plaid shirt and khaki trousers.

He scanned our faces as if looking for a clue to our visit. "If you're selling something, I'm not interested. If you want to tell me about your religion, I'm definitely not interested. However, if you've come from the Publishers Clearing House to award me five thousand dollars in cash every week for the rest of my life, I'm listening." He grinned and winked at Sonia.

She chuckled and pointed to me. "Hi, Melroy. You remember Martha, right? Lives on the corner?"

I wiggled my fingers in a wave.

"Sure thing. I see you've been busy at your house with visitors coming and going."

I introduced Crusher's sister, Fanya, and my sister, Giselle.

Melroy shifted his attention to Fanya. "I saw you and another lady arrive with suitcases on Saturday. Are you from out of state?"

Wow! I guess Sonia isn't the only yenta in the neighborhood.

"New York. I'm here to visit Martha and my brother, Yossi."

"Welcome to Encino." He turned his attention back to me. "What were the police doing at your house on Sunday and Monday? Is everything okay?"

"We had a break-in on Sunday and another one on Monday." I decided to give him only the barest information and not tell him about the abduction. The police told us not to talk about it. "And since you were on patrol Monday morning from four to six, I wanted to know if you saw anything out of place when you made your rounds."

"Nothing out of the ordinary."

"Did you see any movement or lights in my house? Maybe a strange vehicle parked nearby? With or without occupants?"

"I know every car in our neighborhood. There was nothing unusual."

"What about the day before? Sunday?"

"There was something." He rolled his eyes to the right

and looked toward the sky as if searching the data files written in the air above his head. "Let me see. On Sunday morning around eleven, I planted some pink dianthus in my garden. I saw you, your boyfriend, and this lady here leave the house." He gestured toward Fanya. "About an hour later, I opened the door to accept a delivery from Amazon. Did you know they deliver on Sundays? Anyways, I looked up and down the street to see who else was around. You know. To say 'hi' and stuff. The street was empty and quiet. I did notice a blue SUV in front of your house but I assumed there were more visitors. Then I saw two men and a woman leave your house and walk to the car. One of the men carried a suitcase, and it looked like the other two were arguing."

My heart began to flutter. "Are you sure the woman was walking?"

"More or less. I couldn't see much detail at this distance, but I recognized her as one of your guests. And I got the distinct impression she was quite a handsome woman. It's a shame, someone like her. It was barely past noon, but I think she was drunk because she stumbled a couple of times. She appeared to be reluctant to get in the SUV."

She wasn't drunk. She'd been drugged with chloroform. And those were no companions, they were her kidnappers. "What about the men with her? What did they look like?"

His eyes opened wide. "Oh dear. You didn't know them?"

I ignored his question. "What about race? Black, white, brown, Asian? Young? Old?"

"They were too far away to see much detail."

"One last thing and we'll leave you alone. Have the police been around to question you yet?"

"No. And I've been waiting for them to knock on my door so I could tell them what I saw."

It's a good thing I decided to do some investigating of my own. The police never got as far as three houses away from the scene of the crime. Beavers needed to know someone on his team dropped the ball when he was supposed to be conducting a house-to-house.

I gave him my phone number. "Please call if you think of anything else. Anything at all. Big or small."

He waved goodbye and closed the front door.

"Can you believe he didn't have the courtesy to ask us to go in his house?" Giselle's face carried a dark frown.

Fanya's voice became almost a whisper. "I think I know why he didn't ask us in." She waited until she had our full attention. "I saw a black lace garter belt and a pair of red high heels on the living room floor behind him. I'm thinking there's a lady friend waiting for him inside."

"Or," Sonia snarked, "the garter belt and shoes belong to Melroy."

Giselle gasped. "Holy mother of God. I'd like to wipe that image from my mind."

CHAPTER 11

We left Melroy and his black lace garter belt and stopped at the next house, two doors away from mine. Catalina Muñoz, an eighty-year-old widow, opened her door. She wore her long gray hair pulled back in a neat bun at the nape of her neck. Her face displayed the kind of wrinkles testifying to a life fully lived. Her eyes were compassionate and her smile gentle. She peered at me through thick glasses. "Martha? What's been going on at your house? The whole neighborhood is worried." She inspected the other faces. "Hello, Sonia."

I quickly introduced Fanya and Giselle. "That's what we've come to discuss. I wanted to ask you a couple of questions if you're not too busy."

"Come in. Come in." She beckoned with a graceful hand to follow her inside.

A miniature poodle yapped a greeting as soon as we

entered the house. Catalina ushered us to the living room, where the four of us sat on a sofa and matching chairs upholstered in shiny gold damask. Each piece was covered in heavy-gauge see-through plastic slipcovers that crinkled when we sat down.

Giselle ran her hand over the clear, stiff plastic. "I didn't know they still made this awful stuff. You must have a lot of visitors to go to this length to protect your furniture. I'll bet you have a lot of children and grandchildren, am I right?"

Catalina gestured toward the walls. "I can see why you would think so." Almost every square inch was covered with family photos—birthdays, graduations, marriages, baptisms—all neatly framed. "Family is a blessing, but a clean house is also a blessing." She sat in what was obviously her favorite spot, a dark green leather recliner with a white cable-knit afghan folded over the back and no plastic cover. "Now, then. Tell me what's going on."

I told her only about the break-ins. "I honestly don't think anyone else needs to worry. My house was a specific target."

"Whatever for? Do you hang priceless paintings on your walls?" Catalina sighed. "I think we could use some tea." The older woman moved toward the kitchen on confident legs.

Sonia stood and joined her. "Let me help."

Giselle leaned back. "Okay, Fanya, what kind of wallpaper would you hang on these walls?"

Fanya didn't miss a beat. "Stripes. Pale cream-colored tone-on-tone."

Five minutes later, Catalina returned to the living room, carrying a plate of homemade sugar cookies with multicolored sprinkles on top and placed them on the coffee table. Sonia followed behind her, carrying a wooden tray laden with an earthenware teapot and five mismatched mugs, which she also placed on the coffee table. Catalina poured the tea and handed a cup to each of us.

I reached for a cookie. "Can you remember seeing or hearing anything around the time of the break-ins? Even the smallest detail could help us."

Catalina frowned and closed her eyes. "Sunday noon I took Chickee for a walk, like I do every day. We walked past your house and around the corner and ended at the soccer fields."

To the north of our street bordered federal land divided into a number of Little League and softball league fields. To the east, our street stopped at the boundary of Balboa Park, home to tennis courts, a recreation center, a children's play area, and several AYSO soccer fields.

"Did you notice a blue SUV parked at my place?"

"Hmm. I don't recall seeing one, no. But I do remember hearing shouting as I rounded the corner. At first, I didn't know where it was coming from. But then I saw your windows were open and realized the yelling came from inside your house."

My heart sped at the promise of finding a real clue. "What did they say? Could you tell if it was a male or female voice?"

"It was both. She said, 'Don't be ridiculous. How should I know?'"

"And the male voice?"

Catalina tugged at her earlobe. "Something about money. She said something back like 'Just like Ziv.'"

I looked at Fanya to see if she was thinking the same thing I was. "Could she have said 'Just like Ze'ev?'"

The older woman raised a blue mug and sipped. "It could've been. Did I help you at all?"

"It's a start. One last thing: Did the police come to question you?"

She placed her cup on the table. "Yes. They came around on Sunday late afternoon, and I told them the same thing I told you. I asked them what was going on, and they said they were investigating a break-in."

"What about yesterday? Did the police come to your house again?"

"Yes, but I couldn't help. I didn't see or hear anything on Monday."

"If you do remember something else, would you please call me?"

The five of us chatted about the changing climate in California. Sonia helped clean and a half hour after we arrived, we left Catalina Muñoz.

Once we were outside, Giselle reached toward me and brushed some cookie crumbs off my chest. "One more house to go. Who's your next-door neighbor, Sissy?"

"Sister Mae Slocum. She's an assistant camera operator in the TV industry. What they call a number two."

Giselle stopped walking and frowned. "Really? I didn't know they allowed nuns to be cinematographers. And I'm Catholic."

"No, G. Sister is her first name, not a title. Sister Mae. A Southern girl."

"I love odd names," Sonia said. "I once met a National Guardsman named Soldier. You'll like Sister Mae. She's an entrepreneur, like you, Giselle. She has a photography business in addition to her job at ABC TV. Doing quite well."

We pushed our way past the little swinging gate into Sister Mae's fenced yard. Building codes limited the fence height to three feet in the front of the house. The white picket enclosure was more decorative than functional. It certainly wouldn't keep Sister Mae's Great Dane from escaping. I knocked and heard the deep baritone bark of King Solomon on the other side of the door.

"Hush up, King." The dead bolt clicked and the door opened about three inches, enough for Sister Mae to talk. "Oh, hi Martha. I was going to ask you about the police . . ."

Toenails scraped across the hardwood floor.

"Oof." Sister Mae slid sideways and disappeared. In her place a gray creature stood over three feet high at the shoulder and weighed about one hundred and fifty pounds. His tail whipped from side to side and ropy saliva dripped from his mouth. His hair was short and stiff, the opposite of my fluffy cat Bumper's. He nuzzled my hand for attention, so I patted his gigantic head. He leaned into me in response and almost knocked me down.

"Now, King, I told you to behave!" Sister Mae appeared once more. She barely reached five feet tall and looked like her Dane outweighed her by fifty pounds. However, she was stronger than she looked. She had to be, because her job required her to lift heavy equipment. She shoved the dog out of the way. "Sorry. He's a big mama's boy. Always lookin' for attention. I'd invite y'all in, but you'd be taking a big chance. He's not fully trained yet."

I told her about the break-ins.

"Holy moly!"

"Did you notice anything on Sunday? Hear something? See something unusual at my house?"

"Well, you know the police stopped by here and asked me the same questions. I don't mind saying they put the fear of the Lord into me. What if those same people tried to break into my house? Of course, King Solomon would probably lick them to death."

"Can you tell me what you told the police?"

"I said I heard shouting. I thought it was highly unusual since I never heard anything like yelling coming from your house before. I mean, you and your boyfriend are great neighbors."

"Thanks. Could you tell if it was a man or a woman shouting?"

"Both."

She reinforced what Catalina told us.

"Could you make out what they said?"

"Only a little bit." Sister Mae frowned, bit her lip, and closed her eyes. "They were arguing. Then I heard her say, 'Shut up.'"

"Did you get an actual look at any of them?"

"I sure did. About fifteen minutes later, I heard them still arguing, only this time the voices came from the outside of the house. I looked through my front window, and it was the strangest thing. I've probably worked behind the camera way too long, because one of them looked like someone I've seen before."

"Even so, it would help us to have a description. Like age, race, or any identifying details."

"Well, like I told the police, one of them was very military looking. You know, tall, lots of muscle, short haircut. Blond or white—I couldn't tell which. He had a thick neck. The other one was shorter. Thinner. Dark, but not African American. Black hair."

I asked my sister, "Are you writing this down?"

"Yup."

"Go ahead," I urged Sister Mae.

"The woman was gorgeous. She resembled Penélope Cruz. Two men escorted her to the car. The one who looked familiar gripped her upper arm. He looked like one of the minor players on *Grey's Anatomy*. Name of Peter-something. The smaller man didn't look familiar. He carried a suitcase to their blue SUV and stowed it in back while the big one hauled her to the car."

"Did they say anything?"

She squinted and focused on a spot behind my shoulder. "Hmm. She seemed really angry. She said something I couldn't make out. But I clearly heard the big one say, 'All the world's a stage, Hadas.' They seemed anxious to leave, and they drove away fast."

Giselle gasped. "What a bizarre thing to say. 'All the world's a stage' sounds familiar. What's that from?"

"We'll Google it when we get home. Did you hear anything else?" I asked.

"No."

"What about Monday morning? Did you see or hear anything then?"

"Nope. I'm awful sorry, Martha. I wish I could help you more."

"You did great, Sister Mae. Thanks for talking to us. Will you call me if you remember something? Any little thing, no matter how insignificant, might be what we need to know."

"*We*? Are you working with the police?"

"Sort of. Let's say I'm double-checking the facts as we know them."

We walked slowly out of Sister Mae Slocum's yard.

Sonia looked at her watch. "I've got to get ready for an appointment now. Keep me posted." She waved goodbye and crossed the street to her own home.

Fanya kissed the mezuzah by my front door before entering the house.

Giselle sat next to her and pulled out her smartphone. "I'm going to Google *All the world's a stage.*"

We watched as she typed a query with her thumbs. "Wow! Listen to this: *All the world's a stage, and all the men and women merely players. They have their exits and their entrances, and one man in his time plays many parts.*"

Fanya ambled over to the sofa and sat next to her. "It's a real saying?"

Giselle nodded. "Shakespeare. *As You Like It.* Now, why on earth would the kidnappers be quoting Shakespeare?" She shook her head as if to clear out the cobwebs.

Fanya reached inside the neck of her shirt and pulled out a small leather pouch hanging on a long silver chain. She gazed out the front windows, fingering the pouch.

Giselle pointed to the small bag. "What's that?"

"It's an amulet."

"Huh?"

"You know, like a charm."

"What's inside?"

Fanya tugged on a string to open the top of the pouch. She cupped her hand and shook out the contents. "This emerald is for safe travels and the sapphire is to guard against illness."

"You're joking. I mean, how does it work?"

"Look at me," she said. "I arrived safely in LA, didn't

I? Plus, I'm healthy as a horse, *keinehora*. Need I say more? The magic in these objects gets amplified when paired with other charms."

"I don't believe in magic. What's the rest of the stuff?"

Fanya held two very tiny pieces of parchment rolled up, each no longer than one inch. "A protective text is written in Hebrew on one of these miniature scrolls, and symbols from the Kabbalah are written on the other." She lifted a small gold charm in the shape of a hand with a cloisonné blue eye in the middle. "Do you know what this is?"

"I believe Martha once told me. It's a *hamsa*, which means five. As in five fingers.'"

"Correct. It's an ancient symbol. Also called the 'hand of Fatima,' which wards off the evil eye. In the bottom of the pouch are fennel seeds to keep me from getting hurt."

Giselle scoffed. "Hah. This is the twenty-first century. You still believe in those things?"

"Of course!" Fanya put everything back in the pouch.

"Can you prove your so-called magic charms work?"

In typical rabbinic fashion, Fanya answered a question with a question. "Can you prove they don't?" She carefully placed the items back into the pouch and sighed. "We don't even know where to start looking."

I glanced at Giselle. "Shadow uncovered some stuff about the Uhrman Company. Do you think he can dig a little deeper?"

She sniffed. "I thought you disapproved of hackers. Now you're saying it's okay to use his special skills?"

"Believe me, I don't feel right about asking for his help. But face it. Hadas is missing and her chances of being found alive diminish greatly with the passing of time. So, anything we can do to find her is fair game as far as I'm concerned."

Fanya nodded in agreement.

My sister flashed a triumphant smile. "I'll text him right now."

CHAPTER 12

Giselle grabbed her turquoise leather tote and prepared for the drive home to the Pacific Palisades late Tuesday afternoon. "You know how much I hate coming to the Valley, Sissy. I've finally discovered something I hate even more."

"What's that?"

"Going back. Especially during rush hour."

"You know, you're welcome to stay here until the traffic thins. Why don't you have dinner with us?"

She took a deep breath and blew it out again. "I would, but Harold's due home from his trip to Dallas. I want to be there when he arrives." She tossed air-kisses to Fanya and me as she walked out the door. "I'll call you as soon as Shadow's finished his . . . *research*."

I was glad Crusher and I had purchased plenty of vegetables and fruits for his vegetarian sister. She opened the refrigerator, rummaged through the contents, and pulled out bags of produce and shredded cheddar cheese. "Unless you have other plans, I'd like to fix dinner tonight."

"Great!"

"Do you have any pasta?"

I opened the pantry door and pulled out a box of elbow macaroni and a box of angel-hair spaghetti. "Which one?"

"Macaroni."

Fanya chopped onions, carrots, mushrooms, and broccoli and sautéed them in olive oil and garlic. She boiled the pasta in just enough water to cover it. "I don't know why we Americans insist on using energy to heat an entire pot of water when the pasta only needs a little bit of water to cook." She made a cheesy sauce, mixed it with the drained pasta and vegetables, poured everything into a casserole dish, topped it with more grated cheese, and put it in the oven. With a big grin, she closed the oven door. "We'll melt the cheese on top and voilà! Macaroni primavera à la *aglio olio*."

An hour later, Crusher helped himself to yet another serving of casserole. "This is great, Fan. You always did know how to cook."

"Yossi," I said, "did you realize the police failed to complete their house-to-house? They completely overlooked one witness." I repeated what Melroy Briggs observed. "I'm going to tell Arlo."

A shadow passed over his face so quickly I might have missed it. "Do what you have to."

Fanya retired to the guest room, while Crusher cleaned the kitchen, according to our agreement: If one cooked the other cleaned. I turned on the television in time for the final *Jeopardy!* category, "heads of state." The answer was *the first prime minister of modern Israel.* The contestants bent their heads to write questions. One completely blanked and wrote a question mark, one wrote *Who was Golda Meir?* and the third wrote *Who was Moshe Dayan?*

"No, people!" I shouted at the TV. "Ben-Gurion. *Who was David Ben-Gurion?*"

Fanya returned to the living room and watched *Wheel of Fortune*, and I went to my sewing room to be alone and called Beavers.

"Ah. The clever Martha. And to what do I owe this call?"

"Go ahead, be snarkastic. But I have a couple of leads you might be interested in, as well as a heads-up about your investigation. Of course, if you'd rather not entertain new facts about Hadas, I'll go away quietly."

"One can only hope. What do you have?"

Despite myself, I smiled. Sparring with Beavers had become playful and almost fun. I briefly wondered what our lives would have been like if I chose to marry Beavers instead of Crusher. For one, I wouldn't be trying to find my fiancé's kidnapped wife.

I told Beavers about Melroy Briggs. "He actually saw the kidnappers put Hadas in the blue SUV. He lives only three houses away, but the police never came to question him. I thought you should know someone on your team didn't go far enough on the house-to-house search."

"I'll look into it. You said something about new leads?"

"What about this? My neighbor two doors down, Catalina Muñoz, heard Hadas yelling at her kidnappers. She may have invoked her brother's name, Ze'ev. He was

CHAPTER 15

Thursday morning I got a call from Hilda, my elderly uncle's helper. In the back of my mind I'd secretly feared and anticipated the day she'd call with terrible news. Ever since he was diagnosed with Parkinson's, I'd seen him slowly decline both physically and emotionally. My lips went numb with panic. I could barely speak. "Hilda? Is he all right?"

The voice on the other end soothed, "Oh, yes, Martha. I didn't mean to scare you. Isaac wanted me to invite you to lunch today. He wants you to be here at eleven-thirty because he has something to show you first."

Relief swept over me like a warm blanket on a cold night. "Thank God. Can you tell me what this is about?"

"Even if Isaac could forgive me, I could never forgive myself for ruining his surprise. Can you come?"

killed six months ago in a hit-and-run in New York. Still unsolved. I think his death might be connected to her abduction."

Beavers was silent for a moment. "I'm telling you again, this is a complicated investigation of some seriously bad people. Please back off, Martha. I don't want anything to happen to you."

Was he flirting again? I had to admit his words stirred some unresolved feelings. What if I'd chosen the wrong fiancé? "I'm truly flattered by your concern, Arlo."

"Good night, Martha."

Crusher walked into my sewing room. "You talked to Beavers?" His voice betrayed a tinge of disapproval.

My cheeks grew warm. Thank goodness he couldn't read my mind, otherwise he might catch a glimpse of a guilty conscience. "Yes. Arlo appears to be on top of the investigation. But he won't discuss the details with me. Have you talked to him? Learned anything new?"

"Yeah. This is now a federal case."

"Because of the abduction?"

"Apparently there's more to it than a simple abduction. But they won't tell me more since I'm still considered a suspect."

"Have you told Fanya yet?"

He raked his fingers through his once-red beard, now mostly gray. "I doubt she'd be able to shed light on this. Besides, she's naïve for a New Yorker."

"Baloney. You seem to still regard Fanya as your inexperienced kid sister. But she's all grown up now, a woman leading a life of her own choosing. Don't sell her short. She was friends with the Uhrman family, and I'll bet she can tell us more."

We moved to the living room, where Fanya sat in the middle of the sofa.

Crusher sat beside her. "Fan, can we talk for a minute?"

"Sure." She reached for the remote control as the giant wheel turned and clattered. It landed on a glittering silver wedge worth $5,000. Then the TV screen went black. "Is this about Hadas?"

I settled in an easy chair across from my fiancé and future sister-in-law and told her the feds had taken over the investigation of Hadas's disappearance.

Crusher asked his sister, "You've known the family for a long time. Do you have any idea why the feds would be interested in the Uhrmans?"

She shook her head sadly. "No. She talked almost constantly on the five-hour flight from New York. Mostly about herself and the Uhrman Company. Among his other weaknesses, she said Ze'ev had a drinking problem. More than once she sent him home from the business because he showed up shickered. Plus, he was a womanizer and a gambler. Do you think the kidnapping has something to do with her brother's death?"

Crusher rested his hand on Fanya's shoulder. "It certainly looks that way, Fan. You know Hadas better than we do. Any idea who they might be?"

"No. But you're a federal agent, Yossi. Can't you find these things out from your friends in Washington?"

Crusher worked his jaw muscle. "They won't talk to me."

"Why?"

"I'm their chief suspect."

"Still?"

"I'm the husband."

I resolved right then and there to contact Director John Smith of the FBI. Smith had helped me in the past. He knew Crusher. Surely, he could supply information about Hadas and the Uhrman Company. If Smith couldn't help, there was always Shadow, the hacker my sister employed.

CHAPTER 13

Wednesday morning came far too soon. All the stress of the last few days caught up with me. My whole body ached from fibromyalgia and my head pounded with a migraine. I glanced at the clock and groaned. It read eight. Past time to rise. I rolled on my side and pushed myself into a sitting position. The room spun for a few seconds and then stopped. I slowly made my way to the bathroom and the medicine I desperately needed for the pain.

Ten minutes later I sat at the kitchen table with Fanya, sipping my first cup of coffee of the day. "I'm sorry I slept this late. What time did Yossi leave?"

"Early. He was already gone when I got up at five. I'm still operating on New York time." She peered at me for a moment. "Martha, you don't look so hot. Is something wrong?"

I explained how fibromyalgia could flare as a result of stress. "But don't worry. I took some medicine. I should feel better in a half hour or so."

"You know what this is, Martha? It's a curse! Someone has cursed you with the *ayin hara*, the evil eye."

"You mean someone is sticking pins into a voodoo doll with my name on it?" I chuckled. "Sorry, Fanya, but I don't believe in that stuff."

"I wish you'd take this more seriously. Who has it out for you?"

"I have no idea. No one."

"From what Yossi says, you helped put a few bad guys in jail. One of them probably threw the curse. But I've come prepared. There are things we can do to reverse the effects."

"As long as it doesn't involve giving up chocolate."

Fanya barked a laugh. "That would be an epic curse, right? But seriously, you've got to wear a sapphire. I do. It's in the amulet I showed you yesterday. It'll cure you and keep you from getting sick in the first place."

"How do you come up with these things?"

"Have you heard of the ephod, the breastplate the high priest wore in the holy temple?"

"Vaguely."

Fanya grinned, showing the gap in her front teeth. "It contains twelve stones, one for each of the twelve tribes of Israel. Each stone has special properties. Sapphire is the stone you need right now."

"You speak as though the breastplate still exists."

"*Halevai*. Nobody knows what happened to it or to the *aron hakodesh*, the holy ark. They say when the destruction of the temple was imminent, the priests hurried to a secret place underground below the temple and hid the sacred items."

Despite my doubts about using charms or magic, I was impressed by Fanya's knowledge of the somewhat arcane superstitions and practices within Judaism. "I have a little sapphire ring my bubbie gave to me right before she died. Will that do?"

"Perfect. Wear it all the time. And wear amethyst, too. Demons and spirits don't like amethyst."

I did a mental inventory of my jewelry box. "I don't have an amethyst."

"I highly recommend you get one."

Despite my protests, Fanya insisted on helping me with the breakfast dishes and tidying the house. "You're obviously still in pain, despite the drugs you take. Besides, I'm glad to help."

At noon, she prepared a vegetable salad with hard-boiled eggs and cheese. She produced a small plastic bag filled with something black. "I brought these with me."

"They look like dead flies."

She sprinkled a few on the salad. "They're black mustard seeds. Good for stiff muscles and joints and inflammation."

The ringing of my cell phone interrupted our conversation. One glance at the screen told me the caller was Giselle. "I've put you on speaker. I want Fanya to hear. I hope you're calling with news from Shadow because I feel we're back at square one with no place to go."

"Then this is definitely going to advance us to square two. Remember Shadow found out the Uhrman Company had been bleeding cash?" She didn't wait for an answer. "Well, it seems Ze'ev secretly withdrew cash from the business."

Fanya leaned forward to get closer to the phone. "Are you sure? Uhrman Company was everything to Hadas. She wouldn't have allowed Ze'ev to hurt the business in any way."

My gut told me we were on to something important. "Maybe she didn't know about those cash withdrawals."

"How could she not know?" Fanya frowned and blinked rapidly at the phone.

Giselle's voice came across the phone loud and clear. "Didn't Hadas tell you Ze'ev was the numbers guy? He could've hidden his theft from the business by some sort of deception, like keeping an extra set of books. Isn't it suspicious that the reversal of fortune in the business co-incided with his death?"

"My thoughts exactly, G. I've been asking myself the same thing since she disappeared." I turned to Fanya. "On the long plane ride to LA, you said Hadas never stopped talking. Did she confide anything about her brother besides his addictions to wine, women, and wa-gering?"

"Hmm." Fanya closed her eyes briefly as if to reach some memory. "I already told you about Ze'ev's drinking problem. Hadas also discovered he owed serious money to some mobbed-up bookie. After Ze'ev's death, Hadas cleaned out his desk and found a bunch of betting tickets shoved in the back of a drawer. He never bet less than a thousand dollars at a time."

"Now we know where the money from the business probably went," Giselle said. "Anyway, that's all I have for now."

"One other thing before you go, G. Your guy Shadow said six months ago, right after Ze'ev died, there was a sudden infusion of capital into the business. Do you think he can discover where the cash came from?"

"I'll ask. Talk to you soon."

After the call ended, Fanya shook her head. "*Oy va voy!* What does all this mean?"

"The more I learn about Ze'ev, the more I think it's possible his death wasn't an accident."

Fanya gasped. "Are you talking about murder? God forbid!"

"As horrible as it sounds, he could've been killed over money—gambling debts or theft from the business or both. And there are still a couple of nagging questions. Hadas said she recently changed her will, making Yossi her sole heir. If both of them die, God forbid, who is next in line to take over the Uhrman Company? Hadas didn't have children, but what about Ze'ev? Did he have kids?"

"Nine."

"So why didn't Ze'ev's family inherit his half of the business?"

"Oh my gosh, you're right. Hadas never once mentioned Ze'ev's family."

"I think it's time to call my friend at the FBI."

Director John Smith was technically not my friend. Especially since Crusher still called him "sir." However, since Smith and I had successfully worked together in the past, perhaps he'd help me once more. I carried my cell phone to my favorite chair in the living room and scrolled through my contacts under the letter "S" and turned on the speaker so Fanya could hear our conversation.

"Hello, Martha. I was wondering when I'd hear from you. Can I assume this call is about the abduction of Mrs. Hadas Levy from your home over the weekend?"

"Jeez. How did you know? Are you wiretapping me?"

"No. Abductions are the business of the FBI."

"Are you working with the LAPD?"

"The federal government likes to collaborate with local agencies to solve complex crimes. This is one of them."

"If you already know about Hadas, you must also know she's still married to Yossi. He can't get any information on the case because they say he's a suspect."

"And technically, you are as well."

"I think you know how absurd that sounds."

"You know, Martha, I have always thought of you as a reliable witness—even a friend at times. I still remember the wonderful meal at your home." Smith referred to a time in the past when Crusher brought him home for Sabbath dinner and we called each other by our first names.

"A friend? As in I'll-show-you-mine-if-you-show-me-yours kind of friend?"

"Exactly. I have a great deal of respect for your sleuthing abilities. I wouldn't be surprised to learn you've already been rummaging around for clues."

How could I tell him what I knew without compromising Giselle and Shadow? "As a matter of fact, I have. Ze'ev Uhrman was taking cash out of the business. Probably gambled it away. After his death, Hadas found some betting tickets of his. He never placed a bet under one thousand dollars."

"And you know this, how?"

"Hadas told Yossi's sister, Fanya, during a five-hour plane ride from New York."

"Hmm. Gambling and betting tickets? The sister failed to mention tickets in her statement. Anything else?"

"I feel certain Hadas's abduction and her brother's death are connected. I just don't know how. Not yet. But

I'm beginning to believe his death was no accident. Now I've shown you mine, it's your turn. What can you share with me?"

"I'm impressed as always. You are very perceptive. Officially, I can't throw standard procedure out the window and let you in on the investigation, as if you were a sworn officer assigned to this case. But I can reveal the FBI shares your view about a connection between the hit-and-run and the sister's abduction."

"Then I'm on the right track? Good. There's something else. I wanted to make sure you knew Yossi was at the beach with me and his sister, Fanya, when Hadas was abducted."

Smith coughed. "You know a person doesn't have to be present at a crime to be responsible for it. It's called conspiracy. Murder for hire."

"*Murder?* You think she's dead?"

"As time passes without a ransom demand or communication of any kind, I'd have to say it's a strong possibility. If only we knew why she was abducted, we might find her before it's too late."

I sighed. "I'm honestly at a loss."

Smith waited a beat before responding. "The best way to prove your and Levy's innocence is for the FBI to find Mrs. Levy—dead or alive—and arrest the people who took her. As skillful as you are in gathering intel, Martha, I'm asking you to step back and let us do our job."

"Can I help it if I'm a very sympathetic listener? People find me irresistible. They tell me stuff they might not tell an officer of the law, such as yourself. Apparently, Fanya is also a good listener because during the flight to LA, Hadas talked nonstop about the business and how she wanted Yossi to resume their married life and go back to New York with her."

"Interesting detail about the marriage. How did that make you feel?"

"What do you think?"

"Can you see how the police might conclude the marriage thing gives you a motive to arrange for Mrs. Levy's disappearance?"

"Don't be ridiculous. I'm more interested in who might inherit the business if Hadas is dead and Yossi were in prison for her murder. Do you know?"

"Yes."

"I suppose it's futile to ask you for names?"

"Yes, but I will share this with you. The business will stay in the Uhrman family."

"You mean Ze'ev Uhrman's family?"

He remained silent in a response I could only interpret as assent. Finally he spoke. "One word of caution, Martha. The people behind Ze'ev Uhrman's death and Mrs. Levy's disappearance are your worst nightmare. I can't emphasize too much that any inquiries you make may prompt them to return to your house. And next time, they'll be coming for you."

"Are you saying Ze'ev Uhrman's death was no accident? He was murdered?"

Smith remained silent.

I didn't know if Fanya inspired me, but I crossed the fingers of both hands before I lied to the FBI. "I have no plans to take this any further."

CHAPTER 14

Wednesday afternoon, I led Fanya into my sewing room, and gestured broadly toward my stash of cotton fabric, folded by color groups and sitting on shelves.

Fanya stared at my rather large collection. "Wow. These are beautiful. How do I even begin?"

"What inspires you?"

"I liked the Ohio Star pattern we talked about before. Like the quilt on your bed. But then I found this one I like better." Fanya opened the quilting magazine and pointed to a picture.

The quilt block pattern she chose was the Snail's Trail, also called Whirligig, Ocean Waves, Virginia Reel, and Monkey Wrench. Each block featured spirals of one dark and one light fabric.

"This pattern is a little bit tricky to sew because the bias seams tend to stretch. But I'm sure you have the skills to manage. Snail's Trail is often made with two contrasting colors. Do you want to go with a dark-light design, or would you like to try multicolors for a scrappier look?"

Fanya nodded rapidly. "Definitely two colors. Greens and yellows."

I walked over to the neatly folded piles of fabric sitting on the shelves and grabbed a stack of folded yellow fabrics eighteen inches high. I brought it over to the cutting table, where Fanya sat. I returned with an equally tall stack of green fabrics.

"Wow! How many different fabrics do you have, anyway? There must be dozens here." In truth, there were at least a hundred different yellows and greens for her to choose from.

"The Snail's Trail block really pops if there is a high contrast between the two fabrics. How big do you want to make your quilt?"

"Definitely for my double bed."

"Okay. You'll need thirty twelve-inch blocks. Five across and six down. Plus borders. For a more interesting look, try not to repeat fabric from one block to the next. Go ahead and pair up thirty greens and thirty yellows."

Fanya bent happily to her task while I sat across the room, opened my laptop, and searched for the Uhrman Company. The last entry on the web page was dated a year ago, when Ze'ev was still alive. "We need to find out more about the remaining Uhrmans. According to my contact in the FBI, one of them will inherit the business. You were friends with the family. Who could that be?"

Still sifting through the fabrics, she replied without looking at me. "Not a clue. Like I said, Ze'ev and his wife, Ettie, had nine children, *keinehora*."

"Would she or her children talk to you?"

"Ettie would, for sure. She still lives in Borough Park. I hung some paper in her living room about three months ago. Gave her a big price cut on account of her husband's recent death."

"Do any of her children still live at home?"

"It was hard to tell. Tons of family photos hung on the walls. She showed me a picture of a granddaughter who died not long ago. Leukemia, poor thing."

"Poor Ettie. I can't imagine anything worse than losing a child."

Fanya held a selection of yellow printed fabrics. Flowers, birds, even stripes and one plaid. "What do you think of these?"

"Great choices. Keep going." I tried dragging the conversation back to the Uhrmans. "Would it be better to telephone or talk to her in person?"

"I could phone her." She carefully handed me a small cut of green fabric with tiny pink and blue flowers. "This is really pretty, but there's not much here. Will this be enough?"

Passionate quilters collected fabric like tchotchkes collected dust. We bought whatever appealed to us and stashed it for future use. Sometimes we bought yardage in anticipation of large projects, but most of the time we bought smaller cuts of a half yard or a quarter yard. Over time, a quilter would accumulate a wide selection of fabric. "I don't think there's enough for one block, Fanya. But you can always fill in the missing bits with another green fabric."

"You're allowed to do that?"

I laughed. "One of the best things about quilting is

there are no rules. You can do whatever you like without being afraid of the quilt police."

I stopped searching for Uhrman information, left Fanya to her sorting, and went into the kitchen to start prepping dinner. By the time Crusher appeared at six, Fanya had finished her selections and we enjoyed a dinner of home-made guacamole and tacos made with ground meat sub-stitute and vegetarian refried beans.

"These are delicious!" Fanya raved.

I told Crusher about Ze'ev's widow, Ettie Uhrman. "Fanya's going to call her tonight. If it becomes neces-sary, could you go back to New York with your sister and talk to Ze'ev's widow? You were his friend, after all."

Crusher reached for his third taco. "I can't go. Your ex-boyfriend told me not to leave town."

"Arlo Beavers?" I forgot about the local police work-ing with the feds. "Since when are you concerned about what the LAPD thinks?"

"Since my boss gave me specific orders to care."

Who could argue?

He scratched the back of his neck. "Let's not get ahead of ourselves, babe. Make the phone call and see what happens."

"My brother's right. I hate to travel unnecessarily. Best not to tempt the evil eye." Fanya vigorously spit three times behind her hand.

We left Crusher in the kitchen for cleanup duties and moved to the living room. She scrolled down the contact list in her cell phone. "What am I supposed to say to Ettie?"

"Begin by telling her you're in LA visiting your brother, Yossi. Don't mention anything about Hadas. I'll be right here with my notepad and pen. I'll write questions for you to ask."

"But Ettie already knows Hadas and I traveled together to LA."

"So, if she asks, tell her Hadas is staying with friends for a few days."

"It's ten in the evening there. Should we wait until tomorrow?"

"No. Hadas is out there someplace and needs our help." Not for the first time, I thought about the irony of my trying to rescue my fiancé's wife.

Fanya nodded and touched the phone icon next to Ettie Uhrman's name, put her on speaker, and got a less-than-enthusiastic response.

"Fanya? It's late. What's the emergency?"

"Oh, hello, Ettie. I'm still in LA visiting my brother." She crossed her fingers. "I forgot about the time difference."

Ettie sighed. "*Nu?* Are you having a good time? How is Yossi?"

"Fine, fine. Everyone is fine. And you?"

I rolled my eyes and motioned with my hand for her to get to the point.

"*Ach.* My sciatical is acting up again. I can hardly walk. Now that Ze'ev, may he rest in peace, is gone, I gotta walk everywhere myself. Zalinski the butcher, Pearl's Bakery, Bank Hapoalim—everywhere."

I scribbled fast and handed Fanya my first note.

"You must miss him very much." Fanya briefly glanced at me.

I nodded encouragement and signaled an OK with my fingers.

"Running to his bookie and *shtupping* other women

was about all he was ever good for, may he rest in peace. Refusing to get married? You're the only smart one in all of New York. Tell me, Fanela, did you and Ze'ev ever . . . ?"

"*Has v'halilah*, Ettie. What a thing to ask."

"Not even once? I saw the way he used to look at you. Oy. Hungry like a dog. May he rest in peace."

Fanya looked at me, eyebrows raised in question marks. I nodded and gestured for her to answer the question.

She said, "Are we being honest here, Ettie?"

"Go ahead. I won't be surprised or mad. Even though the whole family suffered, I'm way past it."

"Okay. If you're sure." She cleared her throat. "It's true he used to proposition me, but I laughed it off. 'You've got a lovely wife and nine children waiting for you,' I used to say. 'Stop being such a putz and go home.'"

Ettie barked a laugh. "Putz? Ha. What did he say?"

Fanya chuckled. "He didn't like it much. But what could he do?"

"Ah, well, to tell you the truth, after the ninth baby, I was glad he got it elsewhere. He was worse than that little *nafke* sister of his. He was a male whore. So *nu*? What about Hadas? Did she persuade your brother to come back to New York?"

Fanya glanced at me. I shook my head and made a cutting motion across my throat. "No way. He's engaged to a terrific woman here in LA. No way would he ever switch partners."

"His girlfriend. She's Jewish?"

"Of course."

"So, what did Hadas do when she found out she couldn't have him?"

"Oh, you know. She went to stay with some friends."

I scribbled another hasty note and shoved it toward Fanya. She looked at it and nodded. "Ettie, when Hadas and Yossi talked, she said Yossi would inherit the business from her. Of course, he's not interested. But I was wondering, if—God forbid—both of them should die, who would the business go to? Do you know?"

"I think Zelig."

"Your son?"

"Yeah. My oldest. He got some big lawyer to help us get back half ownership of Uhrman Company. After Ze'ev died, half of the business shoulda gone straight to us. But Hadas did something sneaky. Now we gotta fight her in court. Oy! I curse the day I ever met such a bunch of gonifs. To think I could've married Rabbi Schechter's son, Aryeh. He's now a big macher in Crown Heights."

"I'm sorry for your troubles, Ettie. God willing, you'll get everything that's coming to you."

"Thank you. Thank you, Fanela. You're a good girl. I'll never forget what you did for me with the wallpaper and such. You were good to me after Ze'ev died. When you get back to New York, you'll have to come to dinner. I've got a neighbor, Mr. Bloomfield. His wife died. He's looking. Maybe you . . . ?"

Fanya opened her mouth and a huge laugh erupted all the way up from her belly. "Ettie! Do you hear yourself? Didn't you tell me a minute ago I was smart to never get married?"

"*Ach*, but this is different. He's a real mensch. Not bad looking either, *keinehora*."

"Ettie, you're still young-ish. Maybe you should think of yourself this time."

"Nah. He's got five children at home who scream all

the time. A bunch of *vilde chyahs*." Fanya grinned when Ettie used the Yiddish term for wild animals. Ettie continued. "They need a mother's loving but firm hand. By the way, did you know an eyewitness finally came forward? He told the police the car that killed Ze'ev accelerated and deliberately swerved to hit him."

Just as Smith said. Ze'ev Uhrman's death was no random accident.

Fanya looked at me with her mouth open. "No, I didn't know."

"Yeah, about three months ago."

I wrote rapidly and handed her my note.

She read it. "Could the witness identify the driver?"

"The police don't give out that kind of information."

Fanya motioned toward my notepad and mouthed the words, "More questions?"

I shook my head.

"Well, I'll let you go, Ettie. Sorry for calling late. I just wanted to see how you were."

"A pleasure to hear from you. Anytime. *A gute nacht.*"

"Good night, Ettie. *Schlaf gesunterheit.*" Fanya ended the call and blew out a puff of air. "Wow! I can't believe what we did."

"Nice job, Fanya. Now we know for sure Ze'ev's accident was deliberate. And we uncovered a possible motive. The car killing him could've belonged to an angry husband or a jilted lover."

"You're right." She opened her eyes wide. "Wouldn't it be something if we solved his murder?"

"As long as the 'something' isn't dangerous."

During the call, Crusher had finished the dishes and silently joined us in the living room to listen to Fanya and

Ettie's conversation. "You handled the call really well, Fan. You and Martha could go into the private detective business together."

"You mean instead of hanging wallpaper?"

"Sure. After Martha and I are married, you could call it Levy and Levy Private Detectives and Wall Coverings."

Everyone laughed but me. "If we get married, I'm not changing my name."

They both stared at me and said together, "If?"

A muted *"mfff moo"* came out of the shapeless lump on the bottom shelf.

I pulled the sheets away from her head. "What did you say?"

"I said, thank you for helping me."

"Really? Well, there is one thing you can do in return for my saving you."

"What is it?"

"Get a divorce."

I covered her head once again, wheeled the cart into the hallway, and took a deep breath. "Here goes nothing."

"Are you kidding? I love surprises. I might bring someone with me."

"Who?"

"I'm not saying. You're not the only ones with a surprise."

For the rest of the morning, I helped Fanya with her quilt. She steam-ironed the yellow and green fabrics. I gave her a tutorial on how to cut accurate pieces with the cutting mat, acrylic ruler with grid lines, and rotary cutter.

"Actually," she said, "I use similar tools when cutting wallpaper. I do what the carpenters do. Measure twice and cut once."

When it came time to hit the road, Fanya opted to stay home and work on her quilt blocks.

I cautioned her. "Don't open the door to any strangers."

She rolled her eyes. "As if!"

I tried to anticipate what Uncle Isaac and Hilda might be conniving. Whatever it was, I upgraded my clothes. Instead of the usual jeans and T-shirt, I opted for a white silk blouse and gray trousers.

At 11:25 I knocked on the door of the modest three-bedroom house I'd grown up in, the house where my uncle Isaac supported my mother, grandmother, and me with his tailor shop on nearby Pico Boulevard. Situated in a neighborhood adjacent to Beverly Hills, the pre–World War II bungalow grew in value over the decades. Some of the homes on the street had been replaced by grand residences with modern finishes. Others, like our house, remained unchanged with plain stucco exteriors and Spanish red tile roofs.

Hilda opened the door with a huge smile and twinkling

eyes. A baby-blue plastic headband kept her short hair from falling in her face. A former nurse, she had lived among and ministered to the health needs of the homeless. Now, in her early fifties, she'd become too old for the rough life on the streets. She jumped at the chance to be my uncle's live-in caregiver, with her own room and three meals a day guaranteed. She wore a clean white apron with a bib over a simple yellow cotton housedress. "Come in, come in. Where's our surprise guest?"

"Turns out she had other plans. I'm afraid it's only me." Something about the living room seemed changed. It appeared more tidy and cheerful than before. I began to take inventory of the familiar items, most of which hadn't been changed in thirty years. I stopped at the front window. The beige drapes with the torn lining were gone. New, white polyester pleated drapes were open to let the sunshine in.

I smiled. "Those new drapes look fabulous. They change the whole feeling in this room. Is this the surprise you wanted to show me?"

She winked. "Take a seat."

While I settled on the sofa, Hilda slipped her hands into a pair of thick red rubber rectangles. Then she lifted her voice and shouted, "Okay, Isaac, we're ready."

My uncle emerged from the hallway wearing a black yarmulke and long, black workout pants made of ripstop nylon. Parkinson's slowed his walk across the floor. *We Are the Champions* was written on the front of his T-shirt under a picture of Freddie Mercury. Uncle Isaac also wore brand-new red high-top sneakers and red rubber boxing gloves. He stopped when he reached Hilda and grinned at me. "How do I look, *faigela*? Like Maxie Rosenbloom, *nu*?"

More like a skinny old ninja. "Who was he?"

"Oy! I guess you're too young to remember. He was a world champion boxer. Jewish."

I couldn't help myself and began to laugh. "Okay, what have the two of you cooked up? What's with the boxing?"

"Hold onto your hat." He chuckled.

"This I've got to see." I settled back in the chair.

He turned to face Hilda. "Okay, coach."

Hilda stood with her feet apart and held the rubber rectangles in front of her. "Give it the old one-two, Isaac."

Uncle Isaac began to slam his gloves into Hilda's hands, yelling "Oy!" and "Oof!"

"Don't forget the feet." Hilda gestured with her chin toward the floor.

In between each punch, my uncle made little dancing steps, chanting "cha-cha-cha."

He soon established the rhythm of his workout, repeating, "Right, left, cha-cha-cha. Left, right, cha-cha-cha."

He stopped after five minutes, breathing heavily. Tiny beads of sweat quivered on his upper lip. Hilda took off her mitts and reached for a plastic squeeze bottle. Uncle Isaac opened his mouth like a fledgling bird and waited for Hilda to squirt water inside.

"Great work, Isaac. You went one minute longer today. Are you done?"

He nodded, still panting.

Hilda removed his boxing gloves and gave him a small hand towel. "We'll do some more tonight." With a smile and a promise of lunch, she retreated to the kitchen.

"Why the boxing? I'm truly perplexed."

Uncle Isaac mopped his face with the towel, then draped it over his shoulders. "The doctor prescribed it.

He said boxing teaches the brain to make new pathways. You know, for balance and mobility. God willing, it will stop the progression of the disease. Could even reverse the effects, *halevai*." It should only happen.

"*Halevai*," I repeated.

"And now, if you'll excuse me, I'll go change for lunch." He turned and disappeared, leaving me alone in the living room. When he returned fifteen minutes later, his step was slightly less hesitant than before. He'd replaced his workout clothes with khaki trousers and a long-sleeved blue shirt. His curly white hair was still wet from a very quick shower. When he bent over to give me a kiss on the forehead, I got a whiff of Irish Spring.

Hilda served large bowls of savory chicken soup with broad egg noodles and matzah crackers.

Uncle Isaac tasted his first spoonful. "Boy! Hilda can really cook, can't she?" He looked at her and smiled. "She's a genuine balabusta, this one."

"Well, you're a great teacher, Isaac." Hilda blew on a steaming spoonful of soup. "Working out gives you a real appetite. And what the doctor said is true. All the punching, stretching, and footwork helps the brain find new ways to control movement."

"Uncle Isaac, can I ask you a question?"

He smiled. "*Nu?*"

"When you owned your tailor shop on Pico Boulevard, did you ever chew on a piece of thread while you were sewing? You know, to keep from losing your wits?"

He scooped another spoonful of soup with a steady hand. "Where did you hear that old *bubbe meiser*?"

I told him about Fanya and her crusade against the evil eye.

"Oy. My mother, your bubbe—may her memory be a

blessing—was from the old school. She sure believed in all of those things. Every morning before I left for the shop, she packed me a good lunch and said, 'Don't forget the thread, Yitzie.' The same thing happened when I came home from work at the end of the day. She always asked, 'Yitzie. Did you remember the thread?'" Yitzie was a nickname for Yitzhak in Hebrew, or Isaac in English.

He sighed. "Your bubbie always knew when I wasn't telling the truth. So, lying wasn't an option. It was easier to gnaw on a piece of thread than face a lecture from my mother about dybbuks and demons."

"What about after she died? Did you continue with the chewing?"

Uncle Isaac shrugged. "By that time, I was so used to it, I did it without thinking."

"And yet, when I started sewing quilts, you never warned me about the thread thing."

This time he laughed out loud. "You're a modern woman, *faigela*. I knew you wouldn't listen to an old superstition."

Hilda stretched her hand in my uncle's direction and touched his arm softly. "Isaac, what was the word your mother called you?"

If I blinked, I would've missed the briefest caress of her fingers. My senses went on high alert. Was something going on between the two of them?

My uncle looked at her with an expression I'd never before seen in him. "In Hebrew, the name Isaac is *Yitzhak*. It means 'He will laugh.' Yitzie is a nickname." The tone of his voice betrayed something deeper. Tenderness? Affection?

As Fanya would say, *Oy va voy and three sholem ale-*

ichems! Something was definitely going on between the two of them.

All during the drive back to Encino I kept thinking about the subtle signals between my uncle and his live-in caregiver, Hilda. Emotions roiled around inside of me like numbers in a lottery drum. He never married or even had a girlfriend. My uncle devoted his whole life to taking care of my bubbie, my mother, and me. I once asked him why he never married. His response was simple and dismissive. "I never met the right one."

After he retired from his tailor shop, his whole social world took place at the senior center on Olympic Boulevard. Every day he met with his *daf yomi* group to study Talmud. Now he was in his eighties and suffered from Parkinson's. What was he thinking? Romance? With a woman young enough to be his daughter? Unbelievable. Or was it?

How could I have misjudged Hilda? Anger stabbed at my vision. I was a fool to trust her. What did she want with an old man like Uncle Isaac? After being homeless for years, she probably wanted security. Like a permanent place to call home. My uncle was more vulnerable now than ever before in his life and easy prey for her seduction. I vowed to replace Hilda with a male caregiver at the soonest possible moment.

I pulled into my driveway around three in the afternoon. In case the kidnappers had come back for Fanya, I searched the street for a blue SUV or black Jeep Cherokee. Everything looked normal. I opened the front door with my key and stepped inside. "Fanya?" I raised my voice.

"In here, Martha."

I dumped my purse on the hall table and joined her in the sewing room. Dozens of carefully cut triangles and squares lay in neat piles on the cutting table. Her toothy grin was enough to convince me she must've been working the entire time I was gone. "I'm done with the cutting and ready for the next step."

"Wow! You have the makings of a true quilt addict. I'm impressed."

"Believe it or not, this wasn't a stretch for me. I'm just not used to measuring to the nearest eighth of an inch."

"Well, now you get to sew all this together. Do you know how to use a sewing machine?"

"Yes."

"Okay. The main thing you need to know is this: All quilters use a fourth of an inch for the seams. It's universal. The presser foot on my machine measures exactly a quarter inch from the outside edge of the foot to the needle in the middle. You shouldn't have a problem lining up your fabrics to sew a perfect seam."

Each block in Fanya's quilt was made with twenty carefully cut shapes. I collected the pieces for one block and arranged them on my design wall. The little bits of cotton fabric easily clung to the white flannel sheet. "Study this arrangement and start sewing outward from the little squares in the middle. Remember to iron the seams as you go along. Let me know if you have any questions."

Fanya swiveled the chair around to face me. "I do have one thing. But it's not about this."

By the expression on her face, I could tell something was bothering her. Taking her cue, I sat in the other chair and said quietly, "I'm listening."

"While you were out, I heard from Hadas."

"She's alive? Thank God! The kidnappers let her use a phone? Did they ask for a ransom?"

Fanya shook her head and held her hand in the universal signal to stop. "It's not what we thought."

"What isn't?"

"The kidnapping."

"Now I'm really confused."

"I'm trying to tell you Hadas wasn't kidnapped after all."

If she'd thrown cold water in my face, I couldn't have been more shocked. "Wait a minute. What about the note the kidnappers left? The one warning *Don't call the police or she dies. Wait for instructions*?"

Fanya leaned back. "The note, the abduction? It was all a fake. The men who took her? Hired actors."

Now we know why one of them said, *All the world's a stage*. Sister Mae Slocum was right. She said one of then looked familiar. Like an actor she'd come across during her career as a cinematographer's assistant. It was a long shot, but I hoped Sister Mae could give me his name.

Fanya continued, "Hadas needed to disappear for a while. She says someone is after her."

"Who? Why?"

"She wouldn't say."

"If she wanted to disappear, why did she call you today?"

"She needs our help. We have to go to her, Martha."

The irony of helping Crusher's wife, Hadas, wasn't lost on me. I sighed, resigned to play the peculiar role of her adversary rescuer once again. "Right. Where's she staying?"

Fanya handed me a slip of paper on which she'd writ-

ten, *Delaware Hotel, Grand Avenue, LA, room 990.*
"She's registered as Jane Smith."

"How original," I snarked.

With afternoon traffic, it took us well over an hour to
reach downtown LA. We pulled in front of the stunning
and historic Hotel Delaware, noted for its elaborate Re-
naissance architecture. I exchanged my car keys for a
ticket from the red-coated valet, and the two of us entered
a grand lobby. Soaring spaces, marble floors, and opulent
furnishings reflected the glamour days of Hollywood.
Kings and heads of state visited the hotel with its vast oriental carpets, dark woodwork, and painted and coffered
ceilings. We headed straight for the elevators and the
ninth floor. Fanya sent a text to tell Hadas we were on our
way to her room.

I pressed the *up* button. As we waited for an elevator, a
worker in a white uniform entered a door marked *Housekeeping.* The elevator bell dinged, the doors opened, and
we entered and punched the button for the ninth floor.
The carpeted hallways completely muffled our steps. If
someone wanted to sneak to Hadas's room and harm her,
no one would hear them coming or going.

As we approached the door to room 990, Fanya said,
"Hadas texted me to knock three times so she'd know
it's us."

After three knocks, a voice on the other side of the
door said, "Who is it?"

Fanya replied, "Fanya and Martha."

The door opened quickly and Hadas motioned for us
to hurry inside the living room of her luxury suite. Fanya
and I moved toward a gray sofa, while Hadas double-
locked the door and opted for one of the two armchairs
upholstered in crimson velvet.

For someone in hiding, the beautiful Penélope Cruz look-alike showed no signs of wear and tear. Her dark hair tumbled in waves to her shoulders, and a sky-blue dress clung to her curves in all the right places. Only the constant movement of her eyes betrayed any anxiety or distress as her gaze darted from Fanya to me and back again. "Thank you for coming. Does anybody else know you're here?"

"I didn't tell a soul. Not even Yossi," Fanya said.

For once, Hadas looked directly at me. "It was good of you to come, Martha."

Ya think? "Do you mind telling us what the heck this is all about?"

CHAPTER 16

Hadas leaned back and folded her hands together in her lap. "I have to stay in hiding. At least until all of this blows over."

"All of what?" Fanya looked as if she didn't know whether the occasion called for salt in the corners of the room or spitting behind her hand. Or both.

"A man is pursuing me. His name's Alexander. I told him I was married. That always worked in the past with men like him. But he wouldn't take no for an answer. Although I couldn't prove it, I sensed someone was following me. Several times I thought I saw him on the street outside my home in New York, watching. I was terrified to leave my house alone, even in broad daylight." As she spoke, she licked her lips repeatedly. Her fear could be real. Nobody could fake such panic.

"Did you report him to the police?" I asked.

"And say what? 'I think I'm being followed, but I can't prove it'? The NYPD is too busy to go after alleged stalkers based on somebody's instincts. No. I decided to escape to LA and ask Yossi to come back to New York with me and scare the guy off. I figured once Alexander got a look at Yossi, he'd leave me alone."

"At least we have that in common," I muttered.

Hadas screwed up her face. "Come again?"

"I hoped once you got a look at me, you'd leave Yossi alone."

She avoided my gaze once more. "I'm being a poor hostess. Would you like a drink? Lots of choices in the minibar."

I stood. "I thought you'd never ask."

She started to rise. "What would you like?"

I motioned for her to sit again. "No, no. I've got this. I'll see what there is."

She pointed to a tiny kitchenette at the end of the living room. "There's a refrigerated minibar next to the sink."

Fanya followed behind me and looked over my shoulder at the contents of the small refrigerator. "I could use some water."

I handed her two plastic bottles of chilled water and scanned the selection of snacks. "Nothing to eat? You're probably hungry after the long ride downtown. I know I am. Surely there must be something kosher here."

Fanya reached for a small package of salted peanuts. "I'll have these."

A price list was posted inside the refrigerator door. Every item was marked up at least seven times above retail. "Here. Take these, too." I handed her a package of M&M'S, a can of Pringles potato chips, and a Hershey's with almonds. I figured they would cost Hadas a bit. I grabbed a Coke Zero and all the other snack items and watched Hadas's face as I spread them on the coffee table in front of the sofa. A hundred dollars' worth, at least. She pressed her lips together in a thin line but said nothing.

I smiled sweetly. "No use letting all this go to waste in the refrigerator." I peeled the wrapping off a Snickers bar and bit into the heavenly chocolate, caramel, and nut confection. "Mmm. I haven't eaten one of these since last Halloween. They're my favorites. Don't you agree? And look. There's even a hechsher on the wrappers." I pointed to a tiny printed symbol signifying the item was kosher.

Hadas recovered quickly and raised an eyebrow. "I've never indulged. Junk food will add pounds to your hips and thighs. But I guess you know that already."

I ignored the dig and sipped my diet cola. You had to draw the calorie line somewhere. "So, Hadas, you were telling us about getting away from Alexander. If you were sure Yossi would scare him off, why did you go to all the trouble and expense of planning your fake abduction? I mean, when did you plan to tell us you were okay? Both the LAPD and the FBI are looking for you, as we speak."

The expression on her face broadcast dismay. "You told the police? I left a note warning everyone not to!"

"So sue me. We were worried about your safety."

She slumped forward, with her elbows on her knees and head in hands. "Oh my God."

I pressed on. "And what, for heaven's sake, was the second break-in on Monday morning supposed to prove?"

Hadas suddenly sat straight, frowning. "There was another break-in?"

Fanya and I looked at each other. "Come on, Hadas.

Admit you sent those actors back for a second go-round of my house."

"I didn't. I swear." By now, her face was ashen. "Alexander. He must be in LA, looking for me. You've got to help me. You can't let anyone know you've seen me today. Not the police and not the FBI." She sprang to her feet and began pacing and wringing her hands. "Do you think you were followed here?"

"I wasn't looking. Did you notice anything, Fanya?"

Her eyes widened. "I might have. I noticed a white Mercedes behind us on the off-ramp of the freeway. When we stopped at the valet stand in front of the hotel, I saw a white Mercedes park in the loading zone right behind us. Do you think it's the same one?"

"What'll I do?" Hadas moaned. "I've got to get out of here." Her eyes welled with tears.

I tried to calm her down. "Surely, if someone followed us, they would've knocked on your door by now."

"Not if they're waiting for you to leave. You've got to help me escape without being seen. Find another safe place where Alexander can't find me."

"Why don't you go to the police?" I asked.

"No!" Hadas raised the palms of both hands. "What do I tell them? I think my New York stalker has followed me to LA, but I have no proof, only a feeling? The police won't do anything. I'm much better off dealing with this on my own."

"*Achalaria* on him!" Fanya spat. "Where's your sapphire, Hadas? And your *hamsa*. Did you remember to carry your charms?"

Hadas reached into the pocket of her dress and clutched a pouch similar to the one Fanya wore around her neck. "I've got everything you gave me right here." She looked straight at me. "Remember, Martha, if Alexander does find me and I disappear, I'll never be able to give Yossi the divorce you want."

Point taken. "Okay. Clearly, we can't take the chance Alexander knows where you are. We've got to find a way to smuggle you out of the Delaware." I scanned the luxury suite, trying to figure out how. "Okay. I have an idea."

They both stared at me.

"Hadas, order room service. Dinner for three. No, make it six. Dinner for six. Order several courses—soup, salad, entrée, and include at least three different wines and every kind of dessert."

Hadas looked at me with mouth open. "Are you meshuga? What are we going to do with this much food?"

"It's not the food I'm interested in. It's the cart they'll bring it on. A nice, big cart. Big enough for someone to hide in. Hadas, do you have a bathrobe I can wear?"

She looked me up and down and the corner of her mouth curled in a wry smile. "You can try, but it might be too small."

The look on my face warned her to go no further. "Get it, please."

She returned with a lacy little number made from pink silk. Hadas and I were about the same height. Except, she wore a size eight and I was several numbers beyond her.

"I see what you mean. Well, it'll have to do." I shrugged into the robe, the two halves refusing to close over my ample bosom. I left my clothes on because the front of me was completely exposed. "Hadas, give me a hundred-dollar bill."

She frowned. "Why?"

"Just do it!"

She disappeared into the bedroom and returned with a bill in her outstretched hand. "Here."

"When the food comes, the two of you hide in the bedroom. Let me do all the talking."

Forty-five minutes later, there was a knock on the door. "Room service."

I motioned for the two of them to move out of sight. Then I looked through the peephole in the door. A server in a white uniform stood behind a stainless-steel cart with a top and a bottom shelf loaded with plates of food covered by silver lids to keep them warm. I unlocked the door and gestured for the woman to enter the suite. She rolled the cart over to the table, unfolded a clean linen tablecloth, and began to unload the dishes.

I waved my hands to stop her. "Please, leave everything on the cart. I'm not quite dressed and I need my privacy. I'll call you when I'm ready for you to take everything away."

She glanced at the coffee table with candy wrappers and an empty tube of Pringles. "Do you want me to clean this before I go?"

"No, no. Those are my appetizers. I'm not through with them yet."

I waved the hundred in front of me and shoved it in her hand. When she saw Benjamin Franklin, she grinned and slipped it into her hip pocket. "My name is Arlene. Next time you need room service, ask for me." She gestured toward the groaning food cart. "Are you expecting guests? I can arrange everything really nice on the table."

Think fast! I can't let her take the cart away.

"I'm so ashamed. My husband left me and I just can't stop eating. You can see what it's done to my figure. I used to be able to close this bathrobe. Please, can we keep this our little secret?"

As I walked her to the door, she stopped and turned toward me. "Men. You know, honey, this is LA. There's a shrink on every corner. Maybe you need somebody to talk to."

"Maybe." I tried to steer her to the door, but Arlene wasn't finished.

She lowered her voice. "I know how you can find great-looking guys who'll show you a good time for a few of those Benjies. Make you feel good about yourself again. I can get a phone number. You know, discreet, like."

I shook my head slowly. "I don't think—"

"Okay. If you don't want to pay, there's always the cowboy bar on Ventura and Laurel Canyon in the Valley. Go after twelve. By then, everyone's pretty hammered. Wear a low-cut blouse and watch 'em try to land on you like flies on honey."

I opened the door. "Thanks, Arlene. You've helped me already. I mean it." I put a finger to my lips. "Remember, our secret."

Arlene walked toward the elevator, patting her hip pocket.

Hadas and Fanya came out of the bedroom, grinning. "You're a really good liar, *keinehora*."

I lifted the lid on one of the plates and discovered a cheese pizza. "Anyone hungry?"

Fanya grabbed a slice and began to chew. "Now what do we do?"

I took off the pink bathrobe, handed it to Hadas, and pointed to the bedroom. "Go in there and remove the sheets from the bed. Then pack whatever you can in your suitcase. You're not coming back, so don't leave anything important. Fanya, you can help me unload the cart."

The two of us began to stack the covered plates of food, beverages, and place settings on the table. Every once in a while I peeked under a silver lid to see what smelled so good. By the time we finished emptying the cart, I'd sampled the lamb kebab, a spear of grilled asparagus, one pumpkin ravioli, and a bite of chocolate soufflé, still warm from the oven.

Fanya grabbed two steak knives. "These may come in handy." She slid one inside her jeans pocket and offered me the other one.

"Whoa! I never figured you for a street fighter. Even if you do come from New York."

"I trained in Krav Maga. It's a kind of martial art originating in Israel. It makes sense for a woman alone to know how to defend herself. Having a weapon also makes sense."

I'd really misjudged Fanya. Underneath all her superstitious behavior was a clearheaded pragmatist. I accepted the knife and put it in my pocket. Then I stepped into the bedroom to see how Hadas was coming along. A tangled mess of bedding lay on the floor.

She shoved her laptop in the open suitcase on top of the bed and brushed the front of her sky-blue dress. "I think I got everything." She handed me the rumpled white sheets from the bed.

"Do you have anything besides skirts to wear? If it becomes necessary to run, you'll be able to move much faster in trousers and flat shoes."

"The only pants I have are my pajamas."

"They'll have to do. Put them on. What about flat shoes?"

"I brought a pair of loafers."

"Hurry and change and meet us back in the other room." I grabbed several towels from the bathroom, added them to the sheets, and rejoined Fanya in the living room.

Moments later, Hadas emerged from the bedroom, rolling her suitcase, dressed in pink-and-white striped cotton pajamas, a brown sweater, and brown penny loafers. "What's the plan, Martha?"

"You're going to sit on the bottom shelf of the cart, covered in the sheets. I'll pile these other linens on the top shelf and take you to the ground floor. When we first came, I saw a door marked *Housekeeping*. Hopefully we can find our way to an outside door."

"What about me?" In addition to the flashes of light in her eyes, Fanya's cheeks bloomed red, a sure sign of excitement.

"You're going to take the suitcase out the front door of the hotel and retrieve my car from the valet." I handed her the claim check. "Keep your phone open. Once Hadas and I have left the building, I'll let you know where we are and you can come and pick us up."

"You're brilliant. No wonder my brother loves you." Fanya took the suitcase from Hadas and disappeared down the hallway.

Hadas sat on the bottom shelf of the cart and shivered a little. "This metal is cold."

"Here. Sit on this towel. Now, bend your knees and wrap your arms around your legs. I'm going to wrap these around you." I bundled the sheets around her until she was completely covered. I unfolded the rest of the towels and placed them in a lump on the top shelf of the cart. "Are you ready, Hadas?"

CHAPTER 17

I pushed the cart with Hadas hidden inside through the empty hallway of the ninth floor. By the time I reached the bank of four elevators thirty yards away, a well-dressed couple appeared to be headed out for the evening. They dismissed my presence with one glance and carried on their conversation as if I were invisible. *This must be what it feels like to be a servant.*

The elevator bell dinged its arrival. I waited for the couple to enter before moving the cart toward the open steel doors.

The man frowned at my load of dirty linen. "Take the next car."

As the doors began to close, she said, "What nerve."

Soon, another elevator car arrived with a portly man aboard, holding his phone to his ear. He stepped out into the hallway and continued his conversation as he walked toward his room, stomach taking the lead. He never once looked at me or the cart.

So far, so good.

I rolled Hadas inside the empty elevator and punched a button for the first floor. We stopped on the way and picked up a group of three millennials on the fourth floor. Two young women and a man talked loudly and laughed as they entered the elevator. As soon as the doors slid shut, Hadas muffled a sneezing fit. I quickly raised the crook of my elbow to my face, as if I had sneezed into my arm. The three stopped talking and glared at me.

"Sorry," I said.

The young man wagged his head. "Wear a mask, lady."

Once we arrived on the main floor, I waited for the trio to leave and pushed the cart out of the elevators. I stood for a moment, trying to remember where I'd seen the door marked *Housekeeping*. As I swiveled my head, searching for the door, a man walked rapidly toward me. He wore a dark suit and a brass name tag identifying him as the assistant manager.

Oh crap!

"What do you think you're doing on the main floor?" He pointed to the cart. "Get that thing out of here as fast as you can. And next time take the service elevators to the laundry."

I would if I knew where it was. "I'm sorry. I—I'm new. I thought I was on the service elevator. Now I'm completely lost. Where is it again?"

He pointed to the far end of the hallway. "In the back, of course. You always use the freight elevator in the back, never the ones in front. These are for guests only. Clear?

Clean linen and laundry comes and goes from the base-ment. Never the main floor, and never in the guest eleva-tors."

"Yes, sir. Sorry, sir."

He looked at my T-shirt and frowned. "Where's your uniform?"

Oh no. My heart sped up. "I'm sorry, sir. I didn't have time to change into my uniform. I was told to hurry and get this." I gestured with my chin to the mound of towels on top of the cart. *Please, God, let him believe me*.

"Louise sent you upstairs looking like that?"

"Uh, yes. Louise." *Please, God, make him go away.* "Uh, I think you need to send someone to room six-twelve to clean the mess." I gestured toward the sheets and towels on the cart. "This stuff came from there. A leak in the toilet, I think."

He leaned in close and muttered, "I'll deal with you and Louise later. Now get out of here. I don't want to see your face again. Understand?"

"Yes, sir. I'm going. Sorry, sir."

I began to push the cart toward the freight elevator in back when he ordered, "Wait!"

I stopped and turned toward him. *Oh, dear God, please don't let him stop us*.

"What's your name?"

Without missing a beat, I said, "Hadas, sir. Hadas Levy."

"I'm going to keep my eye on you, Hadas." He turned on his heel and walked toward the lobby.

I resumed pushing the cart to the far end of the hall-way, increasing our speed as we went. A sign next to an elevator read *Employees Only*. I pushed the call button and heard the cables lifting the car from below. The doors slid open. I stepped inside, pushing the cart in front of me. "Okay, Hadas, we're alone right now. Can you hear me?"

"Yeph" came a tiny voice inside the bundle of sheets.

"I have no idea what to expect when we get to the basement. Be ready to run for it if we have to."

The doors slid open to reveal a much more spartan atmosphere; no painted ceilings, oriental carpets, or luxuriously upholstered sofas and chairs. The beige walls looked as if they hadn't been painted in years. The bare floor was unapologetic concrete. Two women wearing yellow uniforms walked toward me, laughing and chatting.

When they were close enough, I said, "Excuse me, but I'm new here. Where's the nearest exit? I need to go outside for a smoke." I pantomimed holding a cigarette in my right hand and smoking.

"Can't you read?" She pointed to a lighted *EXIT* sign above a door halfway down the corridor.

"Ah." I smiled. "Thanks."

I waited until they walked away and pushed the cart toward the exit sign and opened the door. Cold, night air hit my face as I stuck my head outside to see if it was safe to leave. The door opened to the back of the hotel. A small landing with a set of concrete steps led from the basement to the outside. Flattened cigarette butts littered the ground. On the street level, a truck with *Gourmet Meats* printed on the side slowly pulled away from the loading dock. A produce truck waited to take its place. It *beep-beep-beeped* as it slowly backed up to the dock to unload its cargo.

I stepped back inside the basement and threw the linen off Hadas. "It's now or never. Let's go!" She sprang off the bottom shelf and we both escaped through the door to freedom.

I climbed the stairs, practically dragging Hadas behind me. "Don't let anybody see your face. Look down and walk fast."

We threaded our way between trucks and parked cars and finally came to a street. We walked briskly along the sidewalk to a corner where we could read the street signs. I called Fanya on my cell phone. "We're on the corner of Fifth and Olive. A block away."

"I'll find you," she said. "I've got GPS on my phone. Let's see . . ." She paused. "There you are. I should be there within five minutes."

We ducked into the shadow of a locked doorway. "Get the hell outta my bedroom!"

My heart leapt. Hadas grabbed my arm and held on for dear life. I looked into the shadows to find a homeless man with a scraggly beard. He was curled in the fetal position against the door, wrapped in a filthy blanket.

We'd stumbled into the territory of one of the tens of thousands of homeless people living on the streets of LA. Without adequate services and shelters, most of them slept rough. The police were torn sometimes between compassion and enforcing the laws of the city. Chances were this man would be safe from eviction tonight if he remained quietly hidden in the shadows.

"Sorry," I said. "We didn't see you."

He muttered an expletive and spat, barely missing my shoe.

We walked about ten feet away and waited for an anxious fifteen minutes until my future sister-in-law found her way through the maze of one-way streets. I almost shouted with relief when I recognized my little white

Civic pulling over to the curb. I hurried Hadas into the back, while Fanya ran around the car to sit in the passenger side. I took my place in the driver's seat.

"That was awesome!" Fanya twisted around to look at Hadas as she buckled herself in. "You okay?"

I also peered at our fugitive in the rearview mirror. Her arms were crossed in a full self-hug. "I'm cold and I'm hungry."

She's complaining? No thanks for saving her? Like she's a princess and we are her servants?

Hadas looked into the rearview mirror and her gaze met mine. "Thanks."

Well, okay. Maybe she's not such a princess.

"Tell me how you escaped!" Fanya grinned and rubbed her hands together in anticipation. She laughed as Hadas described being able to hear but not see all our encounters. At the end of our story, Fanya asked, "Okay, now what, Martha? Where can we stash Hadas?"

"Hadas should hide in a remote environment, where nobody will think to look for her. I have a wild idea I hope will work. If my hunch is correct, the place we're going to will be ideal."

CHAPTER 18

We made our way through the freeway interchanges in downtown LA and ended on the 101 heading north. I told my passengers to let me know if they thought we were being followed. But all we could see in the darkness of night were hundreds of red taillights in front of us and just as many white headlights snaking by in the opposite direction.

As we approached Encino, Fanya asked, "Are we going to stop at the house? I could use a sweater."

"Afraid not. This'll have to do for now." I turned on the car heater. "He might be watching the house, waiting to pounce on Hadas when we return. We're going straight to the mountains of Ojai. I have friends who run a secluded retreat there. Mystical Feather."

"Ooh, it sounds fascinating." Fanya twisted in her seat again to look at Hadas in the back seat. "Don't you think?"

"I guess." Hadas sounded distracted.

I chuckled to myself. These two were in for a big surprise. "It's kind of a school for mediums and seers."

"*Oy va voy!*" Fanya clutched the amulet around her neck. "They practice magic there?"

"Magic is forbidden in Torah!" Hadas finally spoke up.

"If that were strictly true, why are you carrying the amulet Fanya made for you?"

"I never thought of it that way."

Fanya asked, "You said it's a school? What do they teach, exactly?"

"They have classes in various mystical arts. I took a class in tarot a little while ago. God hasn't struck me with lightning yet. I'm still walking around."

I didn't tell them Mystical Feather had a public image to rehabilitate. Not long ago, we'd discovered more than one dead body and exposed a serial killer. It was all over the news. I also didn't tell them about my almost being murdered at Mystical Feather. What would be the point? The killer was in jail.

Hadas sighed. "Frankly, I don't know what to think anymore. I just want my life to get back to where it was before Ze'ev ruined everything."

"What about Ze'ev?" I asked.

"My brother was sweet, but irresponsible. He only showed up to work occasionally. Keeping the business going fell pretty much on my shoulders."

"What?" Fanya sounded confused. "I thought you loved being in charge of the business, Hadas. Isn't that what you told me on the plane?"

"I did. But I'm talking now about Ze'ev's personal life. He liked to sleep around and, over the years, he managed to attract a string of girlfriends. Most of those relationships ran their course. But there was one crazy woman who wouldn't go away. Gita was her name. Gita showed up in front of the business shouting curses and threats. She even went around to his house several times and bothered poor Ettie. Fortunately, she disappeared from our lives when Ze'ev was killed."

My antennae quivered. "Getting back to this Gita person. How, exactly, did she threaten your brother?"

Hadas yawned loudly. "You know, the usual stuff. 'You'll be sorry you ever met me. I'll kill you for leaving. I'll curse your family.'"

"Did you know an eyewitness told the cops your brother was deliberately run over?"

"Yeah. We found out later."

"When the police told you your brother was deliberately run over, did you tell them about her?"

"Gita? Of course. But by the time they got around to questioning her, she'd left for Israel. Still hasn't come back, as far as I know. Besides, she never owned a car and didn't have a driver's license. I mean, who would give such a crazy person a license to operate a three-thousand-pound vehicle?"

You mean only licensed drivers are known to have run over people? "You said Ze'ev ruined everything for you. How do you mean?"

"Like I told Fanya, running the business without his help I could handle. I even managed to calm Ettie each time she endured a horrible confrontation with Gita. But when Ze'ev died, there was nobody to stand between me and Alexander. That last layer of family protection disappeared, and Alexander could smell vulnerability like a shark smells blood. He started coming after me the day we buried Ze'ev and sat shiva. Fanya was there. The rest you know."

My two passengers sat quietly for a while, listening to soft rock music on the radio.

When we reached the city of Camarillo, I asked if they wanted to stop for food. "I know a place with a long salad bar and excellent pizzas. It's probably safe to stop for a half hour or so."

Hadas spoke from the back seat. "Absolutely. I'm starved. Why didn't we think to take some of the room service with us?"

I took the Lewis Road off-ramp and headed north on Arneill. "We didn't have the luxury of time, remember? Nor did we have space to smuggle it out."

We parked at the end of a long row of cars and fast-walked through the chill night air toward the entrance of Toppers Pizza. Fanya stretched her long legs and arrived at the door before we did and held it open so we could scurry inside the warm and crowded restaurant. We ordered a cheese pizza loaded with almost every kind of veggie. I vetoed broccoli, kale, and zucchini. No sense in ruining a good meal.

Fanya and Hadas headed for the salad bar while I selected a comfortable booth for the three of us. Having a conversation would be difficult in the din. TV sets were mounted high on the walls around the dining area. One screen blasted a basketball game, another showed a surfer riding inside the curl of a huge wave, and yet another ran a commercial for Audi SUVs. Across the room, an entire Little League baseball team laughed loudly and dove across the table for slices of pizza.

A busy server dressed in a black T-shirt delivered our

food. As we ate, I kept rotating my head to check out the windows in back and in front of the restaurant. I tensed at one point when I caught a man dressed in a black hoodie looking our way. My first instinct was to warn the others to run back to the car. But then I remembered my little white Civic was parked at the end of a long row, on the other side of the vast parking lot. We'd never be able to outrun him.

Fanya bit into her pizza and scraped the paper napkin across her mouth. "What's the matter, Martha?"

I put my hand over my mouth in case the guy in the hoodie could read lips. "Don't turn around. I think we're being watched. Black hoodie. I'm going to get the car and drive to the door. When you hear me honk twice, rush outside and jump in the car."

"If we're being watched, it might be too dangerous to go outside by yourself. I've got a different idea." Fanya pushed the sleeves of her shirt up her forearms. "You forget I'm trained in the martial arts. If anyone dares to attack us, I'll make them wish they hadn't!"

Hadas stopped eating. "What if he's carrying a gun, Fanya?"

I began to slide out of my seat and stopped. "Wait a minute. Why do you think Alexander would be armed? I thought he wanted to possess you, not kill you."

"Well," Hadas bit her lip. "I've heard he can be violent when he doesn't get what he wants."

"Violent? Who told you? Has he ever hurt anyone you know of?"

Hadas waved a dismissive hand. "I don't remember where I heard it. But why take chances?"

Something about her voice sounded a tad insincere, like she was making up the story as she went along. Still, her fear and panic in the hotel seemed genuine. There must have been something more she wasn't telling us. "Why are two men after you? Why does Alexander need an accomplice?"

Hadas shivered. "I don't know. You'd have to ask him. Maybe he wants to make sure he can overpower me without a fight. Maybe he hired a private detective to follow me. Maybe he intends to kill me because he figures if he can't have me, nobody can."

Fanya motioned for me to sit back again. "Don't worry. If he does have a gun, I know how to disarm someone. You've got to trust me on this. Let's finish our dinner. Pretend we haven't noticed him. Meanwhile, we'll see if anyone joins him. If it's the same guy Yossi chased from the house Monday morning, he won't be alone."

As Fanya spoke, I noticed how much she was like her brother. Calm, confident, and ready for combat. She might hang wallpaper for a living, but her demeanor reminded me of every federal agent I'd ever known. Could it be she was also an agent disguised as a wall-covering installer? Fanya caught me looking at her and must've read my mind because she winked. *Oh my God. Could it be?*

I sent a text to my friend in Ojai to let him know I was on my way with a friend who needed a place to hide.

He responded almost immediately with a text of his own. **Glad to help.**

We finished our meal and stopped at the restroom before leaving the restaurant. When we emerged, black hoodie was gone.

"Do you think he's outside waiting for us?" Hadas hugged herself and shivered again. "What'll we do?"

I tried to soothe her worries, although I was thinking

the same thing. "Maybe he's some random guy who ordered takeout and left."

Fanya peered over our heads into the parking lot, her gaze sweeping 180 degrees. "On second thought, Martha, I think your idea was the best. Do you still have the steak knife I gave you at the hotel?"

I reached in my purse and showed it to her.

"Good. Carry it in your hand, just in case. Go get the car and I'll stay here with Hadas. She's the one they want, not you."

Once again, I noticed how practiced and professional Fanya's response seemed. Who could she be working for? FBI? Mossad? Or was she merely what she claimed to be: a wallpaper hanger who knew Krav Maga.

CHAPTER 19

I made it to my Civic without interference and drove to the entrance of Toppers. Fanya and Hadas hurried to the car. Once they were inside, we locked the doors. I drove in the direction of the 101 Freeway, taking a circuitous route through residential streets to see if we were being followed. Satisfied we were alone, I entered the stream of cars driving north. Traffic had thinned long ago, and we made good time through the county roads. We transitioned to the 150 north toward the town of Ojai.

The two-lane highway snaked through the dark mountains past ranches, campgrounds, and Thomas Aquinas College. Finally, we turned left on Sulphur Mountain Road.

Hadas asked, "Exactly what do they do in this place, anyway?"

"It's called the Mystical Feather Society. It was started

decades ago by a famous medium and healer, Madam Natasha St. Germain. Her grandson, Andre Polinskaya, runs the place now. He's agreed to let you hide here as long as you need." They didn't need to know I'd saved Andre's life and that he'd do anything for me.

We climbed the mountain until we came to a driveway on our left with a sign illuminated by our headlights.

WELCOME TO THE MYSTICAL FEATHER SOCIETY

We turned and slowly ascended the driveway, tires crunching on the gravel. With the help of the headlights, we could barely make out a sign on a small building:

MYSTICAL FEATHER SOCIETY
BOOKSTORE AND TEAHOUSE
PUBLIC WELCOME

Farther up the driveway we approached a metal gate. A motion-sensor light switched on and illuminated another sign.

MYSTICAL FEATHER SOCIETY
PRIVATE RETREAT
CLOTHING OPTIONAL
INFORMATION IN THE BOOKSTORE

Fanya gasped. "Clothing optional? As in you don't have to wear anything if you don't want to?"

I chuckled. "Yup. But don't worry, it's chilly tonight. We're not likely to see any nudity. At least not outdoors."

"*Oy va voy!*" She spat three times behind her hand. "*Pu, pu, pu!* What're you going to do, Hadas?"

"Do? Nothing. I couldn't care less." Hadas seemed to be miles away.

The gate stood open, allowing us to continue our ascent, which ended in a parking area surrounded by trees—skeletal branches reaching in the darkness. Another motion-sensor light came to life as we parked next to a white passenger van. Fanya retrieved Hadas's suitcase from the trunk while a dark figure carrying a flashlight came down the hill to greet us.

"Martha, I see you made it okay." As he drew into the light, Andre Polinskaya's black hair and high cheekbones appeared, and I relaxed for the first time that night.

I gave him a brief hug. "Thanks for helping us out." I introduced Fanya as Crusher's sister. When I introduced Hadas as Crusher's wife, Andre gave me a questioning look. "It's a long story. I'll leave the telling to Hadas. I'd like to get started back home as soon as possible. I've been running on adrenaline for hours, and I'm exhausted."

"Understood." His voice was surprisingly deep for a man of average height. "Listen, I knew you were coming even before you called. Grandmother Natasha came to me in a dream last night and told me to help you."

Who was I to argue? I didn't believe in that stuff, but he was sincere enough. I kept my opinions to myself.

Fanya's voice came softly. "I also have such dreams."

Andre snapped to attention. "Really? Are you clairvoyant?"

"I'm not sure." Fanya shrugged. "Mostly it's my bubbie. She's disappointed I'm not married already. And sometimes she warns me when a job isn't safe to take."

Even in the semidarkness, the light in Andre's dark eyes seemed to dance. "What kind of work do you do?"

"Wall coverings. I work by myself, so I have to choose my clients carefully. One time I ignored Bubbie's warning and took on a job for a man with a bad reputation in our neighborhood. Sure enough, as I rolled glue onto a length of ugly green-and-orange–striped paper, he snuck up behind me and groped my chest."

"What did you do?"

Fanya grinned. "I swung around fast, punched his clock and karate-kicked him across the room. Then I took the bucket of glue and poured it over his head and left. From then on, I listened to all of my bubbie's warnings."

Andre barked a laugh and then turned a more sober face to me. "I consulted the tarot before you came, Martha. You need to be very careful. There are forces at work you know nothing about. As for your friend, don't worry. She'll be quite safe here."

I'd hardly call Hadas my friend.

He took the suitcase from Fanya and shone the light on the path to the retreat. "If you follow me, Hadas, I'll show you to your cottage. We have a vacancy at the moment. This is perfect timing."

As she walked back up the hill with Andre, I heard her say, "I still have a business to run in New York. Do you have Wi-Fi here? I'll also need a printer."

My jaw dropped. "Is she for real, Fanya? She didn't even utter one word of thanks. Thanks for your help, thanks for your understanding, thanks for the brilliant escape? What the heck?"

Friday morning I woke at eight, stiff and already tired—even though the clock said I'd slept for nine hours straight. My body was paying me back for the extra stress and long day yesterday. Once again, I was walking proof that fibromyalgia was unforgiving.

I showered and dressed in my jeans and T-shirt and limped into the kitchen, where Fanya, also wearing jeans, sat reading the paper and drinking coffee.

She looked at me and smiled. "Good morning, sleepy-head."

"How long have you been awake?"

She glanced at the clock. "Two hours. I got up as Yossi was leaving. He asked me to tell you he might be home late tonight."

"Darn. Must be important. He never misses Friday nights if he can help it. We almost always have a full house with my daughter, Quincy, and her little family, my sister, Giselle, and her fiancé Harold, and my uncle Isaac and his helper Hilda." I remembered with a sinking feeling in my gut how, during my visit yesterday, I suspected Hilda was developing an inappropriate relationship with my elderly uncle. I dreaded the moment when I would have to confront her. Would I ever find another caregiver as good as her?

"How nice. I miss having a regular family connection. To tell you the truth, I was looking forward to celebrating Shabbat with my brother for the first time in years."

"He might still show."

Fanya sighed. "*Halevai*. It should only happen. Nu? How can I help you prepare for tonight?"

I was grateful for the extra set of hands. The house got clean in half the time, and we finished our food preparations by three.

Fanya dried her hands on a paper towel and looked at the clock. "If there's nothing more to do, I'm going to go in the bedroom and meditate. About an hour."

I kissed her on the cheek. "Thanks again for your help." I cracked open a can of Coke Zero and moved to the living room sofa with my cell phone.

I was relieved to find a text from Crusher. **Home on time tonight. Luv U**

Next, I called my "friend" John Smith of the FBI, who answered after three rings. "Ah, Mrs. Rose. What bon mot do you have for me now?"

"She's alive."

"Hadas Levy?"

"She staged her own abduction."

"You know this, how?"

"She called Yossi's sister, Fanya, and begged for help. Last night we smuggled her out of the Hotel Delaware in downtown LA, where she was hiding from a man named Alexander."

"Where is she now?"

"In a safe place."

"Martha . . ." His voice carried a warning.

"Look. Didn't you tell me the best way to prove Yossi's and my innocence was for you to find Mrs. Levy? Well, we found her on our own. So, you can cross us off the suspect list for her kidnapping, a crime that was never actually committed."

"Where is—?"

I cut him off before he could chastise me again. "We stashed her in a place nobody would know to look. Do you remember the last homicide case we worked on?"

"If the phrase *we worked on* is a figure of speech for you getting in too deep, then yes, I remember."

"Well, she's there. And before you ask, we made sure nobody was following us."

"Who else knows her location?"

"Just Yossi. I told him last night when we finally arrived back home. And Andre Polinskaya, of course. I sense this Alexander guy is the missing link between Ze'ev Uhrman's death and Hadas's present predicament, but I still don't know how."

"What did Mrs. Levy tell you about the man who's after her?"

"He's been hitting on her since the day of her brother Ze'ev's funeral. He's determined to be her lover and won't take no for an answer. When his attentions became too creepy, she escaped to LA with Fanya. She hoped to persuade Yossi to go back to New York with her and scare off this guy for good. I'm pretty sure Alexander was behind the second break-in at my house."

Smith paused. "Hmm. Did Mrs. Levy say anything else?"

"She's concerned Alexander might be armed. She heard he can be violent, although she was vague about details."

"She's not wrong."

"You already knew about him?"

"Yeah, we knew."

"Can't you arrest him?"

"On what grounds? Lusting after a pretty woman? We don't have the evidence a case like this calls for. I'm satisfied Mrs. Levy is safe for now."

"What about me? What if he comes back to my house?"

"Between Levy and his sister, an intruder wouldn't have a chance."

"Wait! Why did you say that about Yossi's sister, Fanya?"

"I hear she's very accomplished at Krav Maga."

How in the world did FBI Director of Counterintelligence John Smith know so much detail about Fanya? "What do you know that I don't?"

He did what he did best. He ignored me. "Speaking of knowing and not knowing, have you informed the local police Mrs. Levy has been found and is out of danger?"

Oh crap. Smith was right. "What should I say? Her kidnapping was just a silly mistake?"

"Levy is her next of kin. Ask him to call the LAPD. He'll know what to say. Don't delay. They won't thank you for wasting more of their time."

I ended the call and sent Crusher a text. **Can you tell Det Beavers H is safe?**

Almost immediately he sent an answer. **Already done.**

CHAPTER 20

At 5:30 Friday evening, Fanya and I, dressed in our Sabbath clothes, were in the kitchen seeing to last-minute food prep. Crusher's Harley roared into the drive-way, and a minute later he bounded in the house and handed me a bouquet of pink roses and kissed me softly.

Before heading for the bedroom to shower and change, he stopped and kissed the top of Fanya's head. *"Ah gutten* Shabbos, Fanele."

She smiled at her brother's affectionate greeting and responded in the Yiddish they both grew up with. *"Ah gutten* Shabbos, Yossi. It's been a long time since we've managed to be together on a Friday night."

At six, my daughter, Quincy, and her little family were the first to arrive. As soon as my infant granddaughter Daisy saw me, she stretched her arms in my direction and smiled. "Baba!"

I pried her out of her father's arms and swept her in circles around the living room. She rewarded me with giggles of delight.

I kissed her fat little cheek. "When I'm very old, you can pick *me* up and dance *me* around the room. Deal?"

"Baba!"

Next to arrive was the Friday foursome, as they called themselves: my sister, Giselle, in a little black dress; her fiancé Harold, still wearing a pinstriped business suit; Uncle Isaac with his embroidered Bukharan yarmulke nestled on top of his white curls, and Hilda in her beige pantsuit. Giselle hugged Fanya as if they were old friends and wished her a happy Sabbath.

Quincy seemed especially pleased to meet Crusher's sister. "I grew up with no aunts or uncles on my mother's side. I was thrilled when my mom discovered she had a half sister. I call her Aunt Giselle. What do I call you? Aunt Fanya?"

"Oh, I love the sound of that!"

I scrutinized Hilda as she helped my uncle step over the threshold into the house. She placed one arm around his shoulders while he steadied himself by grasping on to her other hand. Once inside, he navigated on his own to the living room and sat, with Hilda following close enough to catch him if he stumbled. During this time, I didn't witness any inappropriate touching. Had I been mistaken about Hilda's behavior yesterday?

I leaned over and kissed his cheek. "Shabbat shalom, Uncle."

He returned the greeting. "So *nu*? What's the latest with the wedding, *faigela*? I'm not getting any younger, you know."

I glanced around quickly at the others with a silent plea to keep from telling my uncle anything about Crusher's marriage or Hadas's disappearing act. Considering his frail state of health, I didn't want to alarm my uncle or cause him distress. I smiled. "I think I'm going to ask my friend Jazz to make me a special dress for the occasion. And the cake definitely has to be chocolate with chocolate frosting." I hastily changed the subject. "Uncle Isaac, you seem to be steadier on your feet."

He sat straighter and made a mock bicep curl with his arm. "It's the boxing lessons. I'm training to go a few rounds with Muhammad Ali." He reached over and patted Hilda's hand. "She's a tough trainer, this one. But I'm glad to have her in my corner."

Harold Zimmerman, Giselle's fiancé, removed his black-rimmed glasses and pinched the bridge of his nose. "On the way over here, Isaac told us what he's been doing." He casually wiped the lenses with the end of his tie and slipped them back on. "I boxed a little myself during my squandered youth. It's a great sport."

Fanya nodded. "Boxing is wonderful for balance and toning. Just let me know when you're ready to graduate to Krav Maga, Isaac. I can teach you a trick or two."

I studied Hilda during this exchange. She appeared to be delighted with the casual banter, smiling in all the right places and laughing at Fanya's offer. I resolved to take a more charitable wait-and-see attitude before confronting her.

My bubbie's two silver candleholders with pure white candles sat on the sideboard in the dining room. Joining me there for the blessing were all the other females in the house: Fanya, Giselle, Quincy, holding her baby Daisy;

and even Hilda. I scraped a wooden match over the rough strip on the box and held the flame to the candlewicks until they blazed on their own. Together, we recited in Hebrew what Jewish women all over the world recited to welcome the Sabbath. "Blessed art Thou, oh Lord our God, King of the universe who sanctifies us by Thy commandments and commands us to kindle the Sabbath lights."

Everyone said, "Amen."

I sat at the table next to Uncle Isaac as he recited the kiddush welcoming the Sabbath and blessed the wine and the challah. When he finished, Fanya and I brought the food from the kitchen. I remained standing to get everyone's attention. "Tonight's meal is dairy. I've baked salmon in a creamy hollandaise sauce. In addition, Fanya prepared a special vegetarian entrée with potatoes, beans, couscous, and yogurt."

The table erupted in a flurry of oohs and aahs as serving spoons clinked against the dishes and plates.

Giselle filled her fork with the savory mixture from Fanya's recipe. "Have they found the body of Yossi's wife yet? Hadas?"

I could've kicked her for mentioning anything about Hadas in front of my uncle. He knew nothing about the break-ins. He didn't even know about the complication of Crusher's marriage. I clenched my jaw and spoke through my teeth. "You know, G, this really isn't the place to discuss such things."

Quincy scooped a little bit of soft potato on her fingertip and fed it to an enthusiastic Daisy, who sat on her lap. "What's the big deal? Noah told me all about it, Mom." She looked at Crusher. "I think it's hilarious you're still married to someone else."

I sat back and closed my eyes to avoid seeing my uncle's reaction. I didn't have to wait long. His fork clanked as it dropped on his plate.

I opened my eyes in time to watch tremors ripple through his hand. "Yossi? This is true? You're married?"

Crusher slowly raked his fingers through his short beard and nodded. "I thought it had been taken care of years ago, Isaac. An annulment. I even signed the papers, but they were never filed. Now she's dealing with a personal crisis. When it's resolved, she'll finally be able to give me the divorce we agreed on thirty years ago."

"So what's this talk about finding her body? Is she alive or is she dead, God forbid?"

"I promise you she's very much alive, Uncle." I reached over and grabbed his hand, which continued to shake inside mine. I hated the way Parkinson's was robbing him of a tranquil old age. "She's keeping a low profile until her crisis is resolved."

"Crisis, *shmisis*. I may be old, *faigela*, but I'm no *shmendrik*. I want the truth. Tell me the truth."

Giselle spoke again. "Wait. I'm confused. I thought Hadas was kidnapped from this house by a couple of bad guys who chloroformed her and broke in a second time the next day. Now you're saying she's alive, like you know it for a fact. Is she? Alive?"

I took a deep breath before telling another lie. "I spoke to Hadas on the phone yesterday. She wanted to apologize for any misunderstanding. She wasn't kidnapped. She left willingly with a couple of friends. As soon as she can straighten out a few problems back at her New York office, she'll give Yossi a divorce." The words slipped out of my mouth as smooth as butter. I must admit I was proud of my growing ability to massage the facts at the drop of a hat.

I interpreted the expression blossoming on Fanya's face as admiration. She knew more than anyone else at the table what really happened. Her lips quivered as though she was trying to suppress a smile.

"I'm glad someone's amused," I muttered out of the corner of my mouth.

She quickly covered her face with her napkin and coughed. I heard the yip of laughter underneath and poked her arm.

Later in the evening, after everyone had gone home and Crusher was busy washing dishes, Fanya and I sat in the living room enjoying our second helping of my favorite dessert—key lime cheesecake.

I eyed my empty plate with regret and licked the fork. "You know, I don't trust Hadas as far as I can throw her. She's done nothing but lie. She lied to Yossi thirty years ago, and she lied about her abduction. I think she's still lying."

Fanya wrinkled her forehead. "You don't believe anything she said?"

"Hadas is a master manipulator. I have a strong feeling she's holding back on us. I mean, look how she lied about her marriage to Yossi all these years. She led people to believe she'd been abandoned. And remember when she talked about Alexander? Well, something about her story seemed contrived. The more questions I asked, the vaguer her answers became. Like she was making up things on the fly."

Fanya cut a petite bite of cheesecake. "Why do you think she came to LA in the first place?"

"I wish I knew. I think she spoke the truth when she

said Ze'ev ruined her life. What I want to know is how do you make a leap between her good-for-nothing brother and a creepy guy who's stalking her? I think we should take a closer look at Ze'ev. Who nursed a grudge powerful enough to kill him? We know he gambled and stole from the business. That certainly gives Hadas a motive."

Fanya took one last bite of her cheesecake and placed her empty plate next to mine. "True. But Hadas told me he owed money to some Mobbed-up guys. Maybe they killed him."

"Maybe. But dead men don't pay their debts. Ze'ev was more valuable to them alive." I paused for a moment. "On the other hand, Hadas could've uncovered his thieving and cut her brother out of the business. If so, Ze'ev would no longer have the means to pay off his gambling debts."

Fanya finished the thought. "The Mob could've wasted him to set an example for anyone else tempted to stop paying." Her voice shifted slightly. She sounded less like a perplexed observer and more like professional law enforcement.

I briefly studied my future sister-in-law. She had depth. How much of her flighty, superstitious persona was real? I pushed the thought out of my mind. "Right. Which would explain why the business suddenly operated in the black again once Ze'ev was out of the picture and couldn't steal the business profits anymore. It also might explain why not one penny of the business went to Ze'ev's family when he died."

Fanya nodded. "Ettie said Hadas did 'something sneaky' and now they had to take her to court to get reinstated as half owners of the Uhrman Company. I hate to say it, but this doesn't look good for Hadas."

"No, it doesn't. But Hadas wasn't the only one with motive. We know Ze'ev was habitually unfaithful. That would give his wife, Ettie, a reason to kill him."

Fanya fished for the amulet she wore around her neck and closed her fist around it. "No. That doesn't sound like the Ettie I know. It's more likely the crazy woman Gita killed him. Didn't Hadas say she heard Gita threaten to kill Ze'ev?"

"Yes, but how do we know Hadas is telling the truth? We only have her word that Gita made threats. We should double-check her story. See what Ettie has to say." I inhaled deeply and let it out slowly, contemplating all the possible motives for wanting Ze'ev dead. "And then there's Alexander. Who is he? What does he do? Is he that obsessed with Hadas he killed Ze'ev as part of a strategy to get closer to her? He certainly wasted no time zeroing in on her, starting the day of Ze'ev's funeral."

Fanya counted on her fingers. "How many people had a motive to murder? Hadas, the Mob, Ettie, Gita, and Alexander. Any one of them could've done it."

"We need to find a way to stop Alexander from bothering Hadas. I want her to come out of hiding and give Yossi a divorce."

Crusher, carrying a plate with the last slice of cheesecake, joined us in the living room. "I've been listening from the kitchen. I agree we should keep digging. I'll focus on Alexander. Check NCIC for any priors."

I tried not to stare as he lifted a forkful to his mouth. "Does anyone know his last name? I feel like an idiot. I forgot to ask her that one simple question." I snuck another quick look at his plate, hoping he'd offer me a bite. "And I'll check with Giselle to see if Shadow uncovered more information on the finances of the Uhrman Company."

"What can I do?" Fanya asked.

As the last bite on Crusher's plate disappeared, I sighed and turned to my future sister-in-law. "I'll call Hadas and get Alexander's last name for Yossi. Then we should call Ettie again. We need to confirm Hadas's story about Gita. Between the three of us, we might get lucky enough to uncover a clue pointing to Ze'ev's killer."

Fanya pointed to the ceiling. "From your mouth to God's ears."

I hoped God was paying attention.

CHAPTER 21

Saturday morning I woke determined to make it a true day of rest. I needed a break from our investigation. I entertained visions of the three of us lounging around all day, eating leftovers and enjoying each other's company. Maybe we'd play Scrabble and munch on popcorn. I tied my blue chenille bathrobe around my waist and moved to the kitchen in matching blue slippers. Crusher sat at the table with a steaming mug of coffee. Fanya hummed as she deftly whipped some kind of batter.

"For pancakes." Fanya poured little rounds in a hot skillet and turned them over as they formed bubbles around the edges. Obviously, she didn't observe another one of the thirty-nine kinds of work prohibited on the Sabbath: lighting a fire and cooking. "I hope you're hungry. There's also fresh coffee and some cut-up strawberries."

My first disappointment came when Crusher's cell phone chirped. He read the text and grunted. "Sorry, ladies, but duty calls. Excellent breakfast, Fan. Thanks." He headed toward the bedroom to get his gun and badge and reappeared a few minutes later, wearing a shoulder holster.

"Text me Alexander's last name and I'll look for him when I have time." He kissed me, shrugged into his black leather jacket, and hurried out the doorway.

My second disappointment came when I tried to reach Hadas. My call went to voice mail. I waited for an hour before calling again. When she still didn't answer, my gut told me something wasn't right. I called Andre at ten.

"I haven't seen her today. She didn't show for breakfast. I'll go see if she's okay and call you back."

Twenty minutes later, my phone rang. I touched the green phone icon when Andre's name appeared on the screen. "Did you find her?"

"No. I even went to the bookstore, but she seems to have disappeared."

What? Again? My stomach plummeted. "When was the last time you saw her?"

"Last night at dinner."

"Are her things still in her room? Phone, laptop, clothes?"

"Everything's gone."

Anger boiled in my brain. I wanted to scream, especially after all the trouble we went through to help her. It took every bit of my self-control to speak again. "Was there any sign of a struggle? Any indication she might not've gone willingly?"

"Not that I could see," Andre's voice softened. "But then I'm not a professional."

What a witch! Did she ever intend to give Crusher a divorce?

"Well, what does your famous dead grandmother have to say about it? Can't she tell us where Hadas is?" I immediately regretted my outburst. "Sorry, Andre. I'm just frustrated and angry."

"I understand. Do you want me to do a tarot reading over the phone? It might give you some guidance."

"Thanks for the offer, but I think I'll skip it this time."

I ended the call and went straight to my sewing room, where Fanya worked on her green-and-yellow Snail's Trail blocks—another indication she'd left behind the Orthodox way of life. Sewing together (and ripping apart) were types of work forbidden on the Sabbath.

I stood with my fists resting on my hip bones and spat out my frustration. "Guess what our little Miss Hadas has done now?"

Fanya stopped sewing and cocked her head to the side like a wren eyeing a worm. "Whatever it is, I can tell you're not happy."

"Not happy? I'm beyond pissed off. Hadas lied to us again. She left Mystical Feather sometime between dinner last night and breakfast this morning. Took all her things and snuck off under the cover of darkness. And she's not answering her cell phone."

Still seated in front of my Bernina sewing machine, Fanya turned it off and swiveled on the chair until she faced me. "Oy! I wonder what she's playing at."

I sat in the other chair and crossed my arms. "I wish I knew. You were on the mountain. You saw. She couldn't have pulled off her disappearing act without help."

"Yeah. That place is isolated. It's not like she could walk to the nearest bus stop or call Uber. Maybe she contacted those same two guys who helped her disappear the first time."

"I've been thinking the same thing. I should talk to my neighbor again. Sister Mae thought she recognized one of them. Maybe she'll remember his name. And speaking of names, I was supposed to get Alexander's last name from Hadas so Yossi could run him through the national criminal database. Fat chance now."

Fanya didn't miss a beat. "We still have options. What about your friend in the FBI?"

Bingo! Once again, I was impressed by Fanya's cool thinking. "You're right. I'd forgotten John Smith said they already knew about Alexander. The good news is Smith should know if Alexander has a criminal record. The bad news is I doubt he'll share that information with me. Still, I've got to try."

I opened the contact list in my phone and scrolled to Smith, John. Six rings later, I spoke to his voice mail. "This is Martha Rose again. Hadas Levy bailed in the middle of the night from Mystical Feather. No one knows where she is. Please call me."

Thoughts of a peaceful Shabbat at home evaporated. Anger and frustration became the engine driving the rest of my day. "Okay, Fanya. Can you call Ettie again? I want to check out Hadas's story about Ze'ev's jilted lover, Gita—if she ever existed. That's not something the wife of a cheating husband would forget."

"Um, there's a problem." Fanya cleared her throat. "Ettie's far more observant than we are. She won't answer her phone on Shabbat. We'll have to wait until after Havdalah to talk to her." Fanya referred to the lovely ceremony involving a braided candle, a glass of wine, and some sweet-smelling spices marking the end of the Sabbath and the beginning of the week on Saturday night after sunset.

I glanced at the clock on the wall. "New York is three hours ahead of us. If we call at five our time, it will be eight where she is. Would she answer then?"

Fanya nodded. "We still have five hours to go. I've got plenty to keep me busy in the meantime." She showed me one completed Snail's Trail block. "I've sewn three of these. Only twenty-seven more to go. What do you think?" The yellows and greens spiraled out of the center of the block in a joyful flurry of spring colors.

I took the block and turned it over to observe the precise quarter-inch seams she'd sewn. Then I turned to the front side again and closely examined the points where the triangles came together. All the points were crisp, an indication Fanya knew what she was doing. "I think it's gorgeous. Are you sure you've never quilted before?"

Fanya grinned. "I'm more a maven with wallpaper. But I love the feel of working with cotton fabric."

"You hungry?" I asked.

"Thanks, no. I made a salad. There's some leftover you can have if you want."

"Maybe later. Have fun. I'm going next door." I left the house and let myself through the swinging gate to Sister Mae's front door. King Solomon's deep bark told the world he was doing his job as chief protector of Sister Mae and their property. His baritone woofs drew my curious neighbor to her window. When she saw me, a smile lit her face. Ten seconds later she opened the front door wide enough to stick her head outside.

The petite Sister Mae smiled a greeting. She stood in front of her Great Dane, attempting to keep me from being bowled over by his excited greeting. He managed to push his slobbering muzzle underneath her arm and forward until he could look straight at me, enthusiastic tail thumping against the wall.

"Look him straight in the eyes, like you're the boss," she said.

"Hello, King." I patted the top of his huge head and stared at him.

Sister Mae pushed him back from the door. "Hush up, now. Go play with your toys."

He took one last look at me and withdrew to the inside of the house.

"You seem to be making progress with his training. The last time I was here, he pushed you out of the way to get to me."

She twisted her head to watch his retreat. "Bless his heart. He's as sweet as sugar. One more month and I think I can actually invite people inside the house without King trying to love all over them. Is everything okay?"

"Not really. We found our friend. She was fine, but now she's disappeared again."

"Heavens! Why'd she go and do such a thing?"

"Good question. We think the two people who took her a week ago may have helped her once more. You thought you recognized the big one. I was hoping you might remember his name. You said he looked like one of the minor actors on *Grey's Anatomy*. Peter-something."

She sighed. "I honestly don't know. But I can do an online search. I don't think you'll want to come inside and wait, though. You'd be rassling with King the whole time. How 'bout I call you if I find anything?"

Once back home, I stopped to listen to the sound of my

Bernina sewing machine in the other room humming in fits and starts. It was the music of the busy quilter creating beauty with needle and fabric.

I decided not to interrupt Fanya's sewing. Instead, I made a beef salami sandwich, with slices of the leftover challah and a thin schmear of spicy brown mustard. I opened a can of Coke Zero and installed myself at the kitchen table. As I took my first big bite, my phone rang, John Smith returning my call.

"Your message contained some surprising news, Martha."

"Mmph." I chewed fast and swallowed. "What is Hadas doing, anyway? Yossi and I can't get married until she agrees to a divorce. Now she's disappeared again. We're right back where we started."

"And you should stay there. You're no match for the players in this case."

I was on the verge of whining. "But you're the FBI. You can find anybody. Dead or alive."

"Don't worry. We'll find her."

"Preferably before Yossi and I are too old to care. By the way, do you know anything about a woman named Gita? She's an ex-girlfriend of Hadas's brother, Ze'ev Uhrman."

Smith returned my question with a question. "Is Gita someone I should know about?"

"Only if she's a real person. Hadas said Gita threatened to kill Ze'ev, but frankly, I don't believe anything Hadas says anymore."

"I'll have someone look into it. Thanks for the intel."

"And that's all I get? You could hardly call this the information highway. The data seems to be driving in one direction only. Me to you."

"Well, there is something I can share. You showed a

lot of creativity and quick thinking when you smuggled Hadas from the Hotel Delaware in downtown LA."

I smiled. Praise coming from John Smith was rare. "How did you get the details about our great escape?"

Smith chuckled. "We have eyes and ears everywhere. Someone said you reminded them of an *I Love Lucy* episode. And now I must leave you. Stay at home, Martha. Stay safe."

I hardly responded. I was too busy trying to figure out who the FBI agent in the hotel was who saw our escape. Was it the room service person Arlene? One of the people in the elevator? The hotel manager? The two housekeepers in the basement? Then it dawned on me. If there were FBI agents in the hotel watching us, they must've either followed me there or they already knew where Hadas was.

At four-thirty, I checked on Fanya in the sewing room. She'd been at the Bernina the whole afternoon.

She stopped sewing and smiled at me. "I'm almost finished. Five more blocks to go. Take a look." She gestured toward a neat stack of yellow-and-green quilt blocks, all perfectly sewn with crisp points.

"These are wonderful, Fanya. Your quilt is going to be special. Let's see how these look on the design wall." I carried twenty-five blocks over to the white flannel sheet hanging on my wall. The nap of the flannel grabbed the cotton pieces and hugged them in place. I hung the blocks next to each other and the overall design emerged.

Fanya stood with me and examined the layout. "Wow. Even better than I imagined. I really get how satisfying quilting can be. This hobby could definitely become addictive."

I bristled at her calling quilt-making a hobby. A hobby

implied a part-time interest someone enjoyed when they weren't doing important things in the real world. "Quilting is more than a hobby, Fanya. Think of it as a form of fabric art. Whether you're piecing traditional blocks or venturing into landscapes and portraits, you—the quilter-artist—must design, plan, and execute your creation."

She placed a hand on the side of her face. "Hmm. You're right. Until now, I've always thought of them as just blankets."

"Not necessarily. Quilts can function as both wall art and bed art. Either way, they're meant to be seen, not folded away in the closet."

"Well, this one will look great on my bed."

I glanced at the clock. "It's seven-forty-five in New York. Time to call Ettie."

Fanya turned off the sewing machine, grabbed her cell phone, and followed me into the living room. She put her phone on speaker mode. I grabbed a pen and paper to feed her questions.

Ettie answered on the fourth ring. "Oy, Fanya! *Shavuah tov.*" She uttered the standard greeting for ending the Sabbath, *Have a good week.* "Why am I so lucky to get two phone calls in one week?"

"*Shavuah tov*, Ettie. How's by you?"

"Oh, you know. Good enough for a widow but not as good as it could be. By you?"

"I'm learning a new skill. Yossi's fiancée, Martha, is teaching me how to sew a quilt."

"Mazal tov," she said, chuckling. "Have her teach you how to cook while you're at it. You could become happily married after all."

Fanya looked at me and rolled her eyes. "Listen, Ettie,

I have to ask you about Ze'ev, may he rest in peace. It's something Hadas told me."

Ettie heaved a huge sigh. "Even though he's gone, he still comes back to haunt me. What is it now?"

Fanya's knuckles turned white as she tightened her grip on the cell phone. "There's no nice way to say this. Hadas mentioned that one of Ze'ev's *special friends*, a woman called Gita, used to bother you. Is she right?"

The silence lasted so long, I wondered if we'd been disconnected.

Finally, Ettie growled. "That meshuggenah *nafke* humiliated me." She called Gita a crazy whore. "She showed up shickered in front of my house, stumbling in the street and yelling for all the neighbors to hear. She said he was going to divorce me and marry her."

"Ouch! You must've been really mad."

Ettie's version didn't contradict what Hadas told us. I wrote a question and handed it to Fanya.

She nodded. "Did you ever hear Gita threaten to kill Ze'ev?"

"Not Ze'ev, no. But, God forbid, she did threaten to curse me and my children, *pu, pu, pu*. Why are you asking about him right now?"

"Because someone is threatening Hadas and she's running scared. So, I thought I'd check out her story with you."

I passed Fanya another note.

She glanced at it quickly. "Do you know Gita's last name?"

"Yeah. It's Glassman. Gita Glassman."

"Do you know where she is now?"

"Why would I? When Ze'ev died, she showed up at

his funeral. The rabbi sent several men over to where she stood and made her leave. That's the last I saw of her. Someone said she may have gone to Israel. If so, she's probably lifting her skirts for ten shekels on the streets of Tel Aviv."

Ettie's version seemed to corroborate what Hadas revealed. I handed Fanya another note.

"Ettie, I have another difficult question. Do you know of anyone who would want to kill Ze'ev?"

"Why are you curious about Ze'ev? At this point, does it matter who ran him down? He's gone and we're out in the cold, with no income from the Uhrman Company. You said Hadas was running scared. Do you think the same person who killed Ze'ev wants to kill her, too?"

"The thought did occur to me, yes. Did you ever hear Ze'ev or Hadas mention a man named Alexander?"

"Alexander? The name is familiar. He might've come to pray during the week we sat shiva." She referred to the seven-day mourning period after the death of a loved one. "I have five sons. They make only half a minyan. Because my four sons-in-law couldn't be here every day regular, different men came by each day to help make a full minyan of ten. I saw to it there was plenty for them to nosh on. And wine. You have to reward them with something."

Fanya persisted with our questions. "Do you remember anything else about Alexander? Like, did he seem interested in Hadas?"

"Is he the one she's scared of? *Veh!* I wish I could remember now. You were there sitting with us, Fanya. Did you see anyone like that?"

Fanya glanced at me. "I was too worried about you to notice."

"How about if I ask my Zelig? He might know."

"Your oldest son, yes?"

"Correct! I'll ask him and get back to you."

"Great, Ettie. See if he knows Alexander's full name. Thanks."

Ettie sighed. "Always nice to hear from you. And say hello to your brother. Such a mensch."

"Will do." Fanya ended the call and looked at me. "Now what?"

CHAPTER 22

Saturday evening Fanya and I sat at the kitchen table finishing the leftover vegetarian casserole from the night before when someone knocked on the front door.

My immediate next-door neighbor, Sister Mae Slocum, stood on the porch waving pieces of paper in the air. "I think I found what you're looking for."

"Come in. Come in." I led Sister Mae to the living room and Fanya joined us. "You found out who the two guys were who helped Hadas?"

"That's her name? The one who's missing? I'm terrible with names, but I never forget a face." She handed over the pages, printouts from the internet. "It took some digging. But I found the big blond guy. Remember I said I thought I recognized him from the set of *Grey's Anatomy*? His name is Peter. I searched for him in the IMDb, the Internet Movie Database."

I studied the publicity photo of the blond and overly muscled Peter Hauer. Hauer's professional website revealed he got his start in modeling men's clothes. His résumé cited six small TV acting credits, including a recurring role as a paramedic on *Grey's Anatomy*. The most recent job, a commercial for Gillette razors, happened over a year ago. His agent's name and phone number were listed on the contacts page. "Excellent job, Sister Mae."

"Thanks."

I examined the photo in the second printout. Rocco Fontana was dark-complexioned and slighter than the beefy Hauer. "You're sure this is the other guy?"

"I'm pretty sure. But finding him took a little more digging. I figured Peter might have gotten a buddy to help him. So, I found Peter's Facebook page and scrolled through a ton of photos. I finally found Rocco in one group photo you're looking at, taken in a bar. The people were tagged. That's how I got his name. I clicked on his image, which took me to his Facebook page."

"Wow," Fanya said. "Finding them took a lot of ingenuity."

Sister Mae sighed. "Unfortunately, his page didn't give me much more information. Then I did an internet search. I spent about an hour going from one website to another, like walking along a hallway with a hundred doors on both sides. I finally found the one you're holding in your hand."

I read the third piece of paper. Rocco Fontana's claim to fame was a conviction five years ago for a burglary in LA, resulting in a four-year prison sentence. The expression in his mug shot was defiant. "This is great information. How'd you get it?"

"There's a bunch of online private investigation searches

you can subscribe to. They crawl through public records to find matches." She smiled. "You owe me nineteen-ninety-nine."

"Cheap at twice the price." I passed the pages to Fanya, for a closer look. "This gives us a place to start. But it's Saturday. We'll probably have to wait until Monday to contact Hauer's agent. Hopefully, we'll get enough information to meet the actor in person. And if we have any luck, Yossi will find Fontana's current address in the NCIC database."

Sister Mae clasped her hands in her lap. "The national criminal database? Are you sure you want to talk to someone who's on their list? Won't it be dangerous?"

I glanced at Fanya. She was an expert in Krav Maga. She could probably take on Rocco Fontana with little effort. But how would she match up to the Mr. Universe physique of Peter Hauer? "We only want information. Technically, they didn't do anything illegal. They have nothing to fear from us."

I hoped I was right.

Crusher came home sometime after midnight, snuggled close to me in bed, and almost immediately began to snore. I didn't know how I did it, but, despite the loud noises coming in irregular bursts, I managed to fall asleep again. Sunday morning I woke to an empty bed. He'd left a brief note on the bedside table. *Going out of town again. Luv U!*

"Out of town" was our code for Crusher going undercover, a part of his job with the ATF I hated. Undercover work was dangerous. And even though I knew he could handle himself, I still worried. Plus, I never knew how long he'd be gone. Sometimes he was absent for only a day or two. The longest time he was "out of town" had been for five agonizing weeks.

I needed coffee. I dressed in my usual jeans and a T-shirt and found Fanya and a half-empty pot of Italian roast in the kitchen. I sat across from her at the table, took the first sip of the day, and closed my eyes in pure pleasure.

When I opened them again, Fanya leaned in my direction. "Ettie called me this morning."

"So soon? What did she say?"

"She talked to her son, Zelig. He said Alexander's last name is Koslov. According to Zelig, Alexander visited their home several times during the week after Ze'ev's funeral. Ostensibly to be part of the minyan." Fanya referred to the quorum of ten Jewish men required to recite certain prayers. "But Zelig noticed Alexander seemed to spend a lot of time quietly watching Hadas."

Hadas closely resembled the beautiful Penélope Cruz. I could understand why a man might be captivated. "I hate to admit it, Fanya, but Hadas didn't lie about Gita. And it looks like she also told the truth about why she's running from Alexander."

"Yeah. He sounds like a real creep. *Pu, pu, pu!*"

"By the way, Yossi left me a note this morning saying he had to travel for work, and he doesn't know how long he'll be gone. That means for now, at least, it's the two of us. This is your first time in LA, and I feel terrible. I've dragged you to Pacific Palisades, downtown LA, Camarillo, and Ojai, all in an effort to rescue Hadas. Yet not once did I ask you what you'd like to do."

Fanya chuckled. "Are you kidding? I haven't had this much fun since I was too young to have a period. And you've created a monster because, quite frankly, I'm now hooked on quilting. I've almost finished piecing the top. I'm ready for the next steps."

I grinned. "I think we're going to be the best of friends!" I explained how to make a quilt "sandwich" with fabric for the back, cotton batting in the middle, and her pieced yellow-and-green on top. "We can go to the shop today if you want and get batting and enough yardage for the back of the quilt. Then I'll give you a tutorial on hand quilting."

"What about those longarm machines we talked about? Could I quilt it on one of those?"

"Yes, of course. But you'd need to take a class first. Once you know what you're doing, you can rent the long-arm machine in the back of the shop. Another option would be to simply pay someone with a long arm machine to quilt it for you."

We drove to the Quilt No Guilt shop, located in a nearby San Fernando Valley community. The moment we walked in the store, Fanya's jaw dropped and she stopped in her tracks. Standing together on shelves were hundreds of bolts of cotton fabrics grouped by color or theme. Also on display were a rainbow of threads, sewing notions, how-to books, and specialized tools to help quilters create beautiful pieces of fabric art.

She hastened to an extensive display of precut fabrics and immediately began collecting the little packages. Every quilter had a color or color palate they liked to work with. For me, it was blue. I had more blue fabric in my stash than any other color. Fanya's selections tended toward clear hues, colors that weren't grayed or dulled. Her quilts would be joyous and honest, like her yellow-and-green Snail's Trail. We left the store an hour later with sacks of supplies and lots of fabric, including six yards of a charming yellow calico for the back of her quilt.

We ended our shopping at Aroma Café on Ventura Boulevard, with shaded alfresco seating and lots of vegetarian choices on the menu. We ordered a lunch of *sabich*, a delicious grilled eggplant and hard-boiled egg combo with Israeli chopped salad, hummus, and pita bread.

I could barely hear Fanya's question over the volume of chatter around us. "Once my brother gets a divorce, have you thought about what kind of a wedding you want?"

"*If* he ever gets a divorce, I want a simple ceremony with family and close friends. Giselle and my daughter, Quincy, argued about who will get to be the maid of honor." I laughed once. "It won't be that formal, I guarantee it."

"You and Yossi have been together for a while. Why did you decide now was the time to get married? I mean, nowadays—if you're not too religious—it's no *shanda* to live with someone." She used the Yiddish word for "shame."

I told her about the time a couple of months ago when I was clubbed on the head, tied up, and nearly killed. "When you survive a situation like that, you think about what's important. My priorities changed. I set aside all my fears of failure and finally said yes to a second chance at happiness."

She took a sip of iced tea. "Your first marriage was so awful?"

I half-smiled with a corner of my mouth and rolled my eyes. "I met Aaron Rose when we were thrown in jail for protesting the Vietnam war. He was a med student and I was barely out of high school. Both of us were young and idealistic. I thought we'd change the world together. But all that changed was his attitude. Being a doctor gave him an elevated sense of importance, totally out of proportion with reality. The last betrayal came when I found out he'd been unfaithful. I took our daughter and left him shortly afterward."

Fanya reached over and gave my shoulder a little squeeze. "I've watched the two of you. I think you are Yossi's *beshert*." She referred to the Jewish precept that God has preordained a soul mate for everyone.

From Aroma, it was a short trip home.

Fanya rushed to the sewing room with her purchases and spread her new fabric on the table. "Wow. Look at these. I'm already seeing an Ohio Star quilt in my future."

"Yes, your choices will do up nicely. One thing I like to do is wash my cottons as soon as I bring them home. That way, when I do use them in a quilt, they won't shrink. Plus, it gets rid of extra dye, which might otherwise bleed into the quilt."

"Thanks for the warning. I'll wash everything now."

"Wash your reds and purples separately. Red's the color most likely to bleed."

Late in the afternoon, Giselle called. "Hi, Sissy. You'll never guess what Shadow found out."

"You make your employees work on Sundays? I hope you pay him extra, or give him free gasoline for a year, at the very least."

She gave me a mirthless, "Ha-ha. What can I say? He did this on his own initiative. He likes a challenge."

"Okay. What did he find?"

"Remember he said big money was going in and out of the Uhrman Company ever since Ze'ev Uhrman's death?" She didn't wait for an answer. "Well, some of the money went in as income from sales and ninety percent came out as dividends and expenses paid straight into the bank account of a company called Koslov Associates."

Hadas had said Alexander Koslov was pursuing her for romantic reasons. Once again, I caught her in a lie. How did the Uhrman Company become linked financially with Alexander Koslov? Was this the connection we were looking for? Could he be chasing Hadas because of money, not love? John Smith and Andre Polinskaya were correct. There were forces at work I knew nothing about.

CHAPTER 23

Late Sunday afternoon, while Fanya ironed her newly laundered cotton fabric, I opened my computer and Googled Alexander Koslov. I found an image in a group shot taken in New York, including the Ukrainian ambassador to the United States, the president of the Ukrainian Olympic Committee, and four local businessmen. The caption read, *Ukraine prepares for Winter Olympics*.

A further search found a short article on an English-language webpage about the launch of a Ukrainian national curling team. The opening of a single regulation curling lane in Kiev was made possible through generous donations from Ukrainians living in the US. The article stated:

> *The presence of a specialized curling rink will*
> *solve several tasks at once: Ukrainian athletes will*

have good training conditions, Ukraine will be
able to host prestigious international curling tour-
naments, and ordinary Ukrainians will have a
great opportunity to try their hand at this sport.

Pretty grandiose aspirations for a country with only one lane. It would be like building a bowling center with one lane for the entire population of New York City and LA combined.

I told Fanya what I'd discovered. "Do you think this is the same Alexander Koslov we're looking for?"

Fanya turned away from her ironing and came over to where I sat. "Let me take a look. I sat shiva with Ettie. I might have seen Koslov there without even knowing it." She peered at the photo on my computer and pointed to the image of Koslov. "Yeah, that's him."

"Good. Assuming this is the same guy, we now know Koslov is a Ukrainian businessman living in the US. We also know he must be Jewish if he could pray with the minyan."

Fanya turned back to her ironing. "And he likes curling, whatever that is."

Sunday night I wished Crusher would come home. If there was anything in our relationship making me uncomfortable, it was nights like these spent alone, worrying about his safety. I tossed and turned, thinking first about him and then about how to approach Hadas's "kidnapper" Peter Hauer.

Monday morning I called Giselle and filled her in on a scheme I'd concocted the evening before.

"Sure, Sissy. I'm in."

My next call was to Peter Hauer's agent, Brian "Buster" Dingle. He answered with a high-pitched, reedy voice. "Buster here. How can I help you?"

"My name is Martha Rose . . . enberg with the Miss Manischewitz Wine Pageant. I'm looking to hire a real Schwarzenegger type for a photo shoot. We're featuring thirty beautiful contestants in a calendar for next year."

"Thirty? But there are only twelve months in a year."

I did a mental eye roll. "Some of them will be group shots. The man I'm thinking of must be blond and built like a weightlifter. Someone suggested Peter Hauer. Do you still represent him?"

Dingle's voice turned smarmy. "Ah. Well. Yes. Unfortunately, Peter stopped modeling years ago. He's an actor now. Very much in demand."

"I've visited his webpage, Mr. Dingle. His last credits happened a year ago. Am I correct in assuming he's in between jobs right now?"

Dingle paused. "We're in negotiations with Netflix as we speak. A major deal."

"Until then, how does a thousand dollars sound?"

"Don't forget my ten percent. Twelve hundred."

"Fine. Twelve hundred for a day's work."

"No, no, no. The fee is twelve hundred *per hour*."

"We'll have to audition him first, of course. If our primary investor likes him, I'm sure she'll agree to the price."

"When would you like him to start?"

"This is where our investor lives." I gave him Giselle's address. "Have him meet us at one this afternoon. And for heaven's sake, tell him to be prompt for his audition. If there's one thing she hates, it's people who waste her time, or people who arrive for appointments too early."

"Of course. Goes without saying. Do you want him oiled?"

"I beg your pardon?"

"You know, covered in oil to make his skin shine. Like a weightlifter."

"This is not a Mr. Universe contest, Mr. Dingle. The Miss Manischewitz Wine calendar is almost a sacred institution. Jewish families look forward to picking up free copies from their bank every September, right before Rosh Hashanah. But have him bring a bottle of baby oil just in case."

Fanya listened to my side of the conversation and smiled. "You're really good at lying, Martha. How do you think up these things?"

"It's a gift."

We decided to dress for the roles I'd carefully planned. I wore a gray business suit and Fanya wore black trousers and a jacket and slicked back her hair into a long ponytail. At twelve thirty, we arrived at Giselle's house in the Pacific Palisades. The front yard, planted in rows of lavender, smelled fresh and fragrant in the balmy coastal air.

Giselle greeted us wearing a dark business suit and lots of diamonds. She grinned at Fanya and rubbed her hands together. "Ever since Martha and I found each other, my life has been a lot more fun." Then she looked at me and frowned. "How dangerous is this guy?"

"I don't think we have to worry, G. I wouldn't have asked you to do this if I thought anyone would get hurt. Besides, Fanya's trained in the martial arts. She can protect us if need be."

We moved to the living room, with the carefully hand-plastered white walls, dark wooden beams on the ceiling,

and furniture upholstered in the primary colors of the
French countryside. As a precaution, Giselle stationed
her housekeeper Aria out of sight in the dining room with
a cell phone nearby. "If you hear me say the word *banana*, call the police."

"Yes, missus."

At precisely one, the doorbell rang. Aria, her dark braid
hanging down her back, hurried toward the front door.
We heard him say, "My name is Peter Hauer. I'm here to
see a Mrs. Rosenberg."

Giselle screwed up her face. "Rosenberg? Is that supposed to be you or me?"

"Me!" I whispered.

Aria said, "This way, please."

Footsteps became louder as they neared our location.

Peter Hauer wasn't as tall as I expected. His eyes were
an arresting green, a color not found in nature. His shirt
was the same color as his eyes. The sleeves strained
across his biceps and the open collar looked too small to
button around his prodigious neck. He stopped at a re-
spectful distance of eight feet from where we stood in the
living room and smiled nervously. "Hello."

I walked toward him and extended my hand. "Mr.
Hauer? Thanks for being prompt. I'm Martha Rosenberg."
I glanced at Giselle. "This is Mrs. Cole, our primary investor in the calendar." As part of my plan, I didn't intro-
duce Fanya.

Giselle didn't offer her hand. She gestured toward an
uncomfortable-looking straight-backed chair. "Be seated,
Mr. Hauer."

Hauer waited for us to sit on the more comfortable upholstered furniture before he took the chair. "Thank you

for inviting me to this audition." His tongue seemed to stick to the inside of his dry mouth and I felt a little sorry for him.

"Would you like some water?" I asked.

Relief washed over his face. "Please."

Giselle reached over to the coffee table and lifted a little handbell, which tinkled pleasantly when she shook it.

Aria appeared almost immediately. "Yes, missus?"

Without taking her eyes off an increasingly nervous Hauer, my sister commanded with an imperious voice, "Bring us water."

A smile played on Aria's lips. "Yes, missus."

Aria quickly returned with a pitcher of water with floating lemon slices and melting ice and four crystal glasses on a silver tray. She poured a drink for each of us in turn, starting with Giselle. Hauer was the last to be served and nearly drained the whole thing at once. He glanced at Aria, who refilled his glass and left the room.

Giselle raised her chin slightly. "Now then, Mr. Hauer, you know about our project?"

"My agent, Buster Dingle, explained it to me, yes. You want a male to pose with Miss Manischewitz Wine contestants for a calendar."

I cleared my throat. "Well, I told a little fib to get you here. We really want something else."

He frowned and his eyes darted back and forth between us. "You don't mean porn, do you? I stopped years ago. If that's what you're after, you'll have to pay me double. And you'd have to let me wear a mask. I don't want to screw up my chances for more TV work."

I thought I heard a muffled giggle coming from the dining room. I could barely control my own reaction.

"No, Peter. I can call you Peter, right? Porn isn't why we wanted to see you."

He glared from one of us to the other. "Well, what, then? I brought the baby oil."

I narrowed my eyes. "We want you to tell us where we can find Hadas Levy."

Shock drained the color from his face. "How did you . . . ? So, I guess this isn't an audition?"

Giselle rolled her eyes. "You're quick to comprehend."

He shot out of his chair. "I don't have to tell you jack!"

Fanya rose suddenly, pushed up the sleeves of her jacket and bared her forearms. In two strides of her long legs, she stood in front of Hauer. She towered over him by two or three inches and leaned into his personal space. "Sit down, Mr. Hauer, or I'll break your legs. If you don't believe I'm capable, I invite you to try me."

"*You* take *me*?" He scoffed. "Back off, girly." He raised a meaty hand to push her shoulder.

In an instant, she grabbed his wrist and arm in a pressure lock and twisted them, forcing the stunned body-builder back in the chair. Once seated, she gave an extra backward tug on his wrist, causing him to yell out in pain.

"Be glad you can still walk," Fanya hissed in his ear. Instead of joining us on the sofa, she stood behind him, feet apart and arms folded across her chest.

Hauer massaged his sore wrist. Little beads of sweat appeared on his forehead. "Okay, okay. What do you want to know?"

I sat back on the red-and-white–striped sofa, letting my body sink into the luxurious cushions. "I always like to start at the beginning. You helped Hadas Levy leave my house over a week ago, staged a fake kidnapping, and transported her to the Hotel Delaware in downtown LA. Am I right in assuming the whole stunt was a business deal for which you were paid?"

Hauer used his palms to wipe the sweat from his face, then ran them along his thighs to dry. "Yeah. She paid me and my buddy Rocco a grand each and told us to forget we ever saw her."

"Did she say anything about why she wanted people to think she was kidnapped?"

"Not really. She said some dude was after her and she wanted to lose him. That's about it."

"Why you? How did she find you to begin with?"

Hauer shifted in his chair and took a long drink from his crystal glass. "I knew her from the old days."

"The old days?"

"Yeah. Back when I was modeling in New York. Uhrman Company needed someone really cut for their menswear catalogue. I spent a couple weeks with a photographer and a whole crew. Hadas—Mrs. Levy—was there every day supervising." He sat straighter. "It was E-ticket, man. They said I looked better than Eddy Ellwood."

"Who is he?" Giselle asked.

"For real? He's the best bodybuilder ever. Won Mr. Universe Pro five years in a row. Nobody else comes close. Before or since."

Giselle asked, "So he was like the Tiger Woods of bodybuilding?"

Hauer looked confused. "Eddy Ellwood was a golfer?"

I didn't dare look at Fanya as I tried to maintain a straight face. I rolled my hand in a signal to move forward. "Back to Hadas. Mrs. Levy. Did you become friends? Is that why she contacted you now?"

Hauer smirked. "We had a good thing going for a while. But when she said she didn't want to pay for it anymore? Hey. I know what I'm worth. I knew a guy who ran a male escort service. Said if I ever came to LA, I should look him up. So, I bailed on the big apple and came west."

Aha! The prim little Hadas wasn't that pure after all. She wouldn't be able to complain about spending all those years alone pining for Crusher. In Ettie's world, she was probably accurate if not downright mean when she called Hadas a *nafke*.

"Did you stay in touch? How did she find you?"

"She must've Googled me. I'm on Facebook. I have a webpage. She messaged me and we FaceTimed. Made a plan long-distance. When she got to LA, she texted me her location. I guess that was your house. The rest you know."

"What about the second time she disappeared? Did you give her a ride from Ojai last Friday night?"

He glanced at Fanya, who said, "Just answer the lady."

"Yeah. I went there."

Giselle said, "How much did she pay you to keep quiet this time?"

Hauer stared at the floor in silence.

Fanya slapped the back of his head. "How much?"

"Ow." He raised a protective hand. "She gave me another grand."

"I'll double that." Giselle looked hard at him, as if she were daring him to refuse.

"Two grand?" He brightened.

Giselle nodded and reached for an envelope on the coffee table. She extracted a wad of Benjamins and counted out twenty. Then she looked once at him and counted out another ten. "For your trouble." She pushed the pile of thirty hundred-dollar bills across the coffee table toward him. "Now, where did you take her?"

CHAPTER 24

Hauer reached for the three thousand dollars. He straightened the pile of Benjamins and smiled as he crammed them into his bulging wallet. "I went to Ojai at midnight and drove her to a place in Oxnard by the beach. The house was maybe fifty yards from the sand. Real plush."

I knew of the area, a place called the Silver Strand, where the houses went for seven figures. "There are no hotels around there, only privately owned homes. Did she know someone in the neighborhood?"

"Uh, Hadas doesn't tell me her secrets, you know. But I got the feeling the place was empty because she got the front door key from a lockbox on the side of the house. She made me wait until she knew she could get inside."

"Then what happened?"

Hauer smirked again. "It was late and I didn't feel like driving all the way back to Hollywood. Hadas is still a babe. Know what I mean? So, I asked her if she wanted a little freebie for old time's sake. Figured I could sleep there afterward."

Fanya made a face and looked like she wanted to throw up. Giselle shook her head slowly.

I said, "Did she accept your offer?"

"Gentlemen don't kiss and tell."

He was far away from being a gentleman, but I decided not to pursue the point. I now held plenty of ammunition against Hadas. I didn't need more. "Give me the address where you took her."

Hauer rattled off the street and number. "It's the second house from the corner. Are we done, now? Can I go?"

I rose from the sofa. "You're free to go. Out of curiosity, what are you going to tell your agent, Buster Dingle?"

"Screw him. I'm keeping all the cash. I'll tell him I didn't get the gig."

"And so you know? If you contact Hadas and warn her about this little business deal of ours, I will be forced to go to your agent and tell him about the money you've been making on the side without giving him his ten percent. Then we'll come after you." I pointed to Fanya. "Understood?"

"Whatever." Hauer stood, brushed past Fanya, and slammed the front door on his way out.

"Eww!" Giselle made a face and shivered as if she'd swallowed unsweetened cranberry juice. "What a sleazeball. I feel like I need a shower." She rubbed her arms. "By the way, Fanya, you were terrific. Was that a Krav Maga move you used on him?"

Fanya wasn't listening. She pulled a small packet of salt out of her pocket and began sprinkling it in the corners of the living room, repeating each time, "*Hamsa, hamsa, hamsa, pu, pu, pu* and three sholem aleichems."

I suspected Fanya of being an agent in disguise because of her cool thinking and expertise in martial arts. But as I watched her exorcising demons, I decided she probably was just what she claimed to be, a superstitious wallpaper hanger who knew Krav Maga.

Aria entered the room with her hand over her mouth, shaking with silent giggles. She handed the cell phone back to Giselle, who took one look at her housekeeper and started to laugh out loud. Soon the four of us were howling.

Giselle imitated Hauer. "Eddy Ellwood was a golfer?"

More laughter.

Finally, we sobered enough to talk about our next move.

Giselle said, "I think we should drive to Oxnard before Hadas has a chance to disappear again."

An hour and twenty minutes later we arrived at our destination, a small section of homes with quick access to the beach. Most of the well-kept houses in this community were two-story beach getaways for wealthy families. Many featured one-bedroom rentals on the ground floor. The owners' living quarters were on the second floor, taking advantage of the ocean view.

According to Hauer, Hadas landed on one of the side

streets across from the beach, second house from the corner. We found the address as Hauer described. Giselle eased her midnight-blue Jaguar onto the driveway and turned off the engine. Double garage doors took up most of the front of the house. A small porch with a red door claimed the remainder of the space. The only windows on the front of the house faced the ocean from the second floor.

We knocked on the front door and waited for a minute. When nobody answered, we knocked again. After three tries with no response, I walked back far enough to gaze at the upstairs windows. "Everything's dark. It doesn't look occupied."

Fanya moved toward the side of the house. "Let's go around to the back. There should be windows there." She led the way with determined strides of her long legs.

A bank of windows faced the backyard. We could clearly see inside.

A blond woman in a red halter top stood looking at us for a moment, grabbed something white on a table, and opened a door. Her face was tan and leathery, testifying to a lifetime in the sun. "Hi. Can I help you?"

I stepped forward. "Hi. We're here looking for a friend of ours. She may have arrived over the weekend. Have you seen her?"

The blonde waved a white envelope in the air. "Yes. I talked to her briefly. Nice lady. She said there might be people looking for her. Can I ask your name?"

"I'm Martha Rose." I pointed to my sister. "This is Giselle and this is Fanya."

"Yeah. She said you might come looking for her. Right

before she left, she said if you did come by, I was to give you this letter. She gave me a hundred dollars. I figured it was pretty important." She handed me a sealed envelope with *Martha* scrawled on it.

Crap! Not again. I closed my eyes and wagged my head. "When did she leave?"

"Less than an hour ago. Took her suitcase. She won't be coming back."

"Did you see who gave her a ride?"

"Someone in a white Prius. I think there was an Uber sticker on the window."

"Do you own this house?"

"Heavens no. I rent the downstairs apartment full-time. The owner rents out the top as an Airbnb. I'm used to having people come and go."

"Thanks."

I tore open the envelope as we walked toward the Jag in the driveway. The note inside was short and not-so-sweet: *Martha, Do NOT try to find me. Alexander may be following you.*

"Darn!"

Giselle took the note from my hand and read it aloud. "Well, isn't she the wily one."

Fanya said, "She didn't get to head a big company by being naïve."

I sighed. "Sooner or later, she's going to run out of resources and time." My cell phone chimed in my purse. I pulled it out to see who was calling. "It's Uncle Isaac. I'd better see what he wants." I slid the icon on the screen. "Hi, Uncle Isaac. How are you?"

There was momentary silence on the other end and

then Hilda's voice. "Martha, this is Hilda. It's your uncle Isaac."

My stomach plunged and I stumbled over to the Jag and leaned against it for support. "What? What's happened? Oh my God. Is he okay?"

"He's in the hospital. Cedars-Sinai. He got a dizzy spell, fell, and bumped his head. I called the paramedics right away and they brought him here."

Sour juices rose from my stomach and burned my chest. "Is he conscious? What does the doctor say?"

Giselle and Fanya looked at each other and hurried to my side.

"Yes, he's conscious and not at all happy to be here. He didn't want me to call you. He didn't want to worry you. I waited until they took him to be scanned. That's what's happening right now. The doctor said it could be as simple as low blood pressure or as serious as a mild stroke."

"We're leaving right now from Oxnard. Where in the hospital are you?"

"We're still in the emergency room. I don't expect they'll move him until they know what happened."

"Okay. I'll see you as soon as I get there." I ended the call. Tears stung my eyes and my hands shook. *Oh dear God, please let him live. Please don't take him yet.*

Giselle stretched her hands in front of her and grabbed my arms. "Whoa! What's happened? You look white as a sheet."

By now my whole body trembled. "It's Uncle Isaac. Something's happened. I've got to get to the hospital right away. Drop me off at your house so I can take my car."

Giselle's grip on my arms tightened. "You're in no condition to drive. I'll take you. Which hospital?"

"Cedars-Sinai. It's rush hour. It'll take us at least two hours to get there."

"We'd better get going, then."

The three of us jumped into the Jaguar, Giselle driving, me in the passenger seat, and Fanya in the back. Traffic was beginning to thicken on the freeways. I closed my eyes in frustration with each slowdown and delay. Two hours later we arrived at the hospital, followed the signs to the emergency room parking, and left the car with valet service.

Once the car stopped moving, I wasted no time running into the hospital. Giselle and Fanya caught up with me only when I stopped at the ER admission desk to ask about my uncle. "Isaac Harris. He's here with his caregiver."

The pleasant volunteer in a pink-and-white uniform typed something in the computer. "Are you family?"

"I'm his closest next of kin. Niece. Actually, he raised me. You can say I am more like a daughter." I gestured toward Fanya and Giselle. "These are my sisters."

She looked from my five feet two inches to the almost six feet tall Fanya, the straight auburn hair of Giselle, and back to my wild gray curls. "If you don't mind my saying so, you don't look like members of the same family."

"Do we have to show our adoption papers?" Giselle raised her voice. "I don't think so."

The volunteer blanched at the unexpected outburst and looked back at the computer screen. "He's in radiology now. Why don't you take a seat? The doctor will speak to you as soon as they know anything."

"Oh no," I said. "He came in with his caregiver. If she's allowed to stay with him, then I should be allowed as well. Point us in the right direction."

"I'm sorry, but I can't let all three of you in there. You'll get in the way."

"Fine. They'll stay here, but I insist on going in."

She exhaled loudly and nodded once toward a set of doors marked *staff only*. "Through those double doors. I'll buzz you in."

I pushed through the doors and rushed into the room beyond. People dressed in scrubs with serious faces bustled around me, moving with confidence and purpose. I searched the faces, looking desperately for Hilda.

A young African-American nurse approached me. "Can I help you?"

"I'm looking for my uncle, Isaac Harris, and his caregiver." I gave her a description of the two of them.

"Oh yes. I know who you mean. I don't think he's come back from radiology yet, but she's still here." She pointed to the far end of sick bays. "Last bed."

I thanked her and rushed to the end of the room. The green curtains of the last bay were open. Hilda was sitting in a chair, hands folded in her lap, head bowed, lips moving in silent prayer. She hadn't heard me approach. I cleared my throat to get her attention.

"Thanks for calling me, Hilda. Even though he didn't want you to. You did the right thing. How long has he been gone? Did anyone say when he'll be back?"

"I'm glad you're here. They took him for a brain scan right before I called you." She looked at her watch. "Maybe two hours ago. They didn't know how long it

would take. Something to do with overcrowding in the
ER today."

"Tell me exactly what happened."

Hilda shifted her weight in the chair. "It was after
lunch. He usually likes to take a little nap right after eating. Did you know he could sit in a chair and doze off at
will?"

I chuckled. "I've always admired his ability to do
that."

"Anyway, he slept for about twenty minutes while I
cleaned the lunch dishes in the kitchen. When I finished,
I went into the living room to check on him. He woke up,
smiled, and said he felt like going for a walk."

"Does he normally take walks?"

"Yes. I go with him, of course. Since Isaac's been
boxing, he seems steadier on his feet and he enjoys the
fresh air. He started to get out of the chair, but when he
stood, he collapsed and fell unconscious to the floor."
She paused and shivered a little. "I was so scared. I immediately called 911. They were at the house within a
few minutes."

"Was he still unconscious when they arrived?"

"He came round as they hooked him to a heart moni-
tor. And they let me ride in the back of the ambulance.
Isaac was very adamant about my not calling you. But as
his next of kin, you have a right to know. I called you as
soon as I could. I gave them a list of his meds. I always
carry one with me wherever we go. Just in case."

How could I think this woman would take advantage
of my elderly uncle? She was clearly upset and seemed to
care deeply. Maybe I should give her the benefit of the
doubt. When she touched him tenderly, maybe it wasn't

about seducing him. Maybe she was merely sending a message of comfort.

"Well, I can take up the vigil now and give you a break. Giselle and Yossi's sister, Fanya, are in the waiting room. I'm sure they'd be grateful to hear from you about what happened."

"Thanks. I could use a break." Hilda's shoulders sagged and her eyes were moist. "I simply didn't want him to come back to an empty room."

I sat in the chair Hilda vacated and pulled out my cell phone. I sent messages to my daughter, Quincy, and to Crusher, telling them about Uncle Isaac. Then I sent a group message to Lucy, Birdie, and Jazz, advising them I might have to cancel quilty Tuesday tomorrow.

In the quiet of the sick bay, I kept thinking about all the wonderful things my uncle did for me over the years, beginning with the fact he supported three generations of women: me, my mother—his sister, and my bubbie—his mother. He stepped into the role of father and protector with a selfless determination to keep our little family to-gether.

I'd never seen my uncle Isaac with a girlfriend. As a young girl living at home, I'd never witnessed him leav-ing for a date or bringing one to our home. What must his life have been like without the intimacy of a romantic re-lationship? How lonely he must've felt, for a man as sweet as Isaac. If he and Hilda developed feelings for each other, who was I to object? Wasn't I one of the pri-mary reasons that kept him from marriage and a family of his own?

Shortly after I sat down to wait, my uncle Isaac was wheeled back to the ER, an IV bag on a pole attached to the wheelchair. When he saw me, he sighed. "Oy. *Faigela*, I told Hilda not to call you."

"She did the right thing, Uncle. Don't you dare scold her."

"Where is she now?"

"I'm giving her a break. She's in the waiting room with Giselle and Fanya."

"How is she? You should've seen her go to town, *faigela*. She didn't panic. Knew all the right things to do. She's really something, that one."

I studied his face, trying to decode the feelings behind his words. He obviously relied on Hilda. And his admiration was also plain to see. I still wondered if there was more to their relationship than competent caregiver and grateful patient.

The tech helped him out of the wheelchair and back onto the bed, being careful to maneuver around the IV line snaking from his arm to a clear plastic bag hanging on a pole.

"Ach. I'm sure this is nothing."

"And if it is something, God forbid." My voice began to shake.

"I'm old, *nu*? These things happen." He paused. "What? Are you crying?"

Tears streamed down my cheeks and I choked back a sob. "You'd rather be alone? You'd rather think nobody cared about you?" I pulled a tissue out of a box on a shelf next to the bed, blotted my face, and blew my nose. "I could name a hundred people right now who love you."

"Wait until the doctor tells us why I fainted. Let's not go planning the funeral yet."

I laughed through my tears and reached for his hand. The skin on his smooth fingers was warm to the touch.

His grip was still strong. His hands used to comfort me, for as far back as I could remember, resting on my head while he recited a special blessing for me every Friday evening, holding me after I scraped my knee, brushing my hair and braiding it for school in the morning, measuring me for a winter coat, hugging me at my high school graduation.

Please God, don't take him yet.

CHAPTER 25

I sat with my uncle Isaac for over an hour, waiting for the doctor. I summoned the nurse I first encountered and asked when we'd know the test results. Her nose and mouth were covered by a pleated blue face mask. A pair of dark, weary eyes pleaded for understanding. "I know it's tough to wait and not know what's happening. But honestly, we've been hammered today with an unusual volume of serious emergencies. I promise the doctor will come to see you as soon as she's free."

I felt guilty for abandoning Giselle, Fanya, and Hilda in the waiting room. "Three very concerned family members have been in the waiting room for hours without news. I'd like to let them know what's going on, but I'm afraid I won't be able to get back through those locked double doors. I also don't want to take the chance of not being here when the doctor does come."

Her eyes crinkled at the corners, hinting at a smile hidden under her face mask. "Would you like me to go out there and talk to them?"

I gave her the names of my "sisters" with profound thanks.

Before she left, she checked Uncle Isaac's vitals. "Looking good, Mr. Harris. Blood pressure's within the normal range." She entered something on her iPad and headed toward the double doors to the waiting room. Two minutes later, she reappeared though the doorway. When she saw me watching, she gave me the thumbs-up sign.

Finally, a petite Asian woman, wearing green scrubs and carrying her own iPad, walked purposefully into the last bay, where we sat waiting, the young nurse by her side. The woman's name tag with photo ID identified her as Dr. Yuen.

She acknowledged my presence with a brief nod and smiled at Uncle Isaac. "I've got good news, Mr. Harris. Your scan came back clean. Whatever made you faint wasn't in your brain. And your blood chemistry shows everything is within normal range."

While she talked, the nurse removed the IV needle from his left arm, swabbed the area with alcohol, and applied a small bandage.

Thank you, God.

"The note from the paramedics indicated your blood pressure was dangerously low when they got to your house. But I see your latest pressure check here shows improvement."

The muscles in his face eased and his shoulders relaxed. "So why did I faint?"

"Let me check one thing." The doctor slid her fingers on the iPad. "You're being treated for Parkinson's and hypertension, correct?"

"Yes, I am."

"Some of the medications you're taking can cause a sudden drop in blood pressure. Especially in combination. It's very important you review your meds with your doctor as soon as possible. Otherwise, you appear to be in good shape for a man in his eighties. I've written your discharge instructions. Stop at the desk before you go. They'll have some papers for you to sign." She offered her hand for a shake. "Good luck."

He took her hand in both of his. "Thank you, doctor. *A gesunt auf deine keppeleh.*"

She tilted her head like a small bird wanting a closer look. "What does that mean?"

"You should have good health and blessings."

I stepped outside the bay and closed the curtains to give him privacy. Five minutes later, he opened the curtains, fully dressed. "I'm ready to go now."

A young man in yellow scrubs with a name tag identifying him as a patient escort, attempted to install Uncle Isaac in a wheelchair.

"Thank you, young man, but I feel fine. I can walk."

"I'm sorry, sir, hospital rules. I have to wheel you safely out to your car."

We stopped at the nurses' station for the paperwork, then the escort wheeled him through the double doors. As soon as we entered the waiting room, Giselle, Fanya, and Hilda hurried over to his chair. Everyone spoke at once.

He raised his hand and patted the air in front of him.

"Oy! Such a ruckus. I'm fine, *keinehora*. My noggin's tough. The doc says it was probably my medicines making me faint. It's an easy problem to fix." He looked at Hilda. "And boy, am I hungry."

She rested her hand on his shoulder. "I'll warm some nice chicken soup when we get home. Giselle is going to drive us." She glanced at her watch. "It's almost nine. We'll be there in ten minutes. Can you hold out or shall we go to the hospital cafeteria right now?"

He rolled his head gently backward and laughed. "Let me think. Hilda's delicious chicken soup with matzah balls and noodles in ten minutes or hospital food right now?" His good spirits had a calming effect on everyone.

Uncle Isaac rode in the front of the Jag with Giselle. Fanya, Hilda, and I sat in the back. In the last two hours, I'd received texts from the quilty group asking about him.

I texted them all the good news. **Crisis over. Uncle okay. Quilting is a go. C U tomorrow morning.**

Quincy had left three voice mails. I hesitated to call her back at this hour. Normally, she'd still be awake. But with the baby still waking up at night, she grabbed her sleep when she could. I texted her not to worry, that he was fine. Crusher hadn't responded, which indicated he was still undercover.

We made it to their house in ten minutes, as Hilda predicted. Four women fussed over him all the way into the kitchen. Hilda removed a pot of soup from the refrigerator. The knob on the stove clicked twice and the gas burner came alive with a circle of blue flames.

Uncle Isaac sat at the vintage kitchen table with its shiny chrome legs. I touched the gray Formica tabletop and remembered eating Cream of Wheat and coloring in my *Wizard of Oz* coloring book, eating peanut butter sandwiches and dressing my Barbie and, a few years later, using a compass and protractor for my geometry homework. We anchored our lives to that table, lured by mouthwatering smells from Bubbie's cooking and baking. I was only ten when she died. From then on, Uncle Isaac did the cooking when my mother's mental health became too erratic to count on for regular meals. I sighed. Both Bubbie and my mother were gone now. But I could still feel their presence around the table.

"There's enough soup for everyone," Hilda said. "I'm hungry and know the three of you must be, too. We also have some nice twice-baked rye bread and chopped liver from the deli."

Who could argue?

"I'm a vegetarian. I'm afraid I'll have to pass." Fanya sounded apologetic. "But some rye bread with butter sounds good. Do you have any cheese?"

Hilda brightened. "Sorry, I forgot you don't eat meat. I have some fresh egg salad made this morning. Will that do?"

Fanya grinned. "Perfect."

The five of us crowded around the table in celebration mode. My uncle had dodged a bullet for now. I was willing to settle for one small mercy at a time.

By the time we got back to Giselle's house to get my car, it was eleven-thirty. "It's been a very long day and awfully late to be driving back to the Valley. Why don't the two of you spend the night?"

"I'm tempted, G, but I can't. We have quilting tomorrow. Remember? Thanks for driving. I'll see you in the morning."

On the way home, I thought about the note Hadas left for me. How did she know I'd find her? She either had confidence in my sleuthing skills, or Hauer called her, despite my warning, and gave her a heads-up.

I pulled into my driveway forty-five minutes later. Fanya had nodded off during the ride home.

I tapped her on the shoulder. "We're home, Fanya. Wake up."

She opened her eyes with a start. "Sorry, I slept. What time is it, anyway?"

"After midnight."

She stretched and yawned. "Yeah. I must be still on New York time. It's three in the morning there."

Fanya went straight to bed while I refilled Bumper's food dish. The purring ball of fluff rubbed his jaw on my ankle as I poured the kibble.

I hadn't checked my phone since leaving Uncle Isaac's. When I plugged it into the charger, the screen came alive and alerted me to a new voice mail.

"This is Alexander Koslov. Call me."

I pressed the *callback* icon and he answered almost immediately. "Koslov."

"This is Martha Rose."

"We need to talk."

"About?"

"I think you know."

"Not tonight."

"Tomorrow at two. Your house."

"Come alone."

The quilty group should still be at my house. He couldn't overcome so many people, especially one who knew Krav Maga.

"I'm sure you know my address since you broke in a week ago."

I needn't have wasted my breath. He'd already ended the call.

I gave Hadas grudging credit for telling the truth. She said Koslov had been following me.

CHAPTER 26

Tuesday morning I kept turning over in my head the odd conversation with Alexander Koslov the night before. What did he want with me? As Fanya and I made our way through a whole pot of coffee, I warned her about the visitor coming at two.

"Don't worry. I can handle him. Especially if he's coming alone." Her confidence reassured me about the wisdom of welcoming a stalker into my house. I witnessed her "handling" the bodybuilder Peter Hauer without breaking a sweat. I believed she could also handle Koslov.

She offered to take care of the dirty dishes while I ran to Bea's Bakery for two dozen each of *mandelbrot*—Jewish biscotti with almonds—and lace cookies dipped in chocolate. I also added a loaf of rye and a dozen rugelach. We were ready for visitors by ten.

The first to arrive was Jazz, the only male member of our group. He wore a mint green shirt with ivory-colored trousers and tan espadrilles. Zsa Zsa barked once and stuck her little white head out of his green canvas tote bag. She wore a mint green bow in her topknot and a matching dotted Swiss skirt with a bib and shoulder straps to hold it in place. Jazz placed her on the floor and she ran to find her friend and playmate Bumper, my orange cat.

"Martha, it's never too early to start planning for your wedding. Let's discuss your dress. Then I'll need to take measurements." He walked over to the sofa and took his usual place at the end. "And, Fanya, I assume you're going to attend the wedding, too. Would you like me to do your gown as well?" He smiled. "I'd be more than happy to make something bougie, designed exclusively for you. You're thin and you're tall. You'll be much easier to fit." He gasped and covered his mouth with his hand. "Sorry, Martha. You know I love designing for all body types."

Fanya barked a laugh. "Frankly, Jazz, I don't see myself in a ball gown. Ever. Maybe something a little more demure? Like a cocktail dress with sleeves?"

His mouth formed an exaggerated "O." "I've got it! How about black satin trousers to show off those long legs of yours and a matching tuxedo jacket with just a whiff of a lace bandeau underneath? You'd look stunning!"

"If she doesn't want it, I do." Giselle walked in on the middle of the conversation. She took her usual place in the other easy chair. "How about hot pink satin with a black lace bandeau? Very Frederick's of Hollywood."

The three of them tried to top each other with outlandish color combinations until they howled with laughter. Lime green with orange got the biggest hoot.

"What's all the hilarity about?" Lucy and Birdie arrived amid the laughter.

"They were discussing what to wear for my wedding—if it ever happens, that is."

Lucy sat at her end of the sofa and Birdie took the seat in the middle.

Lucy asked, "Why do you say, '*if* it ever happens?' Is there something we should know about?" Lucy took out her Robbing Peter to Pay Paul blocks.

Birdie offered to sew another "flower" for Giselle's endless project, a Grandmother's Flower Garden quilt made with little two-inch hexagons. Birdie gave some of the hexagons to Fanya and taught her how to whipstitch them together with tiny, hidden sutures. Fanya handed each of us pieces of thread to chew on. God forbid we should lose our wits.

I broke the news about how the missing Hadas managed to elude us once again. "Darn that woman! If we don't find her, Yossi can't get a divorce and we can't get married."

The seventy-something Birdie tugged on the end of her long white braid with one purple and one turquoise streak. "Why is she on the lam?" Birdie was a fan of crime dramas and liked to use cop speak, even if it was outdated.

"She believes someone named Alexander Koslov is stalking her."

"Who is he?" Birdie stopped stitching and peered at me over her wire-rimmed glasses.

"He's a missing link in the story of Hadas and the Uhrman Company. He's also behind the second break-in two Mondays ago, I'm almost sure of it. Hadas says he's stalking her. She says it's about unrequited love, but she lied. Her company is somehow involved with him financially. He's probably pursuing her because of money.

"Anyway, I'm pretty pissed off she disappeared for the third time. And I'm exhausted chasing her." I paused for breath. "And now everybody's here, I can tell you Koslov is coming here at two this afternoon. Hadas hinted he could be violent, so I'll understand if you want to leave before he gets here."

I didn't have a chance to finish my sentence. The four of them spoke at once while Fanya and I listened.

Giselle pushed her eyebrows together. "Are you kidding, Sissy? Of course I want to be here. After all, it was my IT guy who discovered the financial connection between the Uhrman Company and Koslov Associates. I'll secretly record the conversation with my smartphone."

"Unfortunately, Birdie and I have to leave at one," said Lucy. "Wish we could stay, but I've got a doctor's appointment."

Jazz sat up straighter. "You always forget, Martha, I took jujitsu classes years ago. I'll stay in case he tries anything funny."

"Okay, okay." I tried to regain their attention. "Koslov must know Fanya is staying here. There's no need for her to hide. Jazz, you and Giselle will disappear in the sewing room out of sight before he comes. I'm pretty sure you can hear everything from there. I don't want to scare Koslov away with too many witnesses."

Giselle said, "If you need our help, just say the word *banana*."

Lucy stopped sewing and rested her hands in her lap.

"What about your uncle? I felt awful getting your text last night. How's he doing?"

Every face turned in my direction. I told them about his trip to the ER at Cedars-Sinai. "Turns out the fainting was probably due to his medications. He's going to get them adjusted. As for his Parkinson's, he's taking boxing lessons to improve his symptoms. Hilda says it's working."

Giselle removed a pad of paper from her Gucci tote bag. "Let's continue to talk about your wedding, Sissy. Tell me, what theme do you want? It's never too early to plan the event with the caterers." She clasped a Montblanc pen in her right hand, ready to take notes.

Birdie raised her hand. "I think we should have an Agatha Christie theme. After all, Martha has solved several murders. We could decorate the setting like an English garden."

"True . . ." Jazz drew out the word. "But here's the thing. Aggie was an old spinster. And she was a knitter, not a quilter."

"Hmm." Lucy tapped her lips with her finger. "Along those lines, how about a Sherlock Holmes theme? Martha is just as clever as he was, and he had the advantage of being a fictional character."

Jazz shook his head. "Nope. Sorry. Holmes was addicted to cocaine. We need to think of a more romantic theme. Something like Rose and Jack's love story in the film *Titanic*." He sighed and gazed into the distance. "We could do a whole nautical theme in luscious tones of blue, green, and turquoise, like the waters of the Caribbean."

"I vote no on the *Titanic* theme," Giselle said.

Jazz sniffed. "Why? I think it's a great idea."

"Jack went down with the ship."

Jazz pursed his lips. "Okay. How about a *Pirates of the Caribbean* theme? We could still decorate with blues and greens, and we could all dress up like pirates and wenches."

Giselle rolled her eyes. "I suppose you'd wear a black patch over one eye and attach a rubber parrot to your shoulder."

Jazz leaned forward. "And I suppose you'd wear a leather bodice and carry a whip."

I chuckled. "Okay, you two. Give me a break. I'm not a starry-eyed girl. Plus, I've been married once before. Themes are for the young and idealistic. I want a simple wedding with my nearest and dearest."

We took a break at noon and Fanya made grilled cheese sandwiches for everyone. Jazz bit into his sandwich and closed his eyes. "So good." He opened his eyes. "I remember eating these as a kid with Campbell's tomato soup."

"You're right," Lucy said. "I'd forgotten how good they are together."

At one, Lucy and Birdie went home.

At one fifty-five Giselle and Jazz disappeared into my sewing room. "Remember," Giselle said, "say the word *banana* if you need us."

At precisely two, someone knocked on my door. I looked through the peephole. A handsome man in his forties stood alone on the porch. His gray suit looked perfectly tailored and expensive. A yellow pocket square over his left chest matched the silk tie with yellow and lavender stripes. His perfectly barbered thick brown hair showed gray at the temples. The dark sunglasses obscuring his eyes caused me to hold my breath.

"Who's there?" I asked, although I knew the answer.

"Alexander Koslov."

"Are you alone?"

"My driver waits in car." He spoke with a heavy accent.

I opened the door to let him in.

CHAPTER 27

I led Koslov to the living room and gestured for him to take a seat. He lowered himself into one of the easy chairs and I claimed the other one. Fanya sat facing us on the cream-colored sofa.

Koslov spoke in a soft but controlled voice. "When you asked me to come alone, I assumed you also are alone. Was I mistaken?"

I couldn't see his eyes behind the mirrored black lenses. "I'll answer as soon as you remove your glasses. It's very rude to hide behind them, especially when you're in someone's home."

He stiffened briefly at my rebuke, then removed his glasses, revealing penetrating blue eyes. His mouth formed an empty smile.

I gazed at those eyes and tried not to blink. "You know

what they say about the word *assume*. It makes an ass out of u and me.'" I pointed to my future sister-in-law. "Fanya flew to LA with Hadas. She's family. If she makes you too uncomfortable, you can leave. You're the one who wanted to talk, not me."

He stared at Fanya. "I know you. From where?"

"At the Uhrman house. You came to pray with the minyan while Ettie and her family sat shiva for Ze'ev."

A blanket of recognition settled on his face. "Ah yes. So it is. You're Ettie's friend."

Fanya said, "Right. Ettie and Ze'ev. And Hadas."

I crossed my arms. "You asked for this meeting, Mr. Koslov. What do you want?"

He glanced at Fanya and gave a small shake of the head as if to say he'd resigned himself to her presence. "I must find Hadas. I think you know where she is."

I hoped Giselle was pointing her smartphone in his direction, recording his every word.

"Is that why you broke into my house two Mondays ago? To find her or find some clue about where she'd gone?"

Koslov paused before answering. "That was regrettable. Two of my loyal associates, they sometimes go too far. My apologies for any inconvenience."

"Why do you need Hadas?"

He glanced again at Fanya. "A personal matter."

I laughed once. "You've been stalking her. She obviously doesn't want to be found. Especially, it seems, found by you. Is this a romantic obsession you have or something else?"

This time it was his turn to laugh. "Dear lady, you shoot straight to heart, don't you? I have many reasons why I need to find her. As I said, they are *personal*." He emphasized the last word, an indication he wasn't about to reveal anything more.

"Hadas said you were following me. Were you?"

He waved a dismissive hand. "Hadas has a way of, shall we say, stretching truth?"

I couldn't argue with him. I'd caught her lying more than once.

"I don't need to follow you. I have other ways to find her."

"So you knew where she was each time she moved?"

He smiled pleasantly. "I can't reveal all my secrets. We barely know each other."

Tiny clicks on the hardwood floor signaled we were about to have a visitor. Jazz's white Maltese Zsa Zsa Galore came prancing into the living room wearing her dotted Swiss pinafore and mint green ribbon in her topknot. She stopped suddenly when she saw Koslov and began snarling and showing her teeth.

His eyes widened. "What is this creature?" He made a movement toward the dog and she began to yip hysterically. He sat back. "You Americans and your animals!"

Afraid Jazz would come out of hiding to rescue her, I got out of the chair and scooped her up. "I'll put her to bed and be right back." I hurried into the sewing room and shoved Zsa Zsa into her father's arms. "Hang on to her," I whispered.

I returned to my chair in the living room. "You admitted to being at Ze'ev's house during the week of shiva. How did you know him?"

"Ze'ev and I do business together."

"What business was that?"

"Investments. Wagering."

"You were Ze'ev's bookie?"

"English is not my first language. But even I know *bookie* is crude word. I prefer to call myself 'entertainment broker.' Ze'ev Uhrman was one of my best customers."

Hadas had told Fanya she found betting tickets shoved in the back of a drawer in Ze'ev's desk—none of them less than one thousand dollars. "Yes, he left behind old betting tickets. Apparently, he liked to bet big."

Koslov narrowed his eyes. "Big bets make big winners."

"They also make big losers. Which kind was Ze'ev?"

"More on losing side."

"Did you know he stole money from the Uhrman Company to make those losing wagers?"

"He did? We did not discuss where he got money as long as he paid."

"When he died, did he owe you any money?"

"He was big loser. What do you think?"

"I think you had him killed."

"I would be very foolish to kill him. Dead men do not pay."

"Sometimes living men don't pay, either. I think Ze'ev got cut off from his source of money. He could no longer bleed cash from Uhrman Company, so, in the end, he couldn't pay. Maybe you killed him to set an example for the other big losers you *entertain*."

Koslov didn't answer. Instead, he steered the conversation back to Hadas. "I know about awkward situation with Hadas and Yossi Levy and you. Why do you help her?"

"Simple. If you know about my situation, then you know Hadas must give Yossi a divorce before he can marry me. Why do *you* want to find her?"

"We have shared interest, Hadas and me."

"Yes, I know about the money from the Uhrman Company being deposited every month in an account called 'Koslov Associates.'"

Koslov regarded me with a new look I couldn't quite read. Was it surprise? Admiration? He sneered. "I won't ask how you know. But I warn you—be careful with what you think you know. False accusations have way of coming back to hurt."

"Are you threatening me?" I turned to my future sister-in-law. "Fanya, I think he's threatening me."

Fanya moved her body as if getting ready to spring and disable Koslov.

He shifted almost imperceptibly away from the sofa as if he, too, could read her intentions. Then he raised both hands, palms outward in a gesture of submission, and half-laughed. "I wouldn't dare to threaten such a brilliant lady and her bodyguard."

Fanya remained on alert, body prepared for an offensive action.

"Don't look surprised, Fanya." Koslov addressed her directly. "Everyone knows you are expert in Krav Maga. You are famous. They still talk about what you did to the man who dared to touch you."

Fanya said, "And everyone knows you're a mamzer, a bookie, a loan shark and basic shtick dreck. I've got one question. How could someone like you show up at Ze'ev's house to pray? May he rest in peace. Do you even believe in God?"

"I show respect for my friend Ze'ev. I am sorry he is killed. For many reasons. One you already know. Dead men don't pay. Another reason I go to my friend Ze'ev's house is for his sister, Hadas. She is beautiful woman. I want to know better."

"Her being married to someone else didn't bother you?" Fanya asked.

"I know all about her so-called marriage and how it happened." He stuck out his chin.

"Who told you?" Fanya frowned.

"Ze'ev was my friend. We talk about many things. I want to find Hadas. Maybe after she divorce Yossi Levy, she marry me."

Oh no! Did Hadas know Koslov's intentions? If so, she might never give Yossi a divorce. "You'll excuse me if I say I don't believe a word of it. I think your connection with the Uhrmans is deeper. Especially because of the monthly transfers of money into your account. Ze'ev was murdered and right afterward, you got a piece of the business. It looks to me like cause and effect."

Koslov moved to the edge of the seat and stood. Fanya did the same, ready to pounce if necessary.

He put his sunglasses on and turned to me. "Does this mean you will not tell me where Hadas is?"

I took my time standing and stepped once toward the man hiding behind his mirrored glasses. "I don't know where she is. I wish I did. But you are correct. Even if I did know where she ran off to, I wouldn't tell you."

I walked Koslov to the front door. He left without another word. He got into the back seat of a black Rolls-Royce limousine and rolled open the window. As they pulled away from the curb, he touched his forehead with one finger in mock salute. I didn't need to turn around to know Fanya was dropping salt into the corners of the room.

Giselle and Jazz emerged from hiding.

"Could you hear?" I asked.

They both shook their heads. Giselle tapped something on the screen of her smartphone and held it for all to listen. We could only hear an occasional word. "I'm afraid we were too far away."

Jazz sniffed. "I told you so. You should've left the phone in the living room, where it was close enough to record everything."

Giselle patted his arm. "Live and learn. We'll do it next time Martha invites a mobster into the house."

I filled them in on the conversation.

Giselle gasped. "So Koslov was Ze'ev's Mobbed-up bookie!"

I nodded. "Looks that way. And here's something else to think about. My FBI contact John Smith said he knew who Koslov was."

"Makes sense," Giselle said, "given the FBI is the agency responsible for catching mobsters."

"Andre Polinskaya warned me there were forces at work I knew nothing about. I dismissed his concerns because he gets all his information from the spirit of his dead grandmother or the tarot cards.

"But John Smith told me the same thing. And now I know what they both meant. Koslov is a mobster. Thanks to Giselle's guy Shadow, we know Koslov gets money every month from the Uhrman Company. What I'd like to know is who opened the door to the Mob?"

CHAPTER 28

Early Wednesday morning I moved to the kitchen for my first cup of coffee in the day. Usually Fanya had a pot going, but today the kitchen was the same as we'd left it the night before. She must've finally adjusted to Pacific Time. I brewed a pot of strong dark roast and drank half of it while she slept.

I kept thinking about the elusive Hadas leaving the beach house in Oxnard on Monday. Where did she go from there? If Koslov could track her as he claimed, why didn't he know where she landed this time?

Hadas expected me to appear at the beach house in Oxnard; otherwise, why would she have left a note addressed to me? Hauer must've warned her we were coming. The woman in the ground floor apartment said Hadas got a ride from Uber. If I could access the same resources as law enforcement, I could find the Uber driver who picked her up from Oxnard and learn where they drove to.

Unfortunately, Crusher was still on assignment. He couldn't help. John Smith at the FBI would never share that information. My son-in-law, LAPD Detective Noah Kaplan, would have a severe anxiety attack if I asked him. Maybe I'd try my ex-boyfriend, LAPD Detective Arlo Beavers. All he could do was say, "No."

Eventually, Fanya strolled into the kitchen, hair still wet from the shower.

I poured a cup for her. "Today it's my turn to say, 'Good morning, sleepyhead.'"

Fanya stretched and yawned. "Yeah. I'm used to rising at six to be at the builders store for supplies by seven, then on to my job by eight." She looked at the clock. "Sleeping in until seven-thirty feels like a huge indulgence." She poured Cheerios into a bowl and added almond milk.

She ate in silence until her bowl was nearly empty. She rested her spoon and sat back. "Boy! I feel like we've been running a marathon this week." She grinned. "Hanging around with you is exciting, but also exhausting."

After we cleared the breakfast dishes, Fanya announced she was ready to sew all the Snail's Trail blocks together and baste her quilt. I showed her how to orient the blocks to create the overall design. Eyes dancing with enthusiasm, she sat at the Bernina and began to assemble her very first quilt top.

I left her in the sewing room as she hummed a tune I

thought I recognized as "Sympathy for the Devil" by the Rolling Stones. Two items filled today's agenda. First, check on my uncle and second, call Beavers. My uncle's welfare took priority over everything else. I called him first. "How are you feeling today?"

"Strong. Like a *junger* mensch." He called himself a young man. "Hilda made a doctor's appointment for this afternoon. We'll take a taxi as usual, but this could be the last time. She's studying for her driver's license. When she gets it, we'll go out and buy a nice car. A new one. She likes the little BMWs."

My stomach did a flip. *What are they thinking? He's not a rich man.* "Aren't they a little pricey for you?"

"Well, Hilda tells me cars are much more expensive nowadays, and I believe her. After all, it's been ten years since I've owned a car. Anyway, I'm thinking maybe an SUV would be more useful. We saw a dandy one at the Cadillac place."

Does she really have so much influence over him? "I think you'd have difficulty getting onto the seat of an SUV because they're too high off the ground. And you'd have the opposite problem with a sporty car like a BMW. The seat is too low; you'd have trouble getting out of the car and standing. You'd be better off looking at a practical sedan like a Prius or a Civic."

"We'll see, we'll see."

How can I derail this runaway train? "Do you think I can talk to Hilda for a minute?"

"Sure."

I heard him move toward the loud humming of a vacuum cleaner. He said something I couldn't hear over the thundering motor.

The noise stopped abruptly and Hilda spoke. "Hi. You want to speak to me?"

"Just checking in. He's seeing the doctor today?"

"Right. To adjust his meds. Do you want me to call you afterward?"

I heard my uncle in the background. "*Ach*. She worries too much."

Hilda spoke away from the phone. "That's because she loves you, Isaac."

"Yes, please," I said. "Call me and let me know what the doctor says."

"Will do. By the way, Isaac bought me a smartphone and put me on his plan. Let me give you the number. Now you can reach me directly whenever you want."

"He also tells me he's going to buy a car to get around in."

"Yes. He spends a lot of money on taxis. I think he figured it wouldn't be any more expensive to buy a car."

"He's not a rich man, Hilda. He cannot afford a BMW or a Cadillac. I'd appreciate your not encouraging him in that direction. The gas, insurance, and maintenance alone would be prohibitive. Not to mention monthly car payments."

Hilda paused for a moment. "I understand. Nothing's going to happen until I get a driver's license anyway. When I do, I promise to involve you in any decision-making."

We ended the call on a very cordial note, but something began eating at me once more. My uncle was spending more money since Hilda moved in: new drapes for the living room, a smartphone for Hilda, and soon the biggest purchase—a new car for her to drive. I tried telling myself it was his money to do with as he pleased, but the queasiness still rose in my gut. I should watch them carefully; pay surprise visits to see if things were as tranquil as he claimed.

The sudden worry about my uncle on top of stress from the last two days caused a migraine to claw at my head. First, my scalp tingled, followed by a pounding in my right temple and forehead. Lights amplified the pounding. I closed my eyes to a narrow squint and stumbled into my bathroom for my headache meds. Then I closed the curtains against the daylight and lay on my bed.

Please, God, make this headache go away.

I didn't remember falling asleep. When I woke two hours later, the headache was gone, but I felt slightly dizzy and disoriented. The sewing machine sat silent. Did Fanya finish assembling her quilt top? I rolled out of bed and peeked in the sewing room. It was empty. I continued to the living room. Fanya held a phone to her ear and was frowning.

She acknowledged me with a nod and a wave but continued to talk on the phone. "I don't know what to tell you, Ettie. If the lawyer says everything was kosher, I don't see how you can fight it. Of course, I'm no lawyer. Have you thought about getting a second opinion?"

She paused to listen to Ettie's response, then spoke again. "Well, it's been difficult to keep up with Hadas because she's staying with friends. But the next time I hear from her, I'll definitely ask her to call you." Another pause. "Okay. *Zei gesunt*, Ettie." Be well.

Fanya ended the call and shook her head. "I hate to lie to Ettie. She called me with more bad news. Apparently, the lawyer she and her son Zelig hired said they no longer have a legal right to half the business because of something stupid Ze'ev did. Legally, Uhrman Company belongs only to Hadas."

"Did Ettie say why they no longer have a legal claim? What stupid thing did Ze'ev do?"

Fanya shrugged. "He signed the business over. Didn't say why. But the way Uhrman Company is structured now, Hadas is the sole owner. She fixed it so if she dies, Yossi will inherit as her next of kin. If he dies before she does, the company would revert to the Uhrman family upon her death."

John Smith of the FBI told me the same thing: If both Hadas and Crusher were out of the picture, the business would stay in the Uhrman family. "I wonder what would happen to the order of inheritance if Hadas and Yossi get a divorce. He would no longer be her next of kin, right? Under those conditions, if a divorced Hadas died, wouldn't the company go straightaway to Ettie?"

"That's what the lawyer said."

"Did she say what would happen if Hadas remarried?"

"Good question," said Fanya.

"I'm thinking Hadas would make her new husband next in line to inherit the business." Is that what Koslov hoped for? I began to develop a bit of sympathy for Hadas. Who could she trust? No wonder she wanted Crusher. He was the only man in her life who ever treated her with respect.

"Ettie told me one more thing. She said a woman came to her door and demanded money. It seems Ze'ev fathered her child, a five-year-old girl. The woman said

KNOT READY FOR MURDER

Ze'ev hadn't been very good at giving her money every month, but he promised her a lump sum of two-hundred-fifty thousand dollars upon his death. She wasn't very bright. She thought the money would be automatically paid to her. But after waiting six months for the check that never came from a life insurance policy that never existed, she went to Ettie and demanded the money Ze'ev pledged."

"Did Ettie tell you her name?"

"Yes. Shelly Jacobs. Ettie called her a gold digger."

"Maybe she's the one who killed Ze'ev. Shelly Jacobs had a quarter of a million reasons to see him dead. Poor Ettie. Her husband left behind nothing but trouble, trouble still reaching out from the grave."

Fanya returned to the sewing room to finish assembling her quilt top. It was almost one when I remembered to call Beavers.

"Martha, we've got to stop meeting like this," he chortled. "Your fiancé might think you still have feelings for me."

I ignored him. "Whatever. You know the missing person who ended up not being missing after all?"

"You mean your fiancé's *wife*?" I heard the smug grin in his voice.

"Whatever. She's missing again. I need your help to find her. I think she has a right to be frightened for her life."

"Care to explain?"

"She's being pursued by a Ukrainian mobster from New York. He says he wants to marry her, but I think he really intends to first marry her, then kill her and take over the business. He already seems to have made some inroads."

"And how do you know this?"

"He visited me yesterday."

"Who?"

"Aren't you listening? The mobster. Alexander Koslov."

Beavers laughed outright. "This story is getting to be so much better than I anticipated."

I did a mental eye roll. "Whatever! He's the one responsible for the second break-in at my house, by the way. In case you're still looking for the culprit."

"Oh, yeah. Apprehending your phantom culprit sat at the top of my list."

"Will you listen, please? I found a safe place for her to stay in Ojai. But she left after only twenty-four hours and landed in a beach house in Oxnard. She was there for two days when she left again. Nobody knows where she is. The downstairs neighbor said she called an Uber. We could look at their records and find out where they took her. Then we could go get her and put her into witness protection."

"We?"

I was almost at the end of my rope with Beavers. "Jeez, Arlo. Can't you call Uber? Find out where she went?"

"Ah, Martha. You know, before you telephoned, I was feeling kind of depressed. Discouraged by the size of our homicide caseload and by an epidemic of daytime robberies. Especially worrying for me personally was the early-morning break-in at your house in which nobody was killed and nothing seemed to have been taken. Boy, that really stumped me. But now you've laid it out this neatly, I can see the situation was a whole lot worse than I thought. The Ukrainian mob. Witness protection. Wow. You sure managed to get yourself into another predicament."

"Arlo . . ."

"No, no, let me finish. Witness protection is administered by the Department of Justice out of the *federal* marshal's office. Mobsters are arrested by the *Federal* Bureau of Investigation and prosecuted by the United States Attorney's Office in *federal* court. Do you see a pattern emerging here? We at the local level have too much to do without taking on cases out of our jurisdiction."

"Does this mean you won't help me?"

"I always said you were brilliant. We must chat like this more often. Thanks for calling."

Crap!

I returned to the sewing room and poured out my frustration to Fanya. "Arlo Beavers drives me crazy! I won't get help from the cops. They don't take me seriously. Yossi is gone. He can't help me. And Hadas keeps disappearing." This whole mess was caused by Ze'ev Uhrman, who was now conveniently dead. His signing over the business, and his Mob connection, suggested to me there was much more to the story than either Koslov, Hadas, or even Ettie were willing to tell. "Do you think you can send one more text message to Hadas's phone?"

"Sure. I can always try. But as you know, she probably won't respond."

"She will if she knows Alexander Koslov showed up yesterday looking for her. Ask her what she wants us to tell him if he calls again. Maybe she'll respond."

Fanya reached into her pocket for her phone. She texted Hadas. "What if she doesn't text me back?"

I shrugged. "The next move is hers. Now we sit and wait."

CHAPTER 29

Wednesday evening Fanya and I sat on the sofa eating Ben & Jerry's chocolate ice cream and watching *Jeopardy!* During the break before double *Jeopardy!* her phone chirped. "Hadas answered my text." She handed the phone to me so I could read the message.

Tell A K I've gone back to NY

I punched in a reply.

We need to talk.

I watched the little gray dots dance on the side of the screen, indicating she was writing a reply. After a few seconds, her response popped up on the screen.

Why?

Fanya shifted toward me to better read her phone. "What are you going to tell her?"

"The truth." I began to type an answer.

New suspect in ur brother's death. Told A K to take a hike. U need protection.

Ten seconds later, Fanya's phone rang. I quickly handed it back to her. She enabled the speaker. "Hadas? Martha's here with me. You're on speaker."

"Anyone else there?"

"No. Just the two of us. Yossi's away."

Hadas was silent for a moment. "Who's the new suspect?"

Fanya told her about Shelly Jacobs and her five-year-old child coming to Ettie's house.

Hadas's voice softened. "Yeah, I knew about her. Shelly used to come by the business in hopes of catching Ze'ev for some child support. He wasn't very responsible, as you already know. After he died, she came around to solicit money from me."

"Did you give her anything?" I asked.

"Yeah. A few hundred at a time. I felt sorry for her."

Wow. Maybe Hadas has a heart after all.

Hadas continued, "Shelly told me she was waiting for an inheritance to come through. But she was vague about the details; I only half believed her. I thought she was trying to save face. She's really not very bright. Now you're saying Ze'ev actually promised her a quarter of a million when he died? Hmm. I wasn't aware of a second life insurance policy."

"Second policy?" My antennae stood at attention. "Was there a first life insurance policy?"

"You didn't know? The business carried a million-dollar policy for him. Even after he left, I paid the premiums for his family's sake. Ettie was the beneficiary."

Fanya and I looked at each other in amazement. "Are

you saying Ettie received a million dollars when Ze'ev was killed?"

"That's what I'm saying. I helped her file the claim myself."

"*Oy va voy!*" Fanya wagged her head. "And to think I gave Ettie a deep discount for hanging the wallpaper in her living room. She let me think she was destitute."

My mind raced with this new information. "You both know what this means, don't you? In addition to the litany of complaints against Ze'ev, Ettie had a million reasons to wish her husband dead."

Hadas was slow to respond. "No. I can't accept what you're implying, Martha. Ettie's a natural born kvetch, but she's not a killer. Besides, my brother was deliberately run over and killed by a car. Ettie doesn't drive."

"I know you both have sympathy for Ze'ev's widow, but we can't rule her out. Just because Ettie *doesn't* drive doesn't mean she *can't* drive."

Hadas's voice dripped with impatience. "Is that all you wanted to tell me? Because I need to make a business call to China. It's ten-thirty in the morning over there."

I leaned toward the phone in Fanya's hand. I wanted Hadas to hear me loud and clear. "Actually, I have a much bigger question: Alexander Koslov. We know about the money Uhrman Company pays to his account every month."

Hadas gasped. "How do you know?"

"Never mind how. We also know he was Ze'ev's bookie. Koslov is a Ukrainian mobster. How did he manage to get a piece of your business? And why is he chasing you? What is really going on?"

Hadas sighed audibly. "It's all Ze'ev's fault. And too complicated to explain over the phone."

"If using the phone is your only problem, Fanya and I will come to you. Then you can enlighten us in person. Tell us where."

Fanya fingered the amulet hanging around her neck. "I don't know why you're moving every other day, Hadas, but sooner or later—whoever you're running from—will catch up to you. And you'll have nowhere else to go. We can help, but you need to trust us. Have you forgotten how Martha and I went to such trouble to sneak you out of the Hotel Delaware and take you to a safe place in the mountains?"

"No, I haven't forgotten."

"Then why did you leave there?"

"Even though the three of us were careful, I was afraid we'd been followed. I waited until midnight Friday, when everyone was asleep, and called a friend. Then walked down the driveway to meet him on the road below. He drove me to a place by the beach I'd booked online."

"Yeah," I scoffed. "We talked to your 'friend' Peter Hauer. Why did you leave the beach house in Oxnard?"

"Peter called me. Told me all about your meeting. I knew if he told you where I was, he would probably tell Alexander Koslov. Especially if the price was right. So, I quickly found another place to hide where nobody knew about me."

Now I understood why she left a note for me with the neighbor. Even though we threatened him, Hauer ignored our warning and called Hadas after our meeting to give her a heads-up.

"Are you going to tell us where?" I asked.

The phone was silent.

"Hadas? Are you there?"

"Yeah, yeah. I'm staying at the Marina Vista Hotel, not far from the beach house in Oxnard."

"Under what name?"

"Jane Smith."

How original.

The clock read 7:45. "We can leave now. We should be there by nine."

"No. Not tonight. I have to call China. We'll talk in the morning."

Fanya's voice carried a skeptical edge. "You're not planning to slip away from us again, are you?"

Hadas's sigh traveled wearily over the phone. "I'll be here. Unless Alexander finds me before you do."

True to her word, Hadas called us back on Thursday morning at nine. She sounded upbeat. "Meet me for lunch at one in the hotel lobby. I want to try a nice little Italian restaurant nearby. I'm sure you'll find vegetarian choices on their menu. And if you promise to buy me dessert, I'll tell you everything I know." Her laughter tinkled over the phone like wind chimes made of glass.

I couldn't put my finger on it, but something seemed off. "Why wait? If Fanya and I leave now, we can easily be there before ten-thirty."

"I won't be back before one. If you leave now, you'd have to sit around the hotel lobby and wait for a couple of hours until I return."

Was she planning another getaway? "You're leaving the hotel? Isn't it risky?"

"Nobody but you knows where I am. Besides, I made a very favorable deal with the Chinese last night. To celebrate, I'm going to the mall next door for a little retail therapy and to get my nails done. Don't you love the fact there's a nail salon on every block? The Vietnamese have made a good life in America with fingernails and dough-nut shops."

Oh my God. Does she even realize how racist she sounds?

She continued, "The Filipinos have done the same thing with home health care and paid parking lots. This is a wonderful country for immigrants."

"What about the Ukrainians?" I snapped. "Are they all attracted to the clothing industry, or is that just Koslov's special interest?"

Hadas remained silent for a moment, then sniffed. "I'll see you at one." She ended the call.

Fanya drew back and regarded me. "You seem awfully peeved."

"Where to begin?" I blew out my breath. "She's such a narcissist and drama queen. Not to mention a bigot. She believes everything in life revolves around her. And she's always in crisis. I imagine being her friend is exhausting. How do you do it?"

"In small doses." She smiled. "I only see Hadas occa-sionally and when I do, I make sure ahead of time to have an exit strategy."

"What was your exit strategy when you were on the plane listening to her for five hours straight?"

Her wide grin revealed once more the gap between her two front teeth. "Parachute."

My mood lifted with our laughter. "The only thing I want from Hadas is her divorce from Yossi. She's wel-come to keep everything else in her world."

"*Halevai.*" Fanya punctuated my words.

Fanya and I left Encino before noon. The traffic north on the 101 was light, and we pulled into the Marina Vista Hotel parking lot in Oxnard almost exactly at one. The outside of the hotel looked like a huge waffle, completely devoid of style or art. A vast outdoor mall built to mimic a Mexican hacienda sprawled over several acres adjacent to the hotel. Fanya, who was nearly six feet tall, seemed to unfold as she got out of the car and stood. We ambled through the glass doors and into the lobby. A quick scan of the area revealed Hadas wasn't there.

"If she's skipped again, I'll personally throttle her myself," I growled through my teeth.

We approached the desk and asked if Jane Smith was still registered.

The eager young man in a dark blue jacket typed rapidly on the keyboard and stared at the computer screen. "She hasn't checked out. Would you like me to call the room to tell her you're here?"

"Please," I said.

He lifted the phone to his ear and punched in her room number. After fifteen seconds, he replaced the phone. "She's not answering." He gestured toward the chairs in the lobby. "Would you care to wait or leave a message?"

Smoke must've been coming out of my ears because Fanya took one look at me and responded, "We'll wait." She took my elbow and steered me toward the upholstered chairs in the lobby.

I clenched my teeth. "Crap! She's done it again!"

"Don't give up yet, Martha." She patted my hand. "Maybe Hadas lost track of time. Easy to do when you're shopping."

"Or maybe she was kidnapped for real this time," I growled. "It would serve her right."

Fanya pulled her phone out of her jeans pocket. "I'll give her a call now." She tapped the screen of her smart-phone and listened. Suddenly her face brightened. She looked my way and smiled. "We're here, Hadas. In the hotel lobby. Where are you?" Fanya listened and nodded. "Shall we come and get you? No? Okay. See you in ten."

She replaced her phone in her pocket. "I was right. Hadas lost track of time. But she promised to be here in ten minutes. She's in a mall near the hotel."

Twenty minutes later, Hadas walked through the glass doors, laden with several paper shopping bags. Her beau-tiful Penélope Cruz look-alike face glistened with the effort. The crimson tips of her freshly manicured finger-nails clutched purchases from Nordstrom, Swarovski, Coach, and Victoria's Secret. "Hello, everyone. Sorry I kept you waiting. But when you called, I was paying for my items from Victoria's Secret." She spoke directly to me and winked. "Actually, I took some pictures of myself in the dressing room and texted them to my husband."

What? She sent photos of lingerie—or worse—to her husband? *My Yossi?*

I didn't even try to hide my rage. I wanted to pull her hair. Rip out her eyes. Build a fire right there in the hotel lobby and throw her in it.

Hadas giggled at my reaction. "I'm kidding, Martha." She rattled the packages in her hands. "I'll put these in my room and be back in a jiffy. Then we can go for lunch at Pagliacci's Pasta. My treat. All this running around has made me very hungry."

Fanya smiled at Hadas. "I can hardly wait. By the way, what's your room number? In case we have to come look-ing for you."

"You worry too much," Hadas said. "But to convince you I'm not running away again, I'm on the fifth floor. Room five-twelve."

We watched her disappear into one of the twin elevators.

Fanya made a face. "I must say, I admire your self-control, Martha. Hadas can be a real witch sometimes."

I hardly heard Fanya. I was too busy inventing ways in my head to get rid of Hadas. I took a deep breath and exhaled in one loud sigh. "I wonder what it will take for her to give Yossi a divorce and go away forever."

Five minutes passed. Then ten. I looked at the clock on the wall above the reception desk. "She's taking her sweet time. What's that difficult about putting a few packages in the room?"

"Maybe she needed to use the ladies' room," Fanya said.

When Hadas didn't return after fifteen minutes, my gut began to churn. "Something's wrong."

Fanya took one look at my face and nodded. "I feel it, too. Shall I text her?"

"No time."

We hurried to the elevators.

CHAPTER 30

We poked number five on the elevator keypad. When the bell dinged at our destination, we stepped into a dimly-lit lobby with brown carpet and yellow-and-brown–striped wallpaper.

Fanya made a face. "Look." She pointed to an edge of the wallpaper peeling back slightly. "There's nothing hard about hanging stripes. They either used cheap glue, or they didn't roll it all the way to the edges of the paper. Either way, there's no excuse for such a sloppy job."

A sign with an arrow indicated room 512 was to our right.

We knocked. "Hadas?"

No answer.

Fanya pounded on the door with the side of her fist. "Hadas, if you don't open the door, we're going to get the manager to open it for us!"

KNOT READY FOR MURDER

KNOT READY FOR MURDER 249

Fanya shifted her weight and tensed. "If someone be-sides Hadas opens the door," she whispered, "jump out of the way."

I didn't have to ask why. My future sister-in-law was preparing to defend us.

I heard the squeak of hinges as a door behind us opened slowly. I turned around to see the curious face of a teenaged girl peeking at us from room 511 across the hall.

I forced my face into a smile. "Sorry if we disturbed you. Our friend is sick. We're trying to see if she's okay."

"'kay." The girl lifted one shoulder in a desultory shrug and closed her door.

Fanya knocked again. "Come on. Open the door."

When there still was no response, Fanya said, "She's either gone, or someone's in there with her. I can handle a physical situation better than you. I'll stay here. You go get the manager to open the door."

She was right about handling any physical situation better than me. I took the elevator back to the main floor and hurried toward the reception desk. I ignored the protests of four people waiting in line and went directly to the desk clerk.

"Sorry for interrupting, but this is an emergency. Something's wrong with our friend. We know she went to her room a half hour ago, but now she's not answering the door. We need someone with a key right now."

The young man raised his eyebrows. "Could it be she's taking a shower and didn't hear you?"

"No. She went to her room to drop off some packages and then we were supposed to go out to lunch. Please, can you hurry?"

"One moment." He spoke briefly to someone on the

phone and then turned to me. "Hotel security is on the way." With an apologetic smile he turned back to the woman he'd been helping. "Sorry for the delay."

One minute later, a neatly dressed man with a military bearing and a receding hairline approached "You're the lady who needs help?"

I nodded, comforted by his size and the no-nonsense look on his face. "Fifth floor. Hurry."

Inside the elevator he reached in his trouser pocket and pulled out a fat key ring. A delicate garden of red hair grew on the tops of his fingers. He inserted a small brass key into the override slot and pushed the fifth-floor button. "Do you know what's wrong with her?"

Yes! She's a self-centered, vain, sneaky, miserable witch. I shook my head. "No."

The car lifted nonstop to our destination. We turned right and rushed down the hall.

Fanya stood in front of the door to room 512, shifting her weight from one foot to the other. When we were close enough, she said, "I thought I heard her moan."

The man in the brown suit slid a card with a bar code through the lock mechanism and the door clicked open. He gestured for us to move to the side. "You stay out here for now."

He slowly pushed the door open. "Hotel security, Ms. Smith. Checking to see if you're okay."

She moaned again. He reached under his jacket toward an area adjacent to his left armpit; a place where a shoulder holster would be. "I'm coming in, Ms. Smith." He disappeared into the room.

Low voices mumbled inside, then he reappeared. "She's in here."

We followed him into the dim hotel room. The brown-

and-yellow color scheme continued from the hallway into the room with gold drapes, gold carpet, and a brown bedspread. Apparently, housekeeping cleaned her room while she went shopping, because the bed was freshly made with crisp white pillowcases and the air smelled faintly of Pine-Sol. Hadas lay on top of the bed with an ashen face, clutching her belly.

Brown suit turned to us. "She says she fainted but refuses to see a doctor or go to the hospital. There's no more I can do here, but I still need to write an incident report." We gave him our names and phone numbers. He entered the information in his smartphone and handed us each a business card: James Murphy, Private Security Group.

As he marched toward the door, he said over his shoulder, "Call me if you change your mind about the doctor."

Fanya sat on the bed next to Hadas. "*Nu?* What happened? Did you really faint?"

"I'm fine."

"No, you're not. You're young and healthy." *Pu, pu, pu!* "Something's not right if you're fainting."

Hadas ignored Fanya. She glanced at the business card and frowned. "I'm going to have to find a new place to hide, now the cops are involved."

What? No "Thank you for caring?" No "I'm sorry for dragging you into yet another personal crisis?"

I stood with my fists on my hips and my lips in a straight line. "Well, I'm done chasing after you and your gypsy ways. You're coming back to Encino, where we can keep an eye on you. Once we get home, you're going to tell us everything, and I mean *everything*! Start packing because you're checking out."

Hadas took one look at me and packed her suitcase

without protest. Between the three of us, we managed to carry her luggage and all her purchases to the car in one trip.

On the ride home, Hadas slumped in the front passenger seat. I briefly glanced to my right to check on her. "Are you sure you're fine? Maybe we should stop off at an urgent care clinic and get someone to look at you."

"No!" Her protest was loud. "I already know why I fainted."

"Well, don't keep us in suspense," I said.

Hadas raised a defiant chin. "I'm pregnant."

CHAPTER 31

I tightened my grip on the steering wheel and fought an impulse to drive to the side of the freeway and stop. "How far along are you?"

"Eight weeks."

"So you're keeping the baby?"

Hadas's voice became soft and wistful. "After I miscarried all those years ago, I thought I'd never have another chance. I'm over forty. This is a miracle. Of course I'm keeping this baby."

"Whose baby is it?"

"Mine!"

"Okay." I asked, although I had a fairly good idea of the answer, "Let me put it this way. Who's the father?"

"I think you know."

I looked away from the road long enough to see con-

cern etch wrinkles on her forehead. "Yeah, I think I do."
Was it the man who was desperately pursuing her?

Fanya spoke from the back seat. "Hadas, you need to
be more careful now you're pregnant. For one, you need
to read the Psalms every day and stay away from funerals
and cemeteries."

I glanced at Hadas again.

An amused smile broke through her defenses. "I don't
believe in those old superstitions, Fanya."

"Wouldn't you rather be safe than sorry? There are
simple things you can do to ensure your baby's health."

"Such as?"

"Eat only kosher food, avoid stepping on discarded
fingernail clippings, and keep a ruby on your body at all
times."

Hadas barked a slight laugh. "I won't even ask about
the fingernails. But why wear a ruby?"

"It's a *segulah*, a protection against miscarriage."

"Maybe I need to carry several rubies," Hadas murmured.

I didn't blame her for being scared. She'd lost her first
child in a miscarriage.

Back in Encino, we helped the mother-to-be carry her
shopping bags and suitcase to the guest room. Was it my
imagination, or was her face turning green? She suddenly
clutched her waist with one hand, covered her mouth
with the other, and ran into the bathroom.

Fanya and I looked at each other. "Morning sickness."

We listened to sounds of retching coming from ten feet
away. I almost wanted to sympathize with the unfortunate
Hadas. But I kept thinking about her first pregnancy over
thirty years ago when Crusher offered to marry her and

save the Uhrman family's reputation. During the brief time they lived together, did he witness her morning sickness? Did he comfort her?

Fanya opened one of the dresser drawers she was using and retrieved a bundle of dried herbs tied tightly together with string. She flicked on a plastic lighter and touched it to the end of the bundle until it began to send out the pleasant aroma of sage on the curls of smoke. She walked around the room waving it in the air, reciting, "*Keinehora, keinehora, keinehora.*" Once she banished the evil eye from the guest room, she made a methodical circuit of every room in the house. She ended her exorcism by opening the front door to push out the demons with her last *keinehora* and wave of smoke.

Hadas emerged from the bathroom and asked for water.

I led her to the kitchen and sat her at the table while I drew a tall glass of tap water. "Drink all of this." I plunked the glass on the table in front of her. "You need to stay hydrated."

"Thanks." She held the glass in slightly shaky hands and sipped.

I unwrapped a stack of saltine crackers and arranged some on a plate for her. "Eat these when you begin to feel nauseated." As an afterthought, I handed her a fresh lemon from the fruit bowl on the counter. "Sometimes smelling this will calm your stomach. Scratch the rind a little with your fingernail. The smell will be stronger."

Once I was sure she wasn't going to puke again, I suggested we find a comfortable place in the living room to sit and talk. "It's time to tell us everything. Don't leave out any details."

Fanya put the teakettle to boil on the stove. "I'll make some ginger tea. It's good for the stomach."

Hadas took a deep breath, leaned back on the sofa, and gently clasped her hands over her belly. "I have to stay in hiding. At least until all of this blows over."

"All of what?"

"My brother Ze'ev caused all this trouble. It's a long story."

I looked at my watch. "It's only four-thirty. Take your time."

She nibbled on the edge of a saltine. "My father built the Uhrman Company from scratch. We employed dozens of people. Shortly after I began to work there, I modernized the business."

"We were talking about Ze'ev. You said he was responsible for your current troubles."

"I'm getting there as fast as I can, Martha. But you need to know the history in order to fully understand the present. These are the details you said you wanted."

"You're right. Go ahead."

"At first, my father intended to hand over the business to his only son, Ze'ev. You know how traditional their generation was. But every time Papa gave him something to do, Ze'ev managed to screw it up. The only thing he was good at was numbers, so Papa stuck him in the back office with the accounting."

"But you're running the business now, right?"

"Yeah, but only after Papa realized I'd do a better job than my brother. After Papa's death two years ago, Ze'ev and I inherited Uhrman Company as equal partners, but with me as CEO."

"How did Ze'ev react? Was he upset to discover he wouldn't be running the company?"

"I thought he'd be angry, but I was wrong. He was happy to be in charge of the accounting." She leaned her head against the back of the sofa and sighed. "I should have been more suspicious when our revenue began to dip each quarter. I thought some of our clients were late to pay."

"When did you learn the truth?"

Fanya walked into the room and handed Hadas a cup of steaming ginger tea. "Drink this. It'll help."

Hadas accepted the cup and took a sip. "A year ago. We started to operate in the red. I hired an outside accountant to do a secret audit. Sure enough, he discovered Ze'ev had withdrawn almost a million dollars since Papa's death."

"Ze'ev a gonif?" Fanya called him a thief. "What a shock!"

"Shock? Yes and no. My brother was an addict, Fanya. Gambling, alcohol, and women. When I confronted him, he didn't deny he took the money."

"I'll bet you were relieved," Fanya said.

Hadas swallowed more ginger tea. "I gave him three choices: One, replace the money he stole; two, face prosecution for fraud and embezzlement; or three, sign his half of the business over to me. He couldn't replace the money and he didn't want to go to jail. So, in the end, he had no real choice. He signed over his share of Uhrman Company, making me the sole owner. Two weeks later, he was killed in a hit-and-run. I thought that would be the end of an ugly episode, but I was wrong."

Hadas played with the handle of her cup and broke eye

contact. "A week after the funeral, a handsome, well-dressed stranger appeared in my office."

"Alexander Koslov?" I asked.

She looked at me again. "Right. Alexander said he loaned Ze'ev five hundred thousand dollars but Ze'ev never paid him back. As of six months ago, the added interest boosted the loan amount to over a million."

"Whoa. There are laws against usury, aren't there?" Fanya's eyes sparked with indignation.

"Alexander wasn't a banker. He didn't play by those rules. He was a ruthless loan shark. He said I inherited my brother's debt and he was there to collect."

"That's ridiculous!" Fanya snorted. "No judge in the land would make you liable for your brother's debts."

Hadas took another sip of tea. "Ordinarily, maybe not. But Alexander showed me a note signed by Ze'ev pledging his half of Uhrman Company as collateral for the loan. The date on Alexander's note came before the date Ze'ev signed over his half of the business to me. Alexander said his claim would take precedence over mine."

"What a nightmare." Fanya crossed her arms and huffed.

"You're telling me. I went to a lawyer who basically advised me to settle."

"By settle, you mean pay Alexander Koslov a million dollars?" I asked.

Hadas nodded. "The next time I spoke to Alexander, he said I could buy Ze'ev's note for two million dollars and all my problems would go away. But the longer I waited, the more the interest would pile on."

"Did you tell him *Gei faifen afenyam*?" Fanya used the Yiddish for "go jump in the lake."

"No. When I told him I would have to think about it, these were his exact words. 'Bad things can happen to people who don't pay their debts. Look what happened to your poor brother.'"

I could see how money pressures plagued Hadas and why she chose to run. I also guessed that going into hiding, especially in her delicate condition, provided an island of calm in the midst of all her dramas.

"Alexander gave me a week to get the money. If I couldn't pay him in one lump sum, I could pay over time. With interest, of course."

"Why didn't you go to the police?" By now, Fanya fumed, nostrils flaring.

"Are you kidding? I didn't want to provoke Alexander. I just wanted him to go away. And then I got another shock when, three months after Ze'ev's death, the police told me a 'credible witness' had come forward. They said the car deliberately accelerated and swerved toward Ze'ev. It was awful enough that my brother was killed in a road accident. But murdered? I certainly was not ready for murder."

"Any ideas on who the driver could've been?"

Hadas wagged her head. "As far as I know, the police have made no progress in solving Ze'ev's death."

"But Ze'ev's death and Alexander's threats all happened six months ago. Did you pay the two million he asked for?"

Hadas scowled. "Who has that much cash lying around? Certainly not me. I was still trying to lift the company out of the red. Alexander offered to excuse the debt and eventually destroy Ze'ev's note if I would bring him into the business as a silent partner. He said I could even take a percentage of his transactions. For my trouble."

"Money laundering?"

She looked at the floor and nodded. "I'm not proud of it, but there was no choice. He would deposit large sums of cash into the business account and then I would send cash payments to his Koslov Associates account."

"That's blackmail!" Fanya made a disgusted face.

"So why are you running away now?" I asked. "What's changed?"

"Alexander pressured me to become his lover. He sent flowers every day. He brought me expensive jewelry—which I refused to accept. One day I said, 'If you're really serious about me, there is one thing you can give me which might change my mind.' I didn't think he'd agree, but the next day he handed me the note Ze'ev signed, giving half of Uhrman Company as collateral. I immediately put the note into the shredder."

"Wow!" Fanya said. "No more blackmail."

Hadas raised her eyebrows at Fanya's obvious conclusion. "Yeah. No more blackmail. For the first time in months, I relaxed, knowing Alexander had given me what I really wanted—the business free and clear." She looked at her hands. "In a moment of weakness, I slept with him. Once our affair started, he thought he owned me."

"So that's how . . . ?" I pointed to her belly.

Hadas sighed and gave her belly soft little pats. "I wasn't about to hand over my life or my child's life to him. I needed to act quickly. I made out a will, giving the business to Yossi. In case neither one of us survived, the business would go to Ettie. Then I told Alexander what I'd done."

"Wasn't that risky?" Fanya blinked rapidly.

"A calculated risk. I told him Koslov Associates would no longer receive money from the Uhrman Company."

"Messing with the Mob's money is an extremely dangerous game. How'd he take it?" I asked.

Hadas huffed. "How do you think? He threatened me. That's when I told him my husband was a federal agent. And if he harmed either one of us, the whole federal government would come down on his head."

What an understatement. The feds take it very badly when one of their own is harmed.

"I also let him know I'd been keeping a record of every illegal transaction he made and if anything happened to me, the information would be handed over to the FBI."

I underestimated Hadas. Under the helpless little woman act, she possessed nerves of steel. "You outsmarted him."

She smiled. "He was furious, for sure. He gave me an ultimatum: Destroy the will and hand over the incriminating record or something bad might happen."

"Is that what they were looking for when they broke into my house on Monday?"

Hadas nodded. "I told Alexander the evidence against him was in a safe place. I also informed him I was pregnant. As long as he stayed away from me and the baby, his secrets were safe. But the moment he caused trouble, the evidence would find its way into the hands of the FBI."

"How did he react?"

"Once he learned I was carrying his child, he became obsessed. He claimed he didn't care about the money anymore. He wants us to raise this child. Together."

I finished her thought. "That means as long as you stay married to Yossi, you can use him as an excuse not to marry Alexander?"

Hadas fixed me with a steady gaze. "Exactly."

Great. Now I'd found a new reason to dislike this woman. Once again, she thought only about herself and her latest drama. She used her marriage to Crusher as a way of controlling the latest man in her life, Alexander Koslov. She didn't care about how her actions might affect Crusher or his life with me.

CHAPTER 32

I tried to hide my anger at the selfishness of the woman standing in the way of my happiness. "You can't use your marriage to Yossi as a tactic to deal with Koslov anymore. We're going to see a lawyer friend of mine. You're getting a divorce, Hadas."

Hadas sighed and closed her eyes. "I suppose that's inevitable. And anyway, I'm tired of fighting."

An actual tear slipped down her cheek.

Maybe she's not heartless after all.

We sat in silence for a minute. I didn't doubt Hadas had told us the truth about her situation. But I was still curious how the death of her brother connected to the story. "Tell me more about Ze'ev's death. We know from a witness account that the car deliberately sped up and swerved toward him. Did the police tell you anything more about that?"

Hadas shrugged one shoulder. "They wouldn't say."

"As I see it, there are many people with motive to kill Ze'ev. The reasons for his killing all seem to point to money. Either money he owed, money he promised, or money from his life insurance. Plus, there's also the issue of his sleeping around. Maybe his wife got plain tired of it. Which do you think is more likely?"

"I'm too fuzzy-headed to think about anything right now." Hadas yawned. "I'm so tired I could sleep for a hundred years. And I'm hungry. We didn't have lunch, remember?"

I listened with some amusement as Hadas described the early symptoms of pregnancy: fatigue, nausea, and hunger.

Fanya stood. "I'll fix you something bland to eat. How about scrambled eggs and toast?"

Hadas drained the last of the ginger tea and handed her empty cup to Fanya. "Sure. And I could use more of this."

I glanced quickly at Fanya to see if she resented being treated like a servant. I would've said something if Hadas dared speak to me like that, but Fanya only smiled indulgently and took the cup.

Thirty minutes later, we all sat down to eat breakfast for dinner.

Afterward, Hadas announced, "I'm turning in for the night." She staggered to the guest room and closed the door.

I brewed a pot of PG Tips extra-strong black tea and sat at the kitchen table with my future sister-in-law. I added two teaspoons of sugar and a dollop of milk to my cup. "You know, Fanya, I had a horrible thought. We've assumed Hadas keeps hiding in new locations because she's running from Koslov."

Fanya raised the cup to her lips and blew on the steaming tea. "Isn't that what she told us?"

"I know, but let's assume there's someone or something else she's running from. I mean, I don't believe her life is in danger from Koslov. When he catches up to her, the worst she has to do is face the inevitable confrontation over the child. But she won't have to fear for her life."

"Okay, I'll go along with that. Who else is after her?"

"Suppose whoever killed Ze'ev wants Hadas dead, too. Her disappearing act may be the only thing keeping her alive. We have to wonder, who would benefit from her death?"

"As the will stands now, it would be Yossi. After him, Ettie."

"And after the baby is born?" I asked.

Fanya placed her cup on the table. "Ahh. I see what you mean. Hadas would probably want to change her will and leave everything to her child."

"Bingo! It's possible someone may want to kill her before she brings an heir into the world. Who would benefit?"

Fanya looked perplexed. "According to the will, it's still Yossi. Martha, you can't think my brother's involved."

"No, of course not. But suppose whoever is after Hadas has plans to eliminate Yossi as well?"

"Oy!" She blew out her breath. "That's a big *if.* Ettie would be next in line, but I honestly don't think she's capable of murder."

"Yeah, I know. But it's the only thing making sense right now. I sure wish he would come home. He's always been good about helping me get the information I need to figure stuff out."

"What about Giselle? Doesn't she have someone who can help? Unofficially, of course."

"Of course. I'd forgotten all about Shadow the hacker." Something about Fanya's expression intrigued me. Her face remained neutral, but her eyes said something else. She definitely possessed hidden layers. "I'll call Giselle now."

My sister answered on the first ring. "Hi, Sissy. How are things going with Yossi's wife?"

I told her about driving Hadas back to Encino from the hotel in Oxnard.

When I finished bringing her up to date, she said, "Wow! She must like living dangerously. Personally, I'd stay miles away from the Mob. And if they ever tried to muscle in on my company, I'd march straight to the FBI. Why didn't she?"

"I can't say for sure, but I imagine she felt trapped. At any rate, I'd like to know more about her brother's death. If Ze'ev's killer is after control of the Uhrman Company, he may want to kill Hadas and Yossi, too. She claims the police haven't made any progress on the investigation. But Hadas is a manipulator. I don't know how much of what she says is the truth. Is there any way your IT guy Shadow can access the police file?"

My sister laughed. "For someone who was opposed to hacking, you appear to have come over to the dark side."

I didn't respond at first, because my sister was right. "Okay, I've capitulated. But it's for a good cause."

"Isn't it always?" She chuckled. "I'll put him on it to-morrow. Anything else?"

"Yeah. You and Harold still coming for Shabbat dinner tomorrow?"

"Is Hadas going to be there? I can't wait to meet her after all this high drama."

"She'll be here unless she runs away again."

Friday morning I got an early start and shopped for the food we'd have in the evening. My first stop was Bea's Bakery. I didn't have to wait in line because at seven-thirty I'd beat the Friday crowd preparing for the Sabbath. I breezed in, bought two loaves of twisted challah—one plain, the other raisin—a generous roll of poppy seed strudel, and cinnamon babka. I also bought two dozen *mandelbrot*, Jewish biscotti, to help Hadas with her morning sickness. At eight, I called the attorney who'd helped me out before.

Deacon "Deke" Abernathy's greeting boomed over the phone. "Hey, Martha. Long time no see. How are you?"

I told him about my engagement and the obstacle course we were running on the way to the chuppah, the wedding canopy. "Hadas needs to give Yossi a divorce. Can you draw up the papers? I can bring her in today if you're going to be around."

Deke's laugh was as robust as his greeting. "First of all, congratulations on your engagement. You're bringing me your fiancé's *wife*?" More laughter. "You never disappoint. You manage to get in the most interesting situations."

"You don't know the half of it."

"As it happens, I do have a free half hour at eleven-thirty."

"Great. We'll be there."

I notified Hadas to be ready by ten-thirty for the drive to Deke's office in West LA.

She wasn't happy. "I don't feel well, Martha. What if I throw up in the car?"

"Bring a lemon."

I swapped my jeans and T-shirt for black linen trousers and a white cotton sweater. I asked Fanya if she wanted to come with us.

"I think I'll stay here and get the house ready for tonight. I'll also get a head start on the cooking."

If Fanya were so inclined, she'd make someone an excellent wife. She certainly was turning out to be an excellent sister-in-law and friend.

I hugged her. "Thanks."

Hadas wore a white silk blouse tucked into a gray skirt that appeared to be a little tight around her waist. She slumped in her seat and sulked all the way into West LA. I paid no attention to her attempt to manipulate me into feeling guilty. The beautiful Penélope Cruz look-alike held no power over me.

I parked in the underground garage of Deke's building on the corner of Federal and Wilshire.

Hadas finally spoke in the elevator ride to Deke's tenth-floor offices. "How do you know this attorney?"

"A couple of years ago a girlhood friend died and named me executor of her estate. Deacon Abernathy was her lawyer. We worked together to fulfill the mandates of her will."

The elevator door opened to a plush, glassed-in waiting room with a commanding view of the Pacific Ocean to the west and Westwood Village to the east. I approached the receptionist, a young man with latte-colored skin and hair the color of bleached straw. The last time I'd been in this office, he wore dark eyeliner. Today he'd added shimmering gold eye shadow.

"Hello. I'm—"

He interrupted with a huge smile traveling from his mouth straight to those eyes. "I know." He stood and extended his hand across the desk. "Mrs. Rose. How nice to see you again."

For a moment, I panicked because I couldn't remember his name. I shook his offered hand. "Great to see you, too."

"He's expecting you. Do you remember how to get to his office? Straight down the hallway to the end."

I walked with Hadas along a corridor dotted with original paintings and lithographs of athletes in action. Deke was a big-deal football player at UCLA during the same years I studied anthropology there. Our academic paths crossed only once when we enrolled in the same geography class.

Deke's door was open, and we entered without knocking. A thickset man with a receding hairline stood and came round his desk, with his shirtsleeves rolled up. His forearms were thick and beefy. But the former star athlete had gone soft around the middle, probably thanks to decades of steak dinners and martini lunches.

"Hi, Deke." I grinned and offered my hand.

He gently pushed it aside and gave me a warm hug. "Let me see that ring of yours."

I held out my left hand with the three-karat diamond.

He gave a low whistle. "Very nice."

I introduced Hadas. She acknowledged him with one

nod but didn't offer her hand, a clear indication she wasn't through with her sulk.

He gestured toward a conference table and sat facing the two of us. He directed his first question to Hadas. "Are you a resident of California?"

"No."

He shifted his gaze to me. "A nonresident can't file in California."

My stomach dropped. If Hadas left LA, we might never get her to sign. "But Yossi's a resident. He can file, right?"

"Yes. He could file for divorce as the petitioner, and Hadas would be the respondent."

I wasn't going to leave his office without the papers in hand. "Okay, then. Make out the papers with Yossi as petitioner." I turned to Hadas. "Do you have any issues about being the respondent?"

"No."

Deke clicked open his pen and prepared to write on a yellow legal pad. "Okay. I'll still need some information from you, Hadas." He wrote down all her contact information. "Is this divorce amicable? By that, I mean, do you have any issues you can't resolve? In addition to the petition for divorce, we will file a settlement agreement. Are there any assets you're disputing?"

"No."

I jumped in. "Hadas owns a business in New York. Yossi wants nothing from her and she wants nothing from him." I reached over and gently squeezed her arm. "Am I right, Hadas?"

"Yes."

Deke wrote something on the legal pad. "Then the settlement agreement should pose no problem. Do you have any minor children?"

"No." Hadas glanced at me and touched her belly.

I jumped in. "Hadas is expecting a child, but it's not Yossi's. They were in a sham marriage over thirty years ago and haven't seen each other since." I glanced at Hadas. "She was supposed to get an annulment, but, for reasons of her own, she didn't. This is the first time they've even been in the same room together. They both agree. What's his is his and what's hers is hers. Am I right, Hadas?"

"Yes." Hadas snapped back her answer.

"She lives in New York," I continued. "So, whatever papers she needs to sign should be done ASAP, while she's still in LA. Is it possible to get them prepared this morning?"

Deke sat back and tapped the legal pad with the end of the pen. "This divorce is as simple as they get, Martha. Boilerplate, really. I can get one of the clerks to draft a no-contest petition for dissolution and settlement agreement today. But nothing can be done until Yossi signs the papers. Once he does, we can file and serve Hadas." He smiled at her. "Does that sound like something you can live with?"

"I guess."

Deke wrote down her address and phone number and briefly spoke to someone on his phone. Less than thirty seconds later, a young woman in a navy-blue skirt suit entered the office. He tore off the page from his legal pad and handed it to her. "Drop everything else you're doing and draw up a no-contest petition for dissolution and a marital settlement agreement using this information."

He turned back to us. "We'll messenger these papers to you by tomorrow."

I blew out my breath, the one I'd been holding for two weeks since Crusher first dropped the bombshell about his marriage. "How long does it take for the divorce to become final and he can remarry?"

"In certain cases, as soon as thirty days, plus one from the date the papers are served. Otherwise, it's six months."

Unfortunately, Crusher wasn't around to sign the papers. He would only be available when his undercover assignment ended, and I never knew how long that would be. More than ever, I wished he were here.

We chatted amiably for the next five minutes. I showed Deke a picture of my baby granddaughter, Daisy, and he reciprocated with a photo of his grandson wearing a Pop Warner uniform and a lopsided grin. "The game is in our blood. Tyler wants to play football in college like his grandpa."

At twelve-thirty, we said our goodbyes and drove on the 405 Freeway back to Encino. I was glad Hadas wasn't the petitioner. Who knew if she'd have another change of heart? Thirty years ago, she failed to follow through with an annulment. I didn't want to give her a second chance to "lose" these documents.

We'd crested the Sepulveda Pass when Hadas said, "I feel sick."

Oh, no. "Where's the lemon?" I pressed a button and opened the passenger window. "Fresh air might help. There will be no puking in my car!"

Hadas reached in her purse and fished out the lemon. She scratched the rind with a perfectly manicured scarlet fingernail to release the sharp smell and pressed the lemon against her nose. A moan barely escaped her mouth before she heaved all over the front of her silk blouse and into her lap. "I told you I was sick."

"We're almost home. When we get there, stay seated as you are and I will help you get out of the car."

Ten minutes later, I parked in my driveway, ran around the car, and opened the passenger door. The portion of the passenger seat belt where it crossed her chest would need to be washed, but the rest of the car's interior was mercifully spared. I helped Hadas roll out of the car, took her hand, and led her through the wooden gate at the side of my house and into the backyard. I turned on the garden hose until water flowed out in a soft stream. "Wash the worst of it off with this while I go inside and get you a towel."

Hadas drank some water out of the hose, then squirted it over the slime on her blouse and skirt. "It's cold." She shivered.

"Hang in there. I'll be back in less than a minute." I somehow managed to get Hadas out of her soaking wet clothes and into a hot shower.

Fanya must've worked hard while we were gone because the house smelled like furniture polish and something savory cooking in the oven. "Welcome back. How did the lawyer visit go?"

"He was very encouraging. The papers will arrive tomorrow. We only need to add Yossi's signature and the lawyer will file them in court. Then Hadas will be served and we wait for the divorce to be final. About six months."

I cracked open a can of Coke Zero when music from my phone alerted me to an incoming call from Giselle.

"Shadow was able to get some information for you."

"Good. What did he find out?"

"Apparently the police haven't spent much effort investigating this murder. There weren't many notes in the file."

"Well, Yossi did say the feds took over the investigation, which might explain the lack of paperwork in the police file. Does it say anything about the eyewitness's account of the hit-and-run? Didn't that trigger a more aggressive investigation?"

"Apparently not much. The witness came forward three months after the incident. He couldn't give the police a description of the driver. But he was able to provide enough of a partial plate, which eventually led to a rental car company. The name on the rental contract was Ze'ev Uhrman, and it was dated the day before his death. He used a company credit card to pay."

"That's odd. Hadas told us he was terminated two weeks before his death for stealing money from the company. Why did he still have a valid company credit card? And what about the car? Did it ever show up?"

"Let me see." I heard the sound of papers rustling. "Hold on to those questions. I'll bring the whole file with me tonight and we can study it together."

CHAPTER 33

Friday night, all the usual family arrived for Shabbat: Quincy and her family and the Friday foursome of Giselle, Harold, Uncle Isaac, and Hilda. Our special guests were Fanya and Hadas. Crusher was still undercover.

I presented Hadas to the family one by one. She stood stiff-necked and acted like royalty granting an audience. Even though she was Crusher's wife, almost everyone responded to her graciously. I watched as her defensive posture softened with each warm greeting. Then I caught Giselle studying her with narrowed eyes. Not a good sign.

I placed a brand-new high chair for my granddaughter next to my daughter's spot at the dining room table. Once we blessed the candles and everyone was seated, Uncle Isaac sang the kiddush and prompted Hilda to recite the blessing over the bread.

"*Baruch atah adonai elohaynu melech ha olam, ha motzi lechem min ha aretz.* Blessed art Thou, oh Lord our God, King of the universe, who brings forth bread from the earth."

When she finished, he grinned at her. "This one is a very smart cookie."

Hilda touched his arm ever so gently, gazed into his eyes, and smiled. "I did okay for a shiksa?"

He squeezed her hand. "*Shoin.*" Beautiful.

The skin on my arms prickled. *Oh no. This can't be what it looks like.* I still hadn't managed to get either one of them alone long enough to ask about the nature of their relationship.

Fanya had cooked a cheesy pasta casserole loaded with finely chopped veggies and pinto beans. "The pasta is whole grain. Adding beans makes it a complete protein." She didn't have to persuade people to try it. Everyone piled generous portions on their plates.

Uncle Isaac closed his eyes. "Mmm. This reminds me of my mother's cholent." He referred to the traditional savory stew for Sabbath day. He opened his eyes and smiled at Hadas. "How do you like Los Angeles, young lady?"

"It's a lot more relaxed here. LA doesn't have as many tall buildings as New York."

Then Giselle opened her mouth. "What's it like to be staying in the same house as your husband and his fiancée?"

The entire group fell silent.

I tried to save the moment. "It is an unusual situation, G, but we've managed quite well. Fanya, this casserole is delicious. What exactly is in it?"

Giselle ignored my attempt to change the topic. She

spoke to me but kept her gaze on Hadas. "Really? What do you call having to drop everything to chase her sorry ass all over two counties?"

Hadas remained cool. "That was Martha's decision. Not mine."

Anger spots dotted my sister's cheeks with red as she pinned Hadas in a wrestling match of words. "If I understand the situation correctly, *you* were the one who arranged a phony kidnapping. Then Martha's house was broken into because of you. *You* were the one to call for help in sneaking out of the Hotel Delaware. *You* managed on your own to sneak away from the place Martha found for you in Ojai, and *you* called for help again from the third place you landed. Or was it the fourth?" With each indictment, Giselle's voice rose. "Every time you got into trouble, you took advantage of Martha's good nature. And now here you are again, a guest in her home, eating from her table."

The angry words upset my granddaughter Daisy, and she began to whimper in her high chair. A second later, she screamed for her mother.

Quincy lifted her out of the chair and took her in the living room. "Hush, baby, Mommy's here. *Shah, shah.*"

I wanted to stop Giselle but found myself silently cheering her on. It was Fanya who came to the rescue.

"First, I sautéed the onions with the mushrooms in olive oil. Then I added chopped broccoli, peppers, tomatoes, and carrots." The longer she spoke, the more everyone's faces relaxed. "Then I made a white sauce and added the veggies and a can of pinto beans to the cooked pasta. I heaped on piles of shredded cheese and baked until the cheese melted and the casserole bubbled." She paused for breath. "I'm glad you like it."

Hilda said, "I'd love to have the recipe. I'll make it for Isaac. Could you please give me the recipe before we leave?"

"Sure, although cholent can be prepared many ways: with meat, with potatoes, with anything that can be cooked slowly."

Giselle concentrated on her plate and shoveled in a large bite of casserole. But knowing my sister, she wasn't through with Hadas. Not by a long shot.

After dessert of poppy seed roll and babka, Quincy and her little family were the first to go home.

My daughter carried her sleeping little girl in her arms. "Shabbat shalom, Mom. I don't know how you do it." She gestured toward Hadas with her head.

"I do it for Yossi. For the two of us. I sure wish he were here, though."

The Friday foursome also prepared to leave. Giselle pulled me aside, handed me a folder she retrieved from her bag, and whispered, "I made you a copy of the police report. Obviously, tonight is not a good time to discuss it." She stole a glance at Hadas. "The moment I saw her, I didn't like her."

"Who could've guessed?"

She ignored my snarkasm. "Look at the file and call me in the morning."

When the last guest left, Fanya and I began cleaning.

Hadas yawned. "Looks like the two of you have everything under control. I'm going to bed." She didn't bother to compliment or thank Fanya for cooking an excellent meal. She didn't offer to help us. She walked toward the hallway. "Good night." Her highness was off to bed.

I lifted a dinner plate from the rinse water in the sink

and wiped it dry a little too vigorously. "Fanya, has she always been this self-centered?"

My future sister-in-law screwed up her mouth and nodded. "Always. She was her daddy's little princess. Since the family owned a successful *shmata* business, she came to school with a different outfit every day, it seemed. In the winter, she wore a white rabbit-fur coat and cap. She was spoiled, for sure. But she was also smart. Top of the class."

"What about Ze'ev? What was he like?"

Fanya blew out a puff of air. "Also spoiled. Always carried a pocket full of cash. Compared to the rest of us, he was rich. He wasn't smart or good in school, like Hadas. He was lazy and self-indulgent, but he oozed lots of charm and knew how to use it."

I finished her thought. "Which must explain how he seemed to get away with his bad behavior. But in the end, karma finally caught him. Giselle gave me a copy of the police file tonight. I'm going to look it over and get back to her in the morning."

"Ooh. I'd like to see it, too." She smiled and rubbed her hands together in a gesture resembling a cricket making music with its hind legs.

"Sure. But don't let the princess know what we're doing. I'll study it tonight and then hand it over in the morning."

I wiped clean the apricot-colored marble countertops, the last chore of the evening, and wished Fanya a good night. Then I carried the police file to my bedroom and closed the door, where I could get a good look in private.

Giselle was right. The file on Ze'ev's death was scanty. The list of personal items on the victim's body included a wedding ring, two condoms, and a wallet containing his driver's license, two hundred in cash, and the Uhrman Company credit card he used to rent the car that killed him.

The police file contained almost no information until the eyewitness statement dated three months after the incident. The witness told the detective he'd waited to come forward because he was frightened. But his priest urged him to do the right thing. He'd seen a white car with a rear spoiler deliberately accelerate and swerve toward the victim. After the impact, the driver fled the scene, leaving behind some glass from the headlight and a dying man bleeding out on the road.

He remembered part of the license plate because it bore his initials—Alberto Gomez Acevedo—and the number one: AGA1. He didn't know the make of the car. Although he didn't get a good look, he got the impression the driver was short.

The detective tracked the car to an automobile rental agency. The file contained a copy of the rental agreement signed by Ze'ev, who used the Uhrman Company credit card. The clerk who helped Ze'ev identified him in a photo lineup.

When the police questioned Hadas about the car, she claimed to know nothing about it. She was surprised her brother still used a company card, but, given his history of theft, she wasn't shocked. There was one further note about the vehicle. It was never recovered.

A printout from the credit company listed heavy activity on the same day as the car rental. Ze'ev racked up purchases totaling $3,000 at Best Buy and $4,000 to an online poker game.

The detectives investigated the second lead the witness provided. They reasoned if the driver of the car was short, it could've been a woman, which led them to question all the women in Ze'ev's life who might have a motive to kill him.

The first one they looked at was crazy Gita Glassman, the one who publicly threatened Ze'ev's life. Gita claimed to have been in an all-day adult care facility on the day of his death. Her alibi was corroborated by the art therapist who worked with schizophrenic adults. At the time Ze'ev was killed, Gita was painting a picture of a blue vagina.

Three female suspects remained: his wife, Ettie; the mother of his illegitimate child, Shelly Jacobs; and his sister, Hadas. Ettie claimed to have been babysitting her son Zelig's youngest children. One neighborhood mother confirmed she and Ettie were watching their children play at the park at the time of Ze'ev's death.

Shelly Jacobs was the next to be interviewed. On the day of Ze'ev's death, she was teaching challah baking at her daughter's school, the Bais Sarah Jewish day school for girls. The school's principal and other teachers vouched for Shelly's presence.

The last to be interviewed was Hadas. At the time of Ze'ev's death, she told deputies she'd been in an "intimate situation" at her lover's home. The man backed her story. My eyes gleamed as I turned the page and read his name—Alexander Koslov.

After that, there were no more notes in the file.

I realized one of the alibis couldn't have happened the way she claimed it did. Hadas told the detective that on the day of Ze'ev's murder she'd been in bed with Alexander Koslov. But Hadas couldn't have been with Koslov. They didn't hook up until after Ze'ev's death. I wasn't surprised Koslov, the mobster, lied to the police by giving

Hadas an alibi. Slowly, things began to fall into place: motive, means, and opportunity.

The motive to eliminate her brother was clear. He jeopardized the company she'd devoted her life to. He'd left Uhrman Company with lots of debt she'd somehow have to cover. His life was messy and chaotic, and the people closest to him suffered. Maybe she was tired of rescuing him. Whatever the motive, Hadas was angry enough to kill and smart enough to wait until the right opportunity presented itself. And it did, two weeks after she severed his ties with her company.

How did Ze'ev get his hands on the company credit card he used at the car rental? Hadas ended her brother's access to the company two weeks prior to his death. She would've cancelled any card he might have still possessed.

Yet the company card was found in Ze'ev's wallet when he died. What if she gave Ze'ev the card and asked him to rent a car for her? She was devious and manipulating. Knowing her brother had no income, she could've bribed him in some way, like letting him use the card for his own personal benefit. The printout from the credit card account, showing $7,000 in charges, confirmed my suspicions. Later, when the police discovered Ze'ev's name on the automobile contract, she could deny any involvement.

Poor Ze'ev. He probably thought he'd scored big with the credit card. It likely never crossed his mind his sister planned something else for him. Ze'ev's murder was premeditated and clever. If convicted, Hadas would spend years in prison. I felt sorry for her unborn child, who would take its first breath in jail.

There was one good thing about that sad situation, though. We would know exactly where to serve the divorce papers.

I placed the police file back in the folder and put the folder under my pillow. Tomorrow morning wouldn't be easy to navigate. Confronting Hadas with my suspicions could trigger a violent reaction. After all, she did use a car as a lethal weapon. Still, she was pregnant and no match for the much stronger Fanya, who knew Krav Maga.

I drifted off with a thousand questions roiling around in my head.

CHAPTER 34

Saturday morning, I woke to the sound of an argument coming from the kitchen.

Fanya said, "You're not going anywhere. I won't let you leave this house again."

"You're pathetic, Fanya. No wonder you're not married. Who would have a *mieskeit* like you!" She used the Yiddish word describing an ugly person.

That does it. Nobody calls my sister-in-law nasty names.

I rolled out of bed, threw on my robe and slippers, and marched to the kitchen. Hadas sat at the table, sipping a cup of coffee. Fanya stood at the sink, clutching a dish towel to her chest. From her expression, Hadas's hateful arrow had clearly pierced Fanya's heart.

I glared at Hadas. "What is going on here?" I leaned into her space. "How dare you talk to Fanya like that. If I didn't need your signature on those divorce papers, I'd kick you out of my house this minute. You're a self-centered, coldhearted witch. You use people. You care nothing about hurting others and ruining lives. You even killed your own brother!"

Oh crap, oh crap, and double-crap. How did that slip out of my mouth?

Hadas slowly placed her coffee cup on the table. "What did you say?"

In for a penny, in for a pound. I took a deep breath and jumped into turbulent waters. "You heard me. You duped your brother into renting a car for you, then you used the car to end his life. God only knows what happened to the vehicle afterward. You probably thought you'd gotten away with the perfect murder. But then a witness came forward three months later. By then, you were sleeping with Koslov, so he supported your alibi and confirmed you were with him when Ze'ev was killed. But that was your big mistake, Hadas."

Fanya's mouth gaped as her attention bounced between Hadas and me.

Hadas looked trapped. She licked her lips. "I don't know what you're talking about."

"By your own admission, you didn't begin to see Koslov until *after* Ze'ev died. The first time you saw him was after his funeral and during shiva at Ettie's house. How could you have been in bed with a man you never met on the day your brother was killed?"

Hadas suddenly rose from the table. "I don't have to put up with this. I'm leaving!"

"Oh no, you're not!" Fanya grabbed Hadas by the arm and wrist and twisted them in a pressure lock, like the one she used on Hauer.

"Ouch! Stop it. I'm pregnant. I'm pregnant."

"Then sit down," Fanya ordered. "We're making a citizen's arrest and you're not going anywhere."

Back in the chair, Hadas rubbed her wrist, where Fanya twisted it. "You'll never prove a word of what you said, Martha!"

"It's not my job to prove anything. That's the job of the prosecutor and police. Which I'm calling right now. Watch her like a hawk, Fanya." I returned to my bedroom, closed the door, and phoned Beavers.

"Hello, Martha. What mess have you gotten into now?"

"Stop it, Arlo. I discovered who murdered Ze'ev Uhrman in New York."

"New York? Did you teleport back and forth or do your superpowers allow you to read minds from the comfort of your home?"

"You know, Arlo, sometimes you can be a real jerk. I'm serious. Hadas Uhrman deliberately killed her brother in a hit-and-run." I unfolded all the facts as I knew them. When I finished, the phone was so silent I thought he'd hung up. "Arlo?"

"I'm here. Trying to figure out how you managed to read a homicide report from the NYPD."

"I'll die a horrible death before I reveal my sources. What's important here isn't how I got my information, but whether my conclusions are credible. You need to arrest her and extradite her back to New York."

"I'm not doing anything until I speak to the detective in New York. What did you say his name was?"

I gave him the information. "Don't take too long. Since Hadas knows she's the number-one suspect, she'll take the first opportunity to vanish again. Fanya and I have made a citizen's arrest, but we can't detain her forever."

Beavers ended the call with a promise to contact the NYPD.

I dressed, made my bed, and rejoined Hadas and Fanya in the kitchen. The air was thick with animosity, and I could scarcely breathe. A knocking on the door broke the silence. I looked out of the peephole and saw a FedEx driver with a large white envelope in his hands. I tore open the stiff package. Deke was true to his word. He messengered the divorce documents for Crusher as promised.

I strolled into the kitchen, reading the petition for dissolution of marriage. "The divorce papers have arrived."

Hadas snarled. "If you think I'm going to sign anything now, you're crazy. I'll contest the divorce and drag this thing on for years."

"The only thing you can drag on for years is the settlement agreement. The divorce will go through regardless. And frankly? The dissolution's all I care about."

An hour later, a new white Camry, followed by a black-and-white, parked in front of my house.

Beavers nodded a greeting as I opened the door. "We're here to bring Mrs. Levy to the station."

"You spoke to New York?"

"I did. Turns out the feds took over this case because of the Koslov connection. They're anxious to speak to her, too. Where is she?"

I stepped aside so they could enter. "Kitchen."

He pulled a set of handcuffs out of his pocket, told Hadas to stand, and Mirandized her.

As she was being led out of the house, she screamed, "Now I'll never sign those papers!"

I tried to be a nice person. I was never deliberately mean. But, in her case, I made an exception. I motioned for Beavers to stop. I needed to speak to her. I smirked at Hadas. "Actually, now I think of it, I don't want Yossi to file for divorce."

Her brow wrinkled in confusion. "Huh?"

"Yeah. As it stands now, if you're dead or incapacitated, the Uhrman Company goes to him as next of kin. Right? Didn't you recently put that in your will? I just realized that while you're incapacitated in prison, your husband, Yossi, will move to New York to take over Uhrman Company. And I will join him."

Hadas screamed, "I hate you! I'll kill you!"

I ignored her. "He and I don't really need to be married. I think we'll be more than fine living together as partners. In bed and in business. The cool thing is, while we're in New York, we'll enjoy a more luxurious lifestyle with money from the business. Thank you for helping me see the light, Hadas."

I enjoyed watching her as she struggled in vain to escape Beavers's firm grasp.

Her normally beautiful face became distorted and feral. "Show me those divorce papers," she snarled. "I want to sign them. Right now!"

CHAPTER 35

Seven Months Later

Tuesday morning, I stared at the official document in my hand, the one Crusher received from the lawyer the day before. It stated the marriage between Yosef Benyamin Levy and Hadas Uhrman Levy was now legally and forever dissolved. Crusher and I were free to marry, and I couldn't wait to share the news with my best friends.

Crusher's very tall sister, Fanya, returned to LA for her second visit since Hadas's arrest. She, Crusher, and I shared a bottle of champagne the night before to celebrate his hard-won freedom from Hadas.

Fanya raised her glass. "I'm incredibly happy for you both. L'chaim." To life.

Crusher and I made our own private celebration afterward.

The first quilters to arrive were Lucy and Birdie.

Lucy's orange hair had thinned a little with age but didn't detract from her impeccable appearance. She wore a cerulean blue cotton knit sweater because, as Lucy said, blue made her hair look more "authentic." She greeted me with a kiss on the cheek and a hearty "Hey, girl-friend." Then she handed me a plate of oatmeal cookies. "This is the last of that frozen batch of cookie dough."

Birdie stepped forward and gave me a gentle hug. Pain from her arthritis prevented her from indulging in exuber-ant displays of affection. Well into her seventies, she was all about comfort. From her signature denim overalls and white T-shirt to her Birkenstock sandals, she projected a down-home warmth.

Birdie had always been a free spirit. In addition to the turquoise and purple streaks in her hair, she recently added navy blue to the mix. "Good morning, Martha dear." She handed me a square glass dish with an apple-sauce cake still warm from the oven. "I put in lots of raisins, just the way you like it."

Our friend Jazz Fletcher arrived with his little Maltese, Zsa Zsa Galore. Jazz and I were near the same age, both well into our fifties and sailing toward the next decade. But that was where the similarity ended. Jazz dyed his graying hair brown and worked hard to stay fit while I sometimes struggled to zip up my size sixteen stretch denim jeans. Today he and his dog Zsa Zsa wore match-ing navy-blue outfits. As soon as he removed her from her tote bag, she hurried to find her pal, my cat Bumper.

Jazz gave everyone air-kisses and handed me a pack-age of cut vegetables and a covered bowl of tzatziki, a yo-gurt and cucumber dip. "You should really stick to these, Martha. You want to fit into the wedding dress I'm creat-ing."

Jazz started out his career sewing theatrical costumes. I'd requested a dress styled somewhere in between an Edwardian bustle and a Mary Quant mini. But he wouldn't let me see the design sketches or the fabric he'd selected.

Last to arrive was my sister, Giselle. She wore a white designer pantsuit and accented the look with diamonds. Lots of them. She kissed me on the cheek and handed me a pink box tied with white string. "Éclairs from Benesch." She joined the others, working on their projects in the living room, and began sewing on her Grandmother's Flower Garden quilt.

After I laid out all the goodies on the coffee table and settled everyone with fresh coffee, I cleared my throat to get their attention. "I have some good news."

Everyone stopped sewing and chatting.

As soon as I gained their attention, I waved the paper in the air and grinned. "Yossi's divorce is final."

The group erupted in clapping and whoops of joy.

"*Mozzle tahv*," said Giselle. "Now we can plan the wedding for real. Of course, we'll use the Beverly Hills house." She referred to the famous Eagan estate built by her grandfather with oil money. The main house could comfortably host five hundred people. "You can leave the catering details to me."

"Don't I have a say in the details of my own wedding, G?" I teased my sister's tendency to be the CEO of every situation.

Giselle thought for a second. "Okay, you can choose the colors. But not black and white. It's too cliché."

"And red is bad luck," Fanya said. "I attended a wedding once with red as the theme. The bride fell overboard on the honeymoon cruise to Hawaii. By the time they realized she was missing, it was too late."

Jazz gazed into the distance and waved a hand from side to side, probably painting the picture he saw in his head. "Personally, I still like the idea of soft blues and greens, colors of the warm Caribbean waters. Plus, those colors will be most compatible with your wedding dress."

Lucy took a cookie from the plate she brought and dunked an edge into her coffee. "It's nice to see you again, Fanya. What news do you bring from New York?"

Fanya tugged on the hem of her *Save the Whales* T-shirt. "Hadas is still in custody and Zelig, Ettie's oldest son, visits her occasionally. She's in the process of signing over the business to him. The last I heard, Hadas worked a deal with the DA. She agreed to confess to voluntary manslaughter and serve a minimum sentence of five years in exchange for her testimony against Alexander Koslov."

"What about her baby?" Lucy asked.

Fanya pursed her lips. "When they arrested her, they stripped her of all personal items, including the amulet I made for her. The one with the ruby to protect her against miscarriage." Fanya shook her head slowly. "She lost the baby at twenty weeks. Like the first one thirty years ago. After her miscarriage, they put her on suicide watch. *Pu, pu, pu.*"

Giselle clicked her tongue. "Her failed pregnancy was probably for the best. Her poor little child would've grown up with murderers for parents."

"Is the death of any innocent child ever 'for the best?'" Fanya stirred in her seat. "Maybe the loss of both her pregnancies is punishment enough for Hadas."

I broke the silence, following Fanya's statement. "I have one more piece of news. My uncle Isaac and his helper Hilda were married in a quiet ceremony last Thursday."

"How wonderful, Martha dear." Birdie's smile said it all.

But Lucy's face crinkled again with concern. "Did you know about this? Is she on the up-and-up?"

I sighed. "Yeah, I saw it coming. But I decided I had no right to stand in the way of his happiness. And he is happier than I've ever seen him. They'll continue to live in the house as husband and wife. And when he passes, she'll be able to continue living there."

Giselle said, "Wait. Isn't it your house, too?"

"Who needs two houses? You can only live in one at a time." I glanced to see my sister's wry smile. She owned and used five houses at last count. "He wanted to be sure Hilda never becomes homeless again."

Jazz dipped a carrot stick into the tzatziki. "Personally, I think it's romantic. Imagine finding love for the first time in your eighties."

Giselle nodded. "I agree. Harold and I have driven the two of them every Friday night for Shabbat with the family. At first, they sat far apart in the back seat. Eventually they sat side by side, holding hands. Believe me, I can smell a con artist a mile away. She's no gold digger."

Fanya was quilting a pattern of concentric circles in the Snail's Trail quilt. She smiled broadly, showing the gap between her front teeth. "And now we get to witness another simcha. Martha and my brother are finally getting married."

CHAPTER 36

I paced nervously between the sofa and the king-sized bed in a grand guest suite of the Eagan estate. Quincy, Giselle, Lucy, and Birdie decided they were all going to be my matrons of honor. They chatted amiably, wearing matching pale green dresses Jazz created.

Since Fanya was going to stand with her brother during the ceremony, Jazz made her a black satin pantsuit with a low-cut jacket fitted tightly at the waist and a black lace bandeau underneath. She turned slowly as we admired her unusual wedding attire.

It was five in the afternoon on a Sunday. "Where is Jazz with my dress?"

My daughter, Quincy, belly swollen with her second child, stopped me in mid-stride and grabbed my hands. "Don't worry, Mom. He probably got stuck in traffic."

I was as tightly wound as Giselle's antique French or-

molu clock on top of a gilded bombé chest. "The ceremony is supposed to start at six, and I don't even know if
the dress will fit me." My voice sounded suspiciously
close to a whine.

"We took your measurements, Mom. Remember? Jazz
knows what he'd doing."

"But what if I hate the style? Or the color? You guys
wouldn't even tell me that much. I'm the only one who
hasn't seen my dress."

Quincy's eyes sparkled as she smiled. "You're going
to love the dress, Mom. You'll look beautiful. We all
agree."

Giselle rose from the blue velvet sofa and walked
across an Aubusson carpet to hand me a flute of Dom
Pérignon. "Don't you love the way Antoine did your
hair? It's elegant." My gray curls were artfully arranged
in an updo, leaving my neck bare; a perfect backdrop for
the dangling earrings Giselle loaned me. Studded gener-
ously with diamonds and emeralds, I was sure they cost
as much as a new Lamborghini.

My sister's Beverly Hills hair stylist came to the estate
and did all our hair earlier in the day. Giselle also brought
in a specialist to do our makeup. The lithe Italian with
slender fingers applied hot wax to the fine hairs underneath and between my brows.

Apparently, he was used to insulting his clients and
getting away with it. "How can you live with this *jungle*
on your face?"

"Well," I said, "every six months I send in a safari with
machetes to hack through the undergrowth. One time
they found the lost city of Atlantis."

He roared with laughter. "*Sei molto divertente.* You're
very funny."

Five more minutes passed and still no Jazz. "If he doesn't get here on time, I'll have to wear the clothes I came in." I'd arrived in the morning in jeans and a T-shirt and brought a small overnight bag with the underclothes Quincy told me I'd need, including XXL Spanx. I wore them now underneath a cotton robe. I'd also slipped my feet into the silver Jimmy Choo four-inch heels embellished with hundreds of crystals Giselle insisted I buy. The only thing missing was the dress.

The chattering and laughter of the guests in the first-floor ballroom increased in volume as more and more people arrived. The sound bubbled its way up the stairs and slid under the door into the bedroom.

My stomach did a nervous flip. *This is really happening!* I wrung my hands. "Where is he?"

Lucy fished a small tin pill holder out of her purse. She extracted a yellow tablet and handed it to me. "Take this, girlfriend." She put it in my hand.

"What is it?"

"It's a chill pill. It'll calm your nerves."

I swallowed the pill with a mouthful of champagne. As the minutes ticked by, I could feel my tight muscles relaxing. While we continued to wait, Giselle refilled everyone's glass, including mine. Finally, Jazz hurried into the room, carrying a garment bag. He wore a light-green suit designed to match the matrons of honor.

"Where have you been?" Giselle asked. "The ceremony starts in ten minutes."

He hung the bag over the top of the closet door and unzipped it. "I got waylaid behind a road accident. I tried to call Martha on my phone, but it ran out of juice."

The first glimpse I got of the dress was the color: sparkling greens and blues, like the warm waters of the

Caribbean. Jazz carefully slid the dress off the hanger and brought it to me, which was amazing because there were now two of him. I blinked hard to bring him in focus, but he kept sliding in and out of my vision.

"Well?" He wore a huge grin on both of his faces. "What do you think?"

"Of what?" I could barely concentrate on his words.

"The dress!" He peered closely at me. "Martha? What's wrong with you?"

"Nothing, silly. I'm getting married in a few minutes."

"Stand!" he commanded.

I grabbed his hand and stood, wobbling on the four-inch heels. He helped me step into the garment, a floor-length sheath with a slit in the back. He zipped up the back and the dress settled around my curves like a gentle glove, falling over my shoes to just above the floor. My bubbie's pearls hung above the demure neckline of the bodice. The bare skin of my arms was covered by sleeves made of turquoise chiffon.

I looked at my reflection in a cheval mirror with an ornate gold frame and turned from side to side. The shimmering fabric changed from blue to green and back again with each movement of my body. A wave of deep gratitude pushed up from my chest and into my throat. "I'm beautiful."

I turned to Jazz with tears and tried to hug him.

"No, no!" he said. "You'll wrinkle the fabric. And for God's sake, *do not cry!*"

Giselle hurried over to me with a Kleenex and dabbed at my cheeks. "Stop it, Sissy. Your mascara is running."

My gratitude attached itself to my sister. "You're so good to me, G. I can't imagine my life without you. I love my little sister." I fell against her and began to weep.

Giselle turned to Quincy. "Your mother is drunk. She'll never be able to go downstairs like this. I'll call the kitchen for coffee. We'll force it down her throat if we have to." Giselle headed for the door. "I'll go downstairs and announce a delay. There should be enough hors d'oeuvres and booze to keep everyone happy for a while."

I heard someone say, "She'll never be able to walk in those shoes in her condition." They sat me on the sofa, removed my four-inch heels, and slid my feet into my navy-blue rubber Crocs.

Jazz said, "Now stand, Martha."

"I juss wanna go to sleep."

Several sets of hands grabbed my arms and pulled me to my feet.

Jazz scowled. "Rats! Her hem is dragging on the floor. She won't be able to walk without tripping."

When Giselle returned, they told her about the hem. She called the kitchen and three minutes later someone appeared at the door with a roll of silver duct tape. "We can fold the hem up and tape it underneath."

They sat me on the sofa again. I could feel them tugging on the bottom of the dress. After some ripping and tearing noises, they made me stand. "Okay. She should be able to walk now."

Supported on both sides by two sets of strong arms, they shuffled me back and forth across the floor. The toe of my bulky rubber shoes caught on the edge of the Aubusson carpet and caused me to stumble. After forty-five minutes of coffee and walking, I sobered enough to stand on my own.

I headed for the bathroom. "Gotta go."

Jazz pointed to Giselle. "Go in there and help her with the dress. Make sure she doesn't pee on it."

I walked back into the bedroom on my own.

Lucy looked at her watch. "The wedding was supposed to start at six. It's now seven fifteen. Oh God. This is all my fault. I shouldn't have given you the Valium."

I hated to see my best friend wretched. "No, Lucy. Don't blame yourself. You've been my BFF for more years than I can remember. We've had some great adventures, don't you think? I don't know if I've ever said 'I love you,' but I feel it in my heart all the time."

She lifted a Kleenex out of the box and dabbed her perfect makeup. "I love you too, hon."

Still brimming with deep emotion, I looked at my daughter. "Quincy, my darling, you have brought me such *nachas* over the years. And now you have a growing family of your own." I ran my hand over her belly. "I couldn't have asked for a better daughter. Let me give you a hug." I crushed her against my bosom.

"And I couldn't have asked for a better mom. I'm really happy for you today. You have no idea."

Birdie dabbed at her eyes. "I was never blessed with children. But if I were, I'd want them to be exactly like you, Quincy."

I regarded Birdie's glittering eyes and gentle face. "Birdie, you have become a mother to so many people through your many kindnesses. You're a goddess in the kitchen and a master quilter. You're always willing to try something new. Thank you for being such a good friend over the years. I love you."

Fanya stood quietly, watching us from the corner of the room.

I waved her over. "Fanya, I love your brother *soooo* much. And in the few months I've known you, I've grown to love you, too. I'm so glad we're family."

"I love you, too, Martha. You're a perfect match for Yossi, *keinehora*."

Jazz cleared his throat. "When is it going to be my turn?"

I laughed. "My life would be a lot duller without you, Jazz. You're like the brother I never had, and I truly love you. Did I say thank-you for the dress? It's beautiful. I can feel all the love you put into it."

I was still a little foggy but ready to go downstairs. Before we left the guest suite, I took one last glance in the mirror. Tear tracks made black mascara smudges around my eyes. Several curls fell rebelliously from the top of my head. Duct tape scratched my ankles every time I took a step.

Crusher had been warned about my condition. He met me at the back of the ballroom, looking handsome in his kittel, a ceremonial white robe worn over clothing for special occasions. I was sure it was custom-made because at six feet six inches and three hundred pounds of muscle, nothing about him was ordinary. He'd draped his tallit, or prayer shawl, over his shoulders like a blanket and wore a festive white kippah dotted with sequins. Concern for me was written in every crease of his brow. "Babe. What happened up there?" He pointed upstairs to the guest suite.

A surge of love for him hit me like a tidal wave. "I'm so sorry, Yossi." I told him about the Valium mixed with champagne. "Jazz was so late and I panicked. I'm afraid I made a terrible mess of things." My eyes filled with tears. "You don't deserve this. You deserve to have a beautiful wedding and a bride who isn't still a little tipsy. And you look wonderful."

His face relaxed in a smile. "I'm getting exactly what I

want. Life has never been more complete than it is with you. I don't care about the details."

"This is why I'll always be in love with you," I said. "I've made many mistakes in my life, but marrying you is *not* one of them."

Giselle cleared her throat for attention and shoved a bouquet of white roses in my hands. "Just follow us toward the other end of the ballroom, Sissy, and try not to trip and fall." She smiled and winked. "Everything will be fine. You'll see."

Fanya pressed a small leather bag into my hands. "A *segulah*. For luck." Then she joined the procession of matrons and man of honor.

Fanya's amulet fit inside my dress between my breasts. I clutched the bouquet in one hand and hung on Crusher's arm with the other. We walked slowly toward the front of the ballroom, where nearly one hundred guests stood waiting and watching. My navy-blue Crocs squeaked on the wooden floor, but I didn't care. As far as I was concerned, we were walking on air.

The first person I saw in the crowd of smiling faces was my uncle Isaac. His smile was eclipsed only by the happiness on his new bride's face. How odd that he had to wait until late in life to find his *beshert*. But once I got over my initial shock, I saw what he saw in Hilda: A noble, honest, compassionate woman who loved and admired him as much as he loved and admired her. I believe he saw her as a tabula rasa, a clean slate waiting for him to write their own brief love story.

I had insisted that my one-year-old granddaughter Daisy be allowed to attend our nighttime wedding. I spotted her as she giggled in her father's arms, dressed in a tiny version of the dresses Jazz had made for the wedding party. I knew that somewhere in this huge estate, a little Maltese, also dressed in green, would find her way to the dinner and party afterward. As soon as she saw us walking in her direction, Daisy reached out her arms and grinned. "Baba!"

I waved back and threw her a kiss.

All of my attendants formed a semicircle around the chuppah, the cloth canopy under which Crusher and I would recite our vows. The chuppah was fastened at each corner to a pole, and the four poles were held by our friends: Hector "Malo" Fuentes, our neighbor and Crusher's colleague; Harold Zimmerman, my sister's fiancé; Ray Mondello, Lucy's husband; and (big surprise) John Smith, director of counterintelligence at the FBI.

When Crusher and I stepped under the chuppah, my best friend, Lucy, pointed to the cloth over our heads. "Look."

I craned my neck back to see the surprise my quilty friends must have sewn in secret. The chuppah was a small quilt pieced in the Double Wedding Ring pattern with blues and greens on a field of white. I recognized Birdie's careful handiwork in the colorful flowers and leaves she'd appliquéd around the borders; blues and greens mostly, with soft yellow and lavender. The center of the middle ring featured our names and the date embroidered on white cotton with a blue satin stitch.

I looked at the faces of my friends, all carrying proud smiles. "It's gorgeous!" I could scarcely breathe. "I'm so lucky to have such wonderful friends."

"Fanya!" I leaned toward her and whispered, "Did you remember to put salt into the corners of this room?"

She nodded. "It took me the good part of an hour to get to all the rooms on this floor alone."

I smiled at Crusher, my heart fluttering in my throat. "I guess this is it, Yossi. This is where we make it legal. Unless . . ."

He frowned. "Unless what?"

"Unless you have more wives you haven't told me about."

He let out peals of laughter. "And this, babe, is why I'll always be in love with you."

Please turn the page for a quilting tip from
Mary Marks!

HANDY HINTS FOR HAND QUILTERS

In this age of longarm machine quilting, fewer and fewer quilts are stitched by hand. Let's face it: We can get beautiful and rapid results using the machine as opposed to the dozens (or hundreds) of hours necessary to complete a quilt by hand. Many quilters object to taking that much time, saying, "I don't have the patience."

I get it. I have more unfinished quilt tops than I can possibly finish by hand in this lifetime. But I suggest there is great satisfaction in picking up a needle, biting into the layers of fabric, and letting your mind ramble and roam free. Hand quilting can be a form of meditation or devotion. Most of my finished quilts were given to family and friends. And almost every project was made with someone specific in mind. As I hand quilted, I poured into it my love and concern for that person. And more than once, I was told, "I sleep so much better with your quilt."

So to encourage quilters to try hand quilting, I offer the following hints.

THINGS YOU NEED

- Package of "betweens" needles (The larger the number, the smaller the needle; the smaller the needle, the smaller the stitch.)
- Needle threader
- Grooved thimble that will hold the end of a needle
- Quilting thread with coating to prevent tangles
- Thread cutter
- Hoop or frame that will hold the quilt taut
- Good light

THINGS THAT SLOW YOU DOWN AND TIRE YOU OUT

- Fabric density
- Batting consistency
- Seams and multiple layers of fabric
- Dull needles
- Wrong thimble
- Tangled thread
- Uncomfortable posture, seating

THINGS THAT HELP YOU FOCUS

- Make sure the portion you are working on is clearly marked.
- Give yourself a treat while quilting (i.e., favorite TV show, videos, audiobooks, good music).
- Set achievement goals for each quilting session.
- Try to set aside a regular time each day for quilting.

THINGS TO REMEMBER

- It is not the length of the stitch so much as the consistency and even spacing that makes for pretty quilting.
- Stitching has its own rhythm that will carry you along. Develop a rhythm and you will develop even, fast stitches.
- Stop and admire your work often. Close your eyes and run your hands over the texture of the quilted

fabric. It will inspire you and make you feel good to know that you put that texture there with each loving stitch.

Now go forth and quilt. And don't forget that emergency package of M&M'S.

Connect with

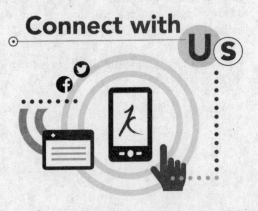

Visit us online at
KensingtonBooks.com
to read more from your favorite authors, see books
by series, view reading group guides, and more.

for sneak peeks, chances to win books and prize packs,
and to share your thoughts with other readers.

**facebook.com/kensingtonpublishing
twitter.com/kensingtonbooks**

Tell us what you think!

To share your thoughts, submit a review,
or sign up for our eNewsletters, please visit:
KensingtonBooks.com/TellUs.

Grab These Cozy Mysteries
from
Kensington Books

Forget Me Knot Mary Marks	978-0-7582-9205-6	$7.99US/$8.99CAN
Death of a Chocoholic Lee Hollis	978-0-7582-9449-4	$7.99US/$8.99CAN
Green Living Can Be Deadly Staci McLaughlin	978-0-7582-7502-8	$7.99US/$8.99CAN
Death of an Irish Diva Mollie Cox Bryan	978-0-7582-6633-0	$7.99US/$8.99CAN
Board Stiff Annelise Ryan	978-0-7582-7276-8	$7.99US/$8.99CAN
A Biscuit, A Casket Liz Mugavero	978-0-7582-8480-8	$7.99US/$8.99CAN
Boiled Over Barbara Ross	978-0-7582-8687-1	$7.99US/$8.99CAN
Scene of the Climb Kate Dyer-Seeley	978-0-7582-9531-6	$7.99US/$8.99CAN
Deadly Decor Karen Rose Smith	978-0-7582-8486-0	$7.99US/$8.99CAN
To Kill a Matzo Ball Delia Rosen	978-0-7582-8201-9	$7.99US/$8.99CAN

Available Wherever Books Are Sold!

All available as e-books, too!

Visit our website at **www.kensingtonbooks.com**